GRAVEDIGGERS
TERROR COVE

Also by Christopher Krovatin

Gravediggers: Mountain of Bones

GRAVEDIGGERS
TERROR COVE

CHRISTOPHER KROVATIN

KATHERINE TEGEN BOOKS
An Imprint of HarperCollins Publishers

Katherine Tegen Books is an imprint of HarperCollins Publishers.

Gravediggers: Terror Cove
Copyright © 2013 by HarperCollins Publishers
All rights reserved. Printed in the United States of America.
No part of this book may be used or reproduced in any manner whatsoever
without written permission except in the case of brief quotations embodied
in critical articles and reviews. For information address HarperCollins
Children's Books, a division of HarperCollins Publishers, 10 East 53rd Street,
New York, NY 10022.
www.harpercollinschildrens.com

ISBN 978-0-06-207743-1 (trade bdg.)

Typography by Carla Weise
13 14 15 16 17   CG/RRDH   10 9 8 7 6 5 4 3 2 1
❖
First Edition

DEDICATED IN SOLEMN MEMORY
OF THE PASSENGERS OF THE *ALABASTER*

ACKNOWLEDGMENTS

Many thanks to Claudia Gabel, who lets my imagination run wild; to everyone at HarperCollins for their tireless support; to Jon Scieszka, Chris Healy, Adam Jay Epstein, Andrew Jacobson, and Nils Johnson-Shelton, for making the Class Acts tour so incredible; and to the many authors who lent their names and reputations to my first Gravediggers book. Much love to the brilliant Kit Reed, for shoving me out the door, and to the infamous Binky Urban, for always watching my back. Special thanks to Lucio Fulci, David Cronenberg, and Ian Fleming, whose sprawling visions taught me the international language of fear.

The Warden's Handbook
by Lucille Fulci

Chapter 6: The Craft

7.b—Discipline Versus Destiny

B lood is the bottom line for being a Warden. Without magic in one's bloodline, it is impossible to control even the most basic forms of karmic enchantment. This is not an opinion; hundreds have slaved away, unable to master the karmic arts due to the simple fact of heritage.

However, Wardens are not born knowing the skills of containment and communion with the energies of the earth. Mastering these abilities takes patience, sacrifice, and extreme discipline. Magic is wild and amorphous, ever changing, and those who do not learn to control their inherited abilities will cause destruction and pain when they accidentally use them. There are countless cases of untrained witches creating epic disasters by accidentally reading the wrong passage or unknowingly playing a sigil-carved instrument (see *The San Francisco Earthquake*, p. 221).

The job of containment requires constant vigilance, focus, and situational awareness. Every sigil must be perfectly carved, and each totem and beacon must be painstakingly crafted. To monitor her chosen plot of cursed earth, a Warden must be able to communicate with the land itself, as well as the flora and fauna therein, to keep herself constantly informed of the whereabouts and activity of the cursed. Indeed, unlike other disciples of the craft, Wardens have little to no room for failure in their role—to break containment is to unleash unspeakable evil upon the world. This constant vigilance means that Wardens must sacrifice the comforts of a "normal" life, such as friendships, romance, or career. It is a hard and often lonely practice, true, but one whose reward is without equal.

That Wardens need to study, train, and dedicate themselves to the cause can seem at odds with other manifestations of karmic energies. The cursed themselves, for instance, are damned by events far beyond their control, and are raised by the dark itself rather than any user of enchantment. Gravediggers feel like a slap in the face to most Wardens, for, as we discussed, Gravediggers aren't taught or trained but are chosen by necessity, their purpose and skill brought into being only when a Warden's containment fails or dark times descend upon a land; eras pass without their presence, but when the balance is tipped by the sins of man, they appear as if from nowhere. Their station, though strengthened by training, is inherently instilled in them, evidenced by the beasts of the wild, which Wardens must learn to speak to, whereas Gravediggers can interact with them almost effortlessly. The Warden is a carefully constructed barrier; the Gravedigger is a time bomb. Like many things about these two classes, we do not fully understand why this is, only that it has occurred this way for eons.

Once again, it is helpful for the two to assist each other. However, Gravediggers clumsily stumble into their roles, committing acts of ignorant destruction and violence that can be later disguised as *cleverness* and *ingenuity*, which only serve to further alienate Wardens, with their hardworking attitudes.

This bluster also attracts outsiders, who assume that the seemingly random occurrence of Gravediggers means that anyone can be at war with the dead; these dreamers, however, usually only have their own interests at heart, and cannot fully comprehend the harm they cause by meddling in affairs beyond their control. . . .

CHAPTER ONE

Ian

"Hurry, Ian!" screams my dad. "They're gaining on you!"

But it's too late. I just *eat* it.

My hands go tight around the edge of the old canvas potato sack, and I hop, man, I hop as fast as my legs'll let me, but it's no use, I can *feel* her coming up behind me, can hear her breathing as she passes me by inches. She does this little minihop, five little hops to my one big hop, and all of a sudden out of the corner of my eye, I see that cloud of black hair come swooping up on me and pull ahead when we're about ten yards away from the finish line. Watching her take the lead, eating her very *dust*, and my dad shrieking like some kind of murder victim jab me with this shot of adrenaline, send me bounding forward in these extra-large hops, but I can tell it's the last thing I should do; the sack is just too constricting, and eventually I trip in it. Next thing I know, I pull my knee up into a tight piece of canvas, my feet tie into a knot with each other, and then the ground flies up to meet me as I fall facedown into the grass, my hands scrabbling to catch me.

As I sit up, I watch the other kids, Tom Richter and Franklin Simms and Katey Price, go hopping past me, doing their best to hold up their ratty canvas sacks, but they were nowhere close to Kendra and me—now just Kendra.

As I climb out of the canvas sack and rise off the grass, I watch Kendra pass the finish line. Coach Arnholt takes her hand and holds it up in the air. "The winner," she announces, "is Miss Kendra Wright!"

The crowd cheers and claps, and Kendra the Queen Brain bows politely, a tight-lipped little smile sitting beneath her wild poof of hair. At first, I have this *sick* feeling in my guts. It's like my dad's eyes weigh a million pounds and they're somehow inside my stomach, and I just have to walk to the end of the finish line and feel them, like a *loser*. Not like a wolf, like a *poodle*.

As I reach her, Kendra folds her arms and raises her chin at me, her smile glowing out of her blushing coffee-colored skin. "Aha," she says, "my vanquished opponent!"

Calm down, don't lose it. This is Kendra, my friend, who I owe in more ways than I can remember. Force a smile. Take deep breaths, like PJ. Look on the bright side—you got to do some running, and you just made Queen Brain's day. Take one for the team, Coach would say.

Coach Arnholt trundles over, all white shorts and visor and that mole on her lip, and she hands Kendra her prize: a huge pink stuffed elephant. Kendra holds it high like a trophy.

"To the victor go the spoils," says Kendra. "Behold."

"You must feel real cool," I tell her, "holding a big stupid plush elephant."

She clutches it tightly to her chest. "I think the word you're looking for is *magnificent.* Or perhaps *radiant.*"

I was looking for *stupid.*

PJ Wilson, our number three, stands on the sidelines, camera in hand, next to my parents. My dad's dressed for the fairway—polo shirt, cap and shades, khaki shorts, white socks and Reeboks, ridiculous mustache—but he looks like he's lost our house and car in a bet, staring straight down. My mom, blond and looking especially thin, smiles at me from next to him, but it's this preppy apologetic smile she always does, where it's about excusing my dad. My best friend, scrawny and

pale in all black like some kind of ar-teest, cackles mani-
acally to himself, glaring into his camera.

Can you believe the scene I'm dealing with? This is
my life when I lose a *sack race at the fair.* Just wait'll I'm
back in basketball and miss a free throw. Dad's going to
kill me (I'd be so lucky).

As Kendra and I reach them, my dad breaks his
loving exchange with his shoes and gives an approving
nod to Kendra, his mouth set hard beneath his mustache. "Good work there, Wright," he says. "You earned
that . . . elephant." He looks at me, and even though he's
got his aviator shades on, I can see his disapproval. "We
need to get your speed back up if you're going to be
playing ball this year. That was subpar."

"Thanks, Dad. Hadn't noticed that."

"Vince, stop it," says my mom. "Honey, you were
great."

"I lost, Mom."

"Winning isn't everything," she says, and then goes
right into, "Kendra, honey, nice job. You wiped the
floor with them."

Fantastic. I glance at PJ, hoping for at least some
dude support, but my wingman is in full-on mad-
professor mode, his big shiny eyes bright and busy as he
messes with the kajillion buttons on his camera. "Please
tell me you didn't get that on tape," I tell him.

"Not only that . . . ," he says, and turns the camera's

screen to us. He presses a button, and a close-up of me tripping and falling plays in super slo-mo. You can see every twitch of my mouth as I realize I'm going down, every *Oh no* running through my head. When I hit the ground, a sound effect blasts like a bomb going off.

Kendra giggles, which is big for her. "Classic."

"When we get home, I'll set it to some really sad opera and send it to you guys," he says, chuckling. His eyes read my face, and he cuts his smile short. "Sorry, man. You did really well, honest."

Pitied by PJ—a fate worse than death. Again, I get that nasty feeling in my core, like I'm so annoyed I could punt PJ's camera into a river, but again, I gotta be chill here. That's old Ian, the Ian who didn't know how good Queen Brain and Jitters Wilson were at having my back.

"I'm starving," I say, trying to shrug off the bad vibe coming off my dad and the complete lameness of losing. "Fried dough?"

"Absolutely," says PJ.

"Vince, maybe you should go with them," says my mom. She's trying to sound casual, but her voice has a hard edge to it.

"They're just walking around the carnival, Emily," he says. "It's fine." But then he turns and gives me another glare from behind those shades. "No leaving the carnival grounds." I can almost hear his eyes narrow. "*No matter how big the deer is.* Got it?"

Whoa. My breath catches in my throat. Next to me, PJ chews his lip and Kendra nods slowly.

Too soon. Way too soon.

The July Fourth Freedom Fair is a big thing in our town. Once a year, our school turns its massive backyard into a carnival to raise money. It used to be kind of dinky, but now everyone in town wants to do something bigger and cooler each year, so suddenly you've got Dr. Sherman the dentist making cotton candy, and Ms. Todd the hairdresser running the fortune-teller tent in a turban. They bring in some carnies so we can have bigger rides—a Ferris wheel, a Gravitron. A great place to eat a ton of candy, go on a ton of rides, puke your guts out, and head home happy.

It's enough to wash away my dad's comment, and soon we're ravenous. We don't know where to start. Before us stretches a mile of food stands covered in flashing lights and red-and-blue streamers.

"Funnel cake or elephant ears first?" asks PJ, reading my mind.

"Funnel cake is more of a dessert," I say. "Let's maybe get a hot dog, then an elephant ear."

"A hot dog wrapped in an elephant ear," says PJ.

"You two are disgusting," says Kendra. "Your stomach lining must be—"

"Wait until I have a hot dog," I tell her. "Then we

can talk about stomach lining."

She smiles. "Most hot dog meat *contains* stomach lining."

"Thanks, Kendra," PJ tells her. "You've somehow managed to *ruin hot dogs*."

That cracks me up, and that gets Kendra laughing, and pretty soon we're all in stitches, but his comment's right: hot dogs now seem awful to me, so we go straight for elephant ears.

The next thing I know, my mouth is full of hot cinnamon-covered fried fat, and all is right with the world. We walk down the grid of the fair, staring into booths, arguing about what we want to do. PJ's talking about an outdoor movie they're showing later, Kendra wants to talk about physics and how Tilt-A-Whirls work, and I'm looking for a booth game involving a fake rifle. It feels good, even if we're each pulling in a different direction. There's kind of a perfect three-way balance to it.

I guess this is our first time doing the carnival together as friends. I mean, we didn't really know each other before—

As we make a turn around the corner of a popcorn and lemonade stand, it comes into view, practically leaping out at us. All three of us stop dead, and I feel panic shoot into the tips of my fingers, giving them pins and needles. Then it spreads up to my heart, then deep into my stomach.

PJ whispers, "Oh, man."

They've always done a spook house—one of those castle-themed cart rides where steam-powered monsters hiss and jump out at you. Sometimes a loud siren goes off or a strobe light flashes. This year, the spray-painted wood façade is a mountain scene, with MOUNTAINS OF MADNESS written over it in bloody letters. Painted on the mountains are vampires in capes, werewolves in tattered flannel . . . and the living dead, rotting corpses with their hands out, screaming silently at the spectator. The swinging door that leads into the ride is painted with a rotting skull laughing.

It's just a little too close for comfort. Because back in—yikes, was it just March?—I wouldn't have even noticed it.

But now, it brings forth this quick flashback, this flicker in my mind, just a single frame that comes back to me every few hours, when we come out of the floor of this cabin, and there, in the light, are the dead, standing around us with their white eyes bulging out of their rotten gray-green skulls and black gore running down their chins. For a second, they just *look* at me, like they've never seen anything like me before, and then all at once, their hands come out and their teeth launch forward, and I hear this moan, deep, from somewhere other than a lung.

I don't know which one is worse—how freaked it

makes me feel, or how excited.

"It's like they know," mumbles PJ.

"They can't know," says Kendra, like she's trying to convince herself. She runs a hand through her puff of hair. "They—it's—they can't. Impossible."

"Do either of you . . . want to go on it?" I ask, the idea making me feel kind of sick, but good sick, pregame sick, like I'm totally on top of what lies ahead of me.

"No way," says PJ immediately.

"No," says Kendra, after considering.

"Yeah," I lie, fighting off the buzzing excitement, "me neither."

The other two turn and trudge off, and I manage to tear myself away from the spook house. After a few silent minutes, Kendra asks PJ, "When's the last time you watched a horror movie?"

PJ shrugs. "Why bother?" he says. "It's just not cool when you know it's real."

PJ glares at his remaining elephant ear like it insulted his mother. This is the new PJ, the dude who came back from the mountain—less terrified, more irritated, not panicked, but peeved by everything that walks, flies, swims, or crawls.

"It's seven fifteen," says Kendra, staring into her phone. "We should get over to the main stage for the raffle."

"Why did you guys put your names in for that,

anyway?" asks PJ as we head toward the center of the fairgrounds.

"Are you kidding?" I tell him. "Grand prize is a week in Puerto Rico! Swimming, soaking up sunshine—why didn't *you*?"

"First of all, because sun poisoning and centipede bites don't sound very fun to me," says PJ, counting off on his fingers. "Thanks, but no thanks." Listen to him, like the beach is his enemy. Nature, like everything else, just ticks him off now. "Second, and more important, because I remember what O'Dea said. The forces of darkness are going to remember us. We're marked. Checked, highlighted. So I'm staying put." He folds his arms proudly. "I won't let the universe have the chance."

"Enjoy your summer at the mall," I tell him, and smile at Kendra. She tries to smile back, but I can see worry in her face, and yeah, I guess PJ has a point.

It didn't really surprise me to find out that there were cursed places all over the world—that's one of the things you learn as a little kid: *Don't go there at night, it's cursed*—but the whole system behind it threw me for a loop. We finally tricked the zombies that attacked us into attacking one another—well, PJ and Kendra melted one—and apparently, that messed with this huge network of karmic energy.

Again, it's weird—a few months ago, when O'Dea, the mountain witch who saved us from walking, flesh-eating corpses, told us that our interfering with her magic force field and destroying all the mountain's zombies made us some kind of special zombie hunters called Gravediggers, it all made sense to me. Of *course* I was a karmically destined zombie slayer. Abso*lutely*. But now it's weird. We can't talk about it with anyone, and if I act like our time on the mountain was an adventure, it's kind of like this big insult to PJ and Kendra.

"You're being paranoid," I say, and nod toward the stage. "Fun in the sun, sandy beaches, lobster rolls. It's going to be great!"

"If being paranoid keeps me alive, then that's fine with me," says PJ.

The main stage is a white riser with a huge American flag hanging behind it. Already, the crowd runs six deep, and we have to nudge and weave our way between the spectators to find my parents up front. The minute we reach them, my mom grabs me by the arm and pulls me close to her, but I manage to pull myself away. Definitely not helping my ego (Kendra says I have a giant one, and she's probably right, as usual).

Principal Jones stands on a cheap platform with the school perfectly centered behind him, poured into his Uncle Sam suit, his cheeks red and his brow shiny with sweat. He still manages to swing his arm in a rootin'-tootin' kind of way and call everyone up to the stage through his blushing and sweating. This carnival is probably too big a moneymaker for the school for him to feel embarrassed about a stupid outfit, but I just hope he doesn't die of heatstroke up there.

"And now," he says into his squealing microphone, "we have the moment you've all been waiting for—this year's raffle." The crowd claps and hoots. "Do I need to remind you that the three students who win this raffle, and their families, receive an all-expenses-paid trip to Puerto Rico?" The crowd claps harder, whistles, screams. All around, kids gape excitedly while parents shift their feet, hoping against hope.

This is it. My time to shine, a little good luck on this crappy day. My dad's hand drops to my shoulder but doesn't squeeze it—not yet, not when I haven't won. I clap my hands together and mumble, "C'mon, let's go, let's win it, Puerto Rico, here I come, big money big money."

"Your cajoling won't increase your chances of winning," says Kendra.

"Hey, you never know," I tell her. "A little karmic interference might be just the ticket."

Kendra shakes her head. "Ridiculous," she says.

Principal Jones pulls a piece of paper from his bucket and unfolds it. "Our first winner is . . . Ian Buckley!"

Finally. Cold and warmth rush over my face at the same time, and without thinking I throw my fists in the air and I hoot like a maniac. My dad ruffles my hair.

"Attaboy!" he growls. PJ shakes his head and crosses his arms, but I ignore it—not even *he* can bring down this mood.

Kendra rolls her eyes, but I catch her mumbling to herself—"Let's win it, let's go, big money big money."

Principal Jones removes a second slip and unfolds it. "Next up is . . . Kendra Wright!"

Kendra throws a fist in the air and whoops, but then she lowers her hand worriedly and looks at PJ, and when I see the expression of utter horror on his face as he slowly lowers his camera, I feel the blood drain from mine.

"Congrats, Wright," says my dad, slapping her on the back. "We're going to have one heck of a party."

My mom smiles at PJ. "Let's hope you're the last one, PJ," she says. "Wouldn't it be great if you three all won this trip together?"

"No, see," says PJ, waving my mom off, his eyes never leaving the stage, "it—it can't be. I didn't put my name—"

"And finally," booms Principal Jones, "Peter Jacob Wilson!"

PJ's words cut short with a little choking noise. My mom and dad pat him on the shoulder and congratulate him, but none of us takes notice. PJ looks at Kendra and me, and we stare back, eyes wide. The carnival around us seems to become a blur as a feeling like little bugs made of ice spreads over my skin.

Because if PJ didn't put his name in the raffle, then someone or some*thing* else did, which means that going to Puerto Rico is probably a bad idea, because the dark forces of the universe are reaching out to us, pulling us together, and shipping us out somewhere dark and cursed (and, sure, that sounds absolutely bananas crazy, I know), but if these forces can wreck our compass on a cursed mountain, if they can bring the dead back to life as hungry brain-eating machines, they can probably write PJ's name on a raffle ticket.

And as PJ goes swamp green and stumbles toward the nearest trash can, and Kendra claps a hand to her mouth and her eyes glaze over, I can't help but feel like I did on the mountain, the last time I really knew how to be Ian, when I climbed rocks and wielded magic dream catchers and deciphered maps and outsmarted zombies like a pro.

And as Dad asks us what's wrong, I can't help but think that, yeah, PJ's right. There's magic here. This was meant to be.

CHAPTER TWO

Kendra

There is no good way to explain to one's parents that they are in grave danger from the occult. Especially when a free tropical vacation is on the line.

All night, my father *careens* (four this week—or was it three? *Come on, Kendra, when was the last time you kept your vocabulary tally? You* know *this*) around his house, making sure he hasn't forgotten anything necessary for the trip—his good swimming trunks, his allergy medicine, his "lucky fishing hat"—while I pace from one room to the next, contemplating a way to convince him that we should not get on this flight to Puerto Rico on Sunday. So far, I've crafted two different falsities—one is that I've come down with some sort of horrible sickness; the other is that I've recently fought with Ian and PJ and don't want to be in their presence anymore. Both of these excuses sound disingenuous when I say them out loud, and if they sound fake to me, my father, with his intuitive mind, will no doubt see right through them, or at the very least dismiss them.

How would I even begin?

Dad, you know the nightmares I've been having the past few months? Well, upon wandering onto a plot of cursed earth during our school trip in March, we encountered a horde of reanimated corpses—zombies, if you will—that we then had to escape from. A witch woman named O'Dea saved us; she's part of a great network of Wardens, whose job it is to protect the world at large from the undead menace. However, after tampering with her magical containment field, we freed a mob of the living dead and then had to destroy them through trickery, cunning, and hot water, which it seems melts dried-up mountainous revenants. But by taking part in their destruction, we marked ourselves as players in the game of cosmic balance, and seeing how close our destination is to the famed Bermuda Triangle, I cannot help but wonder if this vacation is an attempt by the dark powers that be to take us into their decaying arms and bite our tracheas out.

Even thinking it makes me grimace. If someone told

me such a story, I'd call 911. "Dad," I finally babble, groping for the honest truth, "about this trip. Maybe we shouldn't go."

The sound of frantic scrambling from the bathroom stops, and my dad pokes his head out, brow creased, eyes narrowed. "Shouldn't go," he repeats. "On the free all-expenses-paid vacation to Puerto Rico."

"I'm . . . feeling unsure about . . . spending time with Ian and PJ." This is slightly true, but not at all what I mean. Now I'm forced to play the emotional card. I really should have gone with *horrible sickness*.

"What do you mean?" says my father, crossing his bedroom and dropping to a knee before me. His brow is stern, but there is no anger there, only a sort of calm, focused concern. My father shows countless emotions in fractions of degrees of scrunched brow. "You three seemed like best friends when Vince Buckley picked you up here the other night."

Well, Kendra, answer him. You've decided to throw a wrench in the works—better have a good reason for mucking up the machine. Think. What's the exact opposite of the truth? What would a normal twelve-year-old girl say?

"It's just that . . . PJ is . . . incredibly gassy," I say, "and I'm worried he'll embarrass me. On the beach. And Ian is covered with strange-looking birthmarks. It's gross."

. . . I don't know what to say, Kendra. Incredible. Mensa material, this one.

21

My father's brow ripples into a *My God, she's gone insane* tightness, then relaxes knowingly. "Sweetheart," he says, "if you wanted your mother and Herman to go on this trip with you instead of me, you should have told the school when you won the prize."

Great. For two months, nothing but this. "This isn't about the divorce, Dad."

He cocks an eyebrow. "Kendra, talk to me. You know your mother and I still love you very much, right?"

My cheeks go red, and my head swims with overwhelming mortification. I could set myself on fire on the neighbor's lawn, and my father would worry that it would be about the divorce. My mouth opens to try to tell him anything—maybe even the truth—and the brick wall of *the divorce, what this is really about* stops me in my tracks. "Never mind" is all that can come out. Looking at his pained brow makes me cringe, and I turn away, leaving his bedroom. "I'm fine. Everything's fine. Forget I mentioned it."

"Kendra," he calls after me. As I climb the stairs, I hear him mumble, "Does that Buckley boy actually have an abundance of birthmarks?"

In my room, I shut the door behind me and wake up my computer. At least on the web, I don't have to worry about dark forces beyond my control.

And my ridiculous father. My mother, too, both of them.

It still doesn't make sense. Our family was fine—good, even, better than most. The three of us, two cars, a sliding cabinet in the kitchen where one puts cereal—everything added up perfectly. But then, a lot of drama, a move, new furniture, and why?

Not in love anymore.

I suppose that kind of stuff just isn't my specialty. *PJ stuff*, I'm sure Ian would call it. I'm *Queen Brain*, master of logic, solver of problems. It just confuses me, why they had to *make* the problem for us over some fictional state of emotional ecstasy.

Already, my inbox is overflowing with responses to the posts I've put on all my forums this afternoon. Diane from Montreal has some recommendations for sensitive-skin sunblock (PJ asked me about it), and David from Portland has a list of interesting fish he saw during his vacation to St. Thomas. He says the snorkeling is amazing, and that he even saw a sea turtle. My heart flutters with anticipation. While I am worried about this trip, the idea of seeing a sea turtle in the wild is too fascinating to pass up.

Here ya go, IMs Reggie from Georgia as he direct-transfers me a file on shark migration. *Went 4 spring break last year. It was beautiful. Youll luv it down there.*

Thanks, I type back.

Good talking, he types back. *You dont hit the forums much anymore.*

The last part makes me cringe a little. Reggie and I used to email a couple of times a week. This is the first exchange we've had since June—I've just been too busy spending time with PJ and Ian to notice.

The fifth email catches my breath in my throat. Sender: DoubleFeature13. Recipients: myself and ibuckley. Subject: Meeting.

got word from o'd re: trip. meet tonight 8pm at the old graveyard on feather road.
—pjw

Making excuses to my father while wracked with dread has made me lose track of time—it's been over an hour since I checked my email, an unheard-of absence on my part. Which means I should have read this at six, when it was delivered, but I did not. A glance at the clock on my desktop tells me it's 7:25. There's no time to waste.

"Dad, I'm going for a bike ride!" I call as I descend the stairs to the foyer.

My father comes into the foyer and stares down at me, midway through trying on an orange-and-yellow Acapulco shirt. His face, like his body, is all straight lines, standing like prison bars against any nonsense. His brow is a solid horizontal bar, as though drawn with a Sharpie marker.

"Is that right?" he says suspiciously.

Think, Kendra—what would convince your father, master of the poker face, that this idea is anything but uncalled for and dangerous?

"Ian and PJ want to get ice cream," I say. "Also, I need to give PJ some information regarding sunblock."

"There's ice cream in the freezer," he says. "Invite them over."

"PJ only eats soy ice cream," I tell him. "He's lactose intolerant. That's why he's so gassy, you see."

"Kendra," he says, making his sympathetic eyes again. "We have an early flight."

Before I can come up with a rational argument, his eyes spur me into action: "I am feeling self-conscious about your divorce from Mom," I say in an almost robotic tone. "Seeing my friends would be a welcome distraction from this situation."

He rolls his eyes—obviously, I'm being flippant (now that's a vocabulary word), but I've called him on his deepest worry and his broken record routine. "Be back by ten at the latest. Preferably earlier."

"Of course," I tell him and duck out the door. Precious minutes are wasting.

Mounting my bike is still a challenge—I hadn't ridden one since I was seven, before Ian and PJ became my two best friends and biking everywhere became a necessity—but I manage to get going without much wobbling. Over my shoulder, I catch my father in the window and wave to him. Perhaps my *flippancy* (let's do it, new vocab list—there's two, three to go) was a bit harsh, but I have bigger things to worry about, and he's the one who likes to bring up his and mom's separation in every situation possible.

About halfway to Big Stream Road, a bell pulls me back into reality. PJ rides up next to me, his frail little body looking dwarfed by all his pads. I'm wearing a helmet, but PJ's overprotective parents make him wear a padded suit not unlike SWAT gear.

"Any word from Ian?" I call out.

"He said he'd meet us there," gripes PJ. "I hope he doesn't get attacked by zombies on the way."

"PJ, please. For all we know, there's a logical explanation for this."

"Right," he says, rolling his eyes.

Every so often, I glance back at his skinny form biking next to me and marvel how swiftly it happened—the energetic jock, the quiet film kid, and myself becoming easy friends, becoming inseparable. But this is what I mean—we add up. Each of us fulfills a function that the others sorely need, and it helps that they are extraordinary, my friends. They are the best they are at what they do, and with one another's help we survived one of the most terrifying experiences imaginable.

Soon, the streetlights vanish, and we enter a darkened

patch of road, the silver moon our only guiding light. The wrought iron gates of the graveyard grow in the distance, as does Ian's silhouette. He waves as we skid to a halt and lock our bikes to the nearby fence.

"Did we really have to meet in a cemetery?" asks Ian. "Seems a little melodramatic, if you ask me."

"I think you mean *atmospheric*," I tell him.

"Whatever," he says, throwing up his hands. "We could've just met her at the diner."

"That's not her style," says PJ. "Besides, she's probably using the location to show us what kind of situation we're heading into."

Ian jams his hands into his pockets and chuckles darkly. "Great. Last time I visited an old graveyard, its residents came up for a visit."

I push at the wrought iron gate, but a heavy chain with a huge padlock holds it shut. Ian gives the chain a tug, just to make sure it's not simply my feminine weakness barring our way, but still nothing.

"How does she expect us to get in?" asks Ian.

"A good question," I say, taking in the shining black curvature of the fence. "She may be using this as a test of some kind—an obstacle thrown into our path. My first thought is to climb over it."

"I think I have an idea," says PJ. He reaches into his bike basket and unwraps a sheet-covered object to reveal—

"Yecch," moans Ian. "I can't believe you kept that thing."

The severed hand is greenish-brown, but glossy, shining with a coating of wax. The bits of string coming from its fingers are twisted and blackened. The whole thing is terribly macabre (a word from a few months ago, right after the zombie incident) and sends a shudder up my tailbone that ends in a gag reflex.

"It was a gift," says PJ. "You don't just throw away a Hand of Glory." PJ produces a book of matches and holds out the severed hand. "Everybody, grab on. Otherwise, the light will paralyze you."

The thing feels waxy and hideously wrinkled beneath my hand. PJ lights a match and touches it to each of the five finger-candles. At first, typical flickers of flame spring up, but then their light grows, merges, and blurs into a blinding white flash, like ignited magnesium, that seems to fill my heart with a charged giddiness that I can feel radiating off Ian and PJ as well.

Only a handful of people are worthy enough to witness magic in action.

There's a clink as the padlock comes undone by itself, and the chain falls to the ground. The gate swings open with a sickening creak. PJ blows out the Hand of Glory, and suddenly the blinding light is gone, replaced by curling wisps of blue-gray smoke.

"You know, we could use that more often," says Ian

as we enter the graveyard. "We could rob banks, paralyze everyone at school—"

"We're already too deep into the karmic balance,"
I tell Ian. "Using magic will probably only further
upset it."

He makes a sour face. "How do you know? You're
not a Warden."

My hands clench at my sides. Ian should remember
who does the best thinking here.

The old cemetery is bathed in angular shadows cast
by the antique grave markers, their leaning monolithic
shapes and carved crosses like ancient TV antennas
sprouting out of the earth. The grass is overgrown with
neglect, so much so that certain gravestones are almost
swallowed whole, and the long blades crunch loudly
under our feet. A ways off, a few lonely mausoleums sit,
their ivy-covered roofs moonlit but their doors dark and
creepily inviting.

"Maybe I was wrong," says PJ with a sour frown.
"Maybe we should get out of here."

"How old do you think this place is?" hisses Ian.

"Hard to say," I whisper, my mind rushing through
the facts of my town history project from last year,
"but I'd say the last person to be buried here must have
been . . . the early nineteen hundreds?"

"Nineteen oh-two," growls a voice in the darkness.

My nerves light up with raw energy, and all three of

us jump into the air, screaming. Whirling on the source of the sound, I spy a wiry form in gray overalls sitting hunched on a massive tombstone, her eyes glowing eerily out of the darkness.

"You could have simply met us at the gate," I say, annoyed and shaking with adrenaline.

"Just had to make sure," says O'Dea. She spiders down from her perch and steps into the moonlight, her line-covered face gripped in a scowl harder than concrete. Seeing her thin scarecrow form in the graveyard around us—the ratty overalls, the tangle of gray hair, the bony calloused hands—fills me with a chilling unease. Sometimes, recalling our adventure in March makes it seem romanticized, like one of PJ's ridiculous scary movies, full of slavering ghouls and cackling old crones, but seeing O'Dea again in all her wiry no-nonsense ill-tempered resplendence reminds me of how very real it was, how our well-laid plans of defeating the witch, destroying the monsters, and saving the day weren't so cut-and-dried.

"Make sure of what, exactly?" I say to her.

"That you guys have a knack for this sort of thing," she said. "Some dumb kids would've started calling my name like idiots or climbing over the fence. Gravediggers make their own way."

Dumb kids would've climbed over. That would be you, Kendra.

"How's the mountain life treating you?" asks PJ.

O'Dea looks at him, and her sneer becomes a smile that I can't help but envy PJ for receiving. "So much quieter since you guys left," she says. "It's bliss since you killed all those damn zombies and I put up the NO TRESPASSING signs. Haven't had so much as a moan since. Moved back into my cabin, got a cat."

"Nice," says Ian. "Congratulations on rejoining the normal world."

She rolls her eyes. "I still live with a giant dream catcher made of zombie parts, Ian. It's not exactly *Little House on the Prairie*."

"How did you find us?" I ask her, genuine curiosity building within me. "Was there a ripple in the karmic balance? Did PJ visit you as some kind of astral projection?"

"I have a box at the post office," she said. "PJ contacted me right after he won the sweepstakes, saying he smelled a rat, so I wrote him a letter and hitched a ride here." She crosses her arms. "And since I trust his instincts, I'm inclined to believe you're in some real trouble."

When I look at Ian, his irritated frown mirrors my emotional reaction—*trust* his *instincts*? Why is PJ, our resident emotional roller coaster, the one to trust?

"You think that PJ's name being inserted into this raffle was more than just a coincidence," I say. "You believe there's dark magic afoot."

"Absolutely," says O'Dea. "There's no such thing as coincidence for you three anymore. The darkness beckons—you have to answer."

"But what if we just refused to?" I ask. "Wouldn't we be thwarting the bad karma attempting to pull us in?"

"You'd be *shirking your responsibilities*," says O'Dea, looking at me as though I've insulted her. "See, being a Warden is a choice—as long as you have magic in your blood, you get a *chance* to learn the craft. But Gravediggers get chosen by the powers that be."

"But didn't the Wardens just give up on the Gravediggers?" asks PJ. "How could that happen if karma itself picks them?"

"That we did," she said, staring off into the darkness. "There was a scandal about sixty years ago, when some Gravediggers murdered Wardens, and the Council decided on a worldwide campaign among the Wardens, in which we doubled our efforts, recruited every young woman with the right mix of enchanted blood—I was one of those recruits—and forced containment like never before. Gravediggers were chosen out of necessity—so with no breaches of containment, there was no need for them. Then we put a curse on the remaining ones, threatened to kill them if they ever came around." Then those bright blue eyes pan over us, and a strange lightness comes to her voice. "And then, you kids showed up. The fact that you found your way onto my mountain, destroyed all those zombies, and survived to tell about it means that the universe has plans for you. It means that you're needed."

"*Needed*," whispers Ian, nodding. "Like we're superheroes."

"Or *slaves*," grumbles PJ.

As sure as O'Dea sounds, the worm of doubt continues to wriggle within my mind (which image, naturally, leaves me thinking of nothing but zombies). O'Dea seems to be relying too much on this vague magical history to explain our predicament. Some cold hard facts are in order.

"Are you sure we're needed as Gravediggers?" I say, pulling out my phone and bringing up a downloaded PDF. "It might be some other kind of magical interference. My immediate worry is the Bermuda Triangle, given its proximity and history of mysterious magical events—"

"Nah," says O'Dea, waving a hand at my outstretched phone.

"O'Dea, if you'll just take a quick look at this document—"

"The Bermuda Triangle is what we call a sinkhole," she drones, as though any idiot with half a brain would know this. "A weak membrane between our world and a different one. After Amelia Earhart got eaten by it in nineteen thirty-seven—"

"Earhart went down in the Pacific," I note. "Not the Atlantic."

O'Dea shoots me a look that seems to automatically close my mouth. Slowly, she continues. "As I was saying. A group of Wardens and other witches got together and sealed it up in a five-day-long ritual during which two of them went blind and one spontaneously combusted." She glares at me. "You need to trust me here, girl. Don't worry about research. You're a Gravedigger now, not a scholar."

There it is—*girl*, just like she called me on the mountain. The urge to shout the Warden down, to thrust my phone in her face and *make* her read my cold hard facts, rises in me.

And what'll that do, exactly, Kendra? What do you know about magical sinkholes and spontaneous combustion and Amelia Earhart's disappearance? It's just like on the mountain, when you burned O'Dea's dream catcher and released the zombies into the outside world. You pride yourself on your brilliant deductions and scientific know-how, but it appears that counts for nothing. You're just here to fight magically revived corpses, that's all.

PJ must feel me getting angry, because he steps into the argument. "Look, O'Dea, is there anything we *can* do?" he says. "You're telling us it's inevitable that we're going to Puerto Rico, and that Kendra's research isn't helpful." (*Oh, thanks, PJ.*) "So is there some way to at

34

least prepare for whatever we might be faced with?"

O'Dea chews on the corner of her lips. "Right. What doesn't make sense is how your name got entered into the raffle. I didn't smell or sense any zombies when I came here, so I can't imagine the dark forces are using a vessel like they did with that dead girl writing the map of the mountain for you last time. That means there's someone else helping the darkness, which isn't entirely unheard-of. But I don't know island magic—it's got a different history, different ways of doing things. For now, stay aware at all times. Don't get comfortable. Be ready for anything, all the time. Finally—" Suddenly, her head snaps up, and her eyes narrow.

"O'Dea?" asks PJ.

"Did you hear that?" she whispers.

For a moment, the night is perfectly still, and then we hear it—the soft crunch of twigs, and the sound of footsteps charging off into the distance. "HEY!" screams Ian in their direction, and begins weaving between tombstones, but already the sounds are gone, fading into the intense quiet of the churchyard around us.

"Damn," mutters O'Dea. "That mouth-breather might've been our culprit." My stomach clenches at her words, but the Warden seems relatively unfazed, simply putting her hands on her hips and shaking her head. "Well, this is a pickle."

"Do you think we could track him down?" asks Ian, rubbing his hands together.

"Probably not," she says. "Magic can only go so far." She spits and turns back to us. "Well, guys, get your bags ready. It looks like we're going to Puerto Rico."

"We?" I say.

"I certainly can't let you go alone," she says, striding past us. "Gravediggers or not, you're just kids, and no matter how much magic is involved, there's something bigger going on here, something that might involve other Wardens. It'll be best for everyone if I'm there to keep an eye on you."

"But how will you get to Puerto Rico?" asks PJ. "How will we find you?"

"Don't worry about that," she calls back, "I'll find *you*."

And just like that, she walks into the shadows of the woods around the graveyard, and she's gone, another shifting silhouette that eventually joins the curtain of shadows.

"A shame you scared that guy away," I say to Ian.

"What?" says Ian. "Oh, yeah. Well, these things happen." A smile creeps across his face. "Crazy, spies staking us out from the darkness. It's like we're secret agents. Kind of cool, huh?"

"Yeah, a blast," snaps PJ. "Our lives are at stake, Ian."

As we climb back onto our bikes, Ian says, "Remind me, what time's our flight tomorrow?"

"Six in the morning," groans PJ. "And I still have to finish packing. Stupid evil karma, making me go on some dumb vacation." He hops on his bike and rides off.

"You think *this* complaining is bad," says Ian, bounding onto his mountain bike and peddling, "just wait until we get there." He rides off into the dark, leaving me to watch my two best friends, the chaotic blur of instability and confusion filling my head, stomach, hands, and feet. As I ride home to my father, I attempt to map out possible scenarios for the coming days, but my mind draws blank after blank, leaving me hopelessly lost.

CHAPTER THREE

PJ

As I leave the brittle recycled air of the plane and step out into sunny Puerto Rico, the Caribbean reaches out and stuffs a boiled pillow over my face. The sun burns my eyes as it blazes above overgrown mountains, and heat radiates off the concrete in nuclear waves, overexposing my field of vision. As things fade into view, I can see the landscape before me is alive with colors—verdant palms in the distance, sandy browns along the concrete in front of me, a sky so deep blue you could touch it.

"We're all going to die here," I say.

"Please stop saying that," says Kendra. Ian can't stop laughing.

Up until now, our transition from airport to plane, from Wyoming to San Juan, from airplane to airport, has been a nonstop panic of light blue walls and boarding passes. Suddenly, we've got all three of our families standing out on the pavement in inferno-like weather conditions, dragging their rolling bags and checking our car reservation on their smartphones and tablets. The Buckleys both wear shades, caps, khaki shorts, and pastel polo shirts; Ian's dad had three Bloody Marys on the flight and is greeting the sun with a goofy smile under his mustache. Lennox Wright looks cool as a cucumber in his white shirt and shorts, but the hint of a smile on his face is a sign, given his demeanor the whole flight, that he's as excited as a little kid. And then, there's my family—Dad made mostly of glasses and Hawaiian shirt, Mom's messy black hair and freckles on top of her wispy yellow sundress and sandals, my kid sister, Kyra, clutching a picture book to her chest and nervously staring around the San Juan airport.

"Uh-oh," says my mom, glaring at the sun. "PJ, honey, did you put on some—"

"Yeah, Mom, I did it on the plane." By landing, I had so many layers of SPF 50 on me, I must have smelled like a pool house.

"And you brought your sunglasses," she says.

"Yeah, Mom."

"And you're hydrated."

"Mom."

"Samantha," says my dad, "please. He's on vacation." He comes up behind me and squeezes my shoulders, and I try not to cringe too much. "Doesn't this look cool, Pete?" he says. "God, look at those hills, feel that heat. This is going to be so much fun, trust me."

There's real excitement in his voice, and he has an expression of joy that I haven't seen on him in a while. No matter how much I hate this, no matter how much I want to scream my lungs out, I can't be the guy who takes it away from him. So I keep my mouth shut. Which is basically lying to him, about why we're here, about everything.

Words can't truly express how much I hate that. Before, it felt fine, keeping the secret from my family, having this strange adventure that only I knew about. But now they're involved, and that worries me.

As my mother fusses with my poor sister, making sure her backpack's closed and finding her a sun hat, Ian and Kendra sidle up next to me.

"See?" says Kendra. "It's very pretty out here. No need for alarm quite yet."

"*Sure,*" I say, "at least I'm in familiar territory. Where I speak the language. Because of a raffle I *definitely* entered."

"Be cool, man," says Ian. He's dressed like some kind of bowling prodigy—work shirt, cargo shorts,

40

fluorescent-lensed wraparounds. "We've got to relax, not let on anything's wrong. No good in alarming the families. For now, let's just enjoy ourselves."

Enjoy ourselves. When every member of our immediate families is in a place that, for all we know, is cursed. Why am I the only one who's terrified? Why am I the only human being who can see one *single foot* in front of his own *face* and realize the *incredible danger we're all*—

"PJ?" says Ian. "PJ, just calm down. You're turning white."

"Right," I say, taking a deep breath and trying to chase away the worry.

"It's beautiful out," offers Kendra. "Maybe you should get some footage. It might . . . calm you down."

Part of me appreciates the help, and part of me wants to laugh in her face. Footage of the airport? It's a camera, not a pacifier. It doesn't exactly work that way. Still, I force out a smile and a nod for them, hoping to ward off further inquiry. It's not their fault. We're up against a lot here.

Mr. Wright announces our reservation number, and we make our way toward the resort shuttles until we come across a huge white cargo van with a man next to it holding a sign reading RIGHT BUCKLE WILSON. Vince Buckley cracks some joke about how the Buckle family is up a creek, and Ian shakes his head and looks away as his old man guffaws at himself. At least I'm not alone in wanting to punch somebody.

During the shuttle ride from the airport to the resort, I watch the landscape roll by—palm trees, stretches of beach, white-painted houses with red slate roofs, and the ocean, like a green fish with shining scales all along it. Without thinking, I pull out my camera and begin recording, taking in all the blaring colors and pure sunlight of the place, and it feels as though a balm seeps out of its lens and soothes my irritated mind. This, this is the kind of thing I want to shoot. The countryside itself is beautiful, whether or not evil forces bind our trip—this isn't Tampa or Atlantic City, it's *Puerto Rico*, the Caribbean. Taking it in from behind the camera, I see lush vegetation swaying on the sunbaked hills, pastel stucco houses in the foreground, sprawling San Juan skyline in the distance. The camera seems to even channel tastes and smells, and there's spiced sauce and burning palm wood somewhere in the air.

"Say hi." The shot pans, and my dad and little sister come into view in the seat beside me. My dad and sister smile and wave into the camera, looking like an idyllic family. "Say hi, Kyra. Hi, Pete."

"Dad, I don't call him that," laughs Kyra, amused.

Panning across the van, I catch Kendra and her dad, both of their faces lit spectral blue as they stare into their smartphones. As I reach my mom, she messes with her hair as though it'll help and gives me a big, broad smile, and I can't help but smile back. Then, I focus in on Ian, staring intently out the window like a Labrador retriever, his eyes as big as dinner plates, his nose flattened against the glass. Ian Buckley, my perpetual protagonist.

The van slows down due to traffic, and our driver, a round man with light brown skin and a bushy mustache, apologetically tells us a football game has just let out.

"There's football—you mean *soccer*?" Ian gasps. "Dad, can we go to a soccer game while we're here?"

"I don't see why not," says Mr. Buckley. "Your mother would probably enjoy some alone time to hit the spa." Ian's mom moans and clutches a hand to her heart.

Ian looks away from the glass smiling and catches sight of my camera aimed at him. For a split second, I prepare myself for the hand slapped over the lens, but instead he gets this excited smile on his face and salutes the camera.

"And PJ with his camera!" he says excitedly. "Just like old times!"

"Oh, put it away, PJ," gripes his dad, holding the inevitable hand out. "We all just got off the plane—we don't want to be remembered this way."

Ian starts waving his hands and saying "No" in protest, but I've already lowered the camera, and suddenly the harsh acidic world around me—the raging sun, the cramped van on the bumpy road, the overpowering smell of sunblock coming off me—it all comes flying back. My whole body, sweaty from the humidity, sticky from the lotion and still aching from the long flight stuffed in a coach seat, feels uncomfortable and raw, and I can't help but let a scowl cover my face.

My dad pats my leg and flashes a stink-eye over his shoulder at Vince Buckley, but it's little solace. But my scowl is not just at Ian's dad, it's at the whole situation, at *being here*. I made a point of *not* signing up for the stupid raffle so that I *wouldn't* end up getting pulled into some kind of zany adventure.

It didn't use to be like this, before the mountain. Then, I was scared, terrified of the world around me; every bug and spore and poisonous oily plant sent me into a full-on panic attack, and I kept a list in my back pocket of things my mom said to watch out for, every-thing from ticks to black mold, all straight out of the pages of magazines like *Growing Boy* and *A Mother Knows*. Back then, I feared everything. These days, it's like I hate it. All my folks ever wanted me to do was break out of my shell, but once I did, I found out that my skin was red and sensitive and burned at the touch of the world. I could watch horror movies, and they took me somewhere else, somewhere strange and dangerous that I'd never have to experience because these mon-sters were onscreen constructions. But these days, those movies are just coming attractions for my everyday life.

Because make no mistake—the world *will* try to kill you. There *is* danger out there, a horrible world full of dangerous monsters, and it hates you. So it makes sense, doesn't it? To just . . . hate back.

Worst of all, I can't tell anyone. My parents can't know, or they'll put me in an institution. My little sister will freak out if she thinks we might get attacked by the flesh-eating dead. And Ian and Kendra just don't seem to care. They're too busy being the dynamic duo, Ian with his muscles, Kendra with her brains.

"Where exactly are we going?" asks Ian's mom, Emily.

"About thirty minutes outside of San Juan," says Kendra. "Our resort is called Necesidad."

"*Necesidad*," intones Kendra's dad. "Kendra, that means what, exactly?"

"It means *necessity*," says Kendra, almost groaning.

"Some beautiful country out there, huh?" says my dad over my shoulder. "That camera's going to be a life-saver. You're going to have some incredible footage."

"Sure," I say, trying not to wince. He has no idea what could be waiting for us here.

Finally, we roll up to a collection of stately white buildings. The front entrance has a fountain covered with stone angels. Our driver ushers us into a massive marble lobby filled with columns and leather couches, its ceiling high and domed with a stained glass window at the very top. The inside of the lobby is cool, relaxing; piano music plays somewhere in the background, and there's a smell like the ocean and desert. My camera never leaves my hand—this may not be the best footage per se, but it's good filler to take my mind off my impending death. After all, last time, we barely escaped alive what was waiting for us. We were, more than anything else, *incredibly* lucky. And as much as I'd like to believe that we can do that again, I just don't know.

As our parents make their way to the front desk, Ian and Kendra and I spin around and take the place in.

"Whoa," says Ian, "fan-*cee*."

"I'm surprised someone donated a trip to set us up in such a nice resort," mumbles Kendra.

"We're all going to die here," I inform them.

Kendra throws me a pleading stare. "PJ, please," she says. "Can you at least pretend, for now, that you're having a good time?"

Easy for her to say. She put her name in the raffle, despite being our resident genius. I was the only one smart enough to try to stay behind. "Just because it's nicely decorated doesn't mean it's not the belly of the beast."

"Some beast," says Ian, and whistles.

Up in the suite I'm sharing with my sister, I'm in the bathroom, wrestling to try to put on these "frame-supporting" swimming trunks my mom bought for me, and I think I've just found out how to tighten the snap front that's supposed to keep me from garroting my guts in half, when Kyra calls out from the room, "PJ? Are you okay?"

"Yeah," I grunt, "it's just that I think Mom bought my swim shorts from the guy from *Saw*."

"I mean . . . is something wrong?"

I poke my head out to find her staring at me worriedly, like when my mom thinks she already knows what's wrong. Her huge brown eyes glisten like puddles in her round, freckled face, and her mouth is a tiny little inverted U beneath them.

"What would be wrong?" I ask, finally snapping my waistband together and joining her.

"You just seem . . . upset," she says.

"It's nothing," I tell her. "I'm just . . . not used to the heat."

"But this trip," she says, "it's not like that time you got lost in the woods, is it? With the . . . you know."

Maybe I should never have mentioned the zombies to Kyra. I had to tell someone, and she actually loved the bedtime stories, hung on every word as I told her about dangling above a gang of living dead people and crawling around an art room as half of a corpse chased me. But now she's caught me red-handed.

"It's nothing like that," I tell her, "promise."

She's silent for a moment, and then she says, "Maybe we should talk to Mom and Dad."

A firework goes off in my chest, and for a moment it's like the room goes soft-focus, with little white dots swimming in my vision. "No. Don't do that."

"They might be able to help—"

"There's nothing they can—I made it up," I say, waving my hands in front of my face and shaking my head. "It's fake, Kyra. The whole thing was just a story. Don't tell anyone? I lied. It never happened. We just hid in a cave and nearly starved on that mountain. Forget it."

My sister nods obediently, but she still looks like she's going to burst into tears at any moment. There's nothing else I can think of to say. I motion for her to follow me, and we head to the elevator in silence.

We meet the rest of the families downstairs; Ian's folks and Kendra's dad are talking to someone I don't recognize at first. Ian and Kendra wave us over to the families; Ian's now rocking khaki-colored swim trunks and a white shirt, and Kendra's wearing shorts over a bathing suit. They both bite their lips and try not to laugh.

"What?" I ask.

"Dennis, Samantha, this is Ms. Foree," says Ian's mom, motioning to my parents. "She's an activities coordinator who'll be running things with the kids."

"A pleasure," says "Ms. Foree." "I look forward to

getting to know your lovely children."

To be fair, we've only ever seen O'Dea in jeans and flannel, so seeing her like this—Hawaiian shirt, sun hat, cargo shorts, sandals, her wild-woman hair pulled back into a ponytail—is too much. Before I can stop myself, I snort hard with a laugh. Kendra's dad looks at me funny.

"Nothing," I squeak, reeling with giggles. "Had a frog in my throat."

"What's your background in child care?" asks my mother suspiciously.

For a second, O'Dea's face goes blank, but then a weird smile creeps across her face, and she says, "I looked after a group of hellions for a family in Montana. The Wardens. Helped raise their kin for as long as I can remember."

"You seem a little old to be a resort employee," says Mr. Wright.

O'Dea looks for a moment like she might tell him he's a little short for this world, but she manages to force a smile and clutch her black binder to her chest like she's some kind of teenage babysitter. "Well, you know, the kids, eh . . . keep me young at heart."

"Well, just so you know," says my mother, "PJ has some trouble with added gluten and imitation meats, and he can break out in a little dry red patch if he handles too much nut oil. If he gets a little tired, I find these vitamin gummies help. Also, please try to keep him away from most red snapper or beach-caught fish, because I've just read something about tongue-eating lice being a problem in snapper from this region of the world. Oh, and one more thing. . . ." As she pours a handful of vitamin candy onto O'Dea's binder, she leans in and whispers something into the Warden's ear. Though I can't hear what they're saying, both of them look at me at once, O'Dea with a startled expression crossing her face, meaning it's one of three things that I'm not very interested in discussing.

"Okay, that's it," I say. "We're leaving. We're gone. Come on, *Ms. Foree*, let's go enjoy some of those good times you have planned for us." Slowly, after multiple hugs given and kisses blown, our parents let us go.

"Sweetheart?" asks my dad as my sister clutches his leg. "Don't you want to go with PJ?" Kyra looks at me for a moment, expectantly, but I wave them away. If something *does* happen, Kyra can't be in danger. Period.

The minute we get outside the resort, we all pause to drink in O'Dea's new outfit and laugh ourselves silly. O'Dea nods, gritting her teeth, hand on her hip.

"I'm sorry," I moan. "You look great. It's just that . . . *you* . . . in *beachwear* . . ."

"Yeah, yeah," she snaps, "yuk it up."

"How'd you even get to Puerto Rico?" I ask her.

"Oh, it wasn't that bad," she said. "I Wardened my way out here this morning."

"*Wardened?* What does that mean?"

She shrugs. "Simple magic. Hypnotize a few bag checkers, make some supermarket receipts look like a boarding pass . . . Warden stuff. Harmless juju."

"Are you kidding me?" asks Kendra. "You broke the law to get out here?"

"Not my laws," she says. "Besides, my job is to protect the balance and, the way I see it, make sure you kids don't get killed. So I used magic to get out here instead of a credit card. Small price."

"You're ridiculous," I tell her.

"You're one to talk," she says with a sneer. "That's one *nasty* allergic reaction your mom mentioned back there."

My cheeks burn like the sun. Aha. So it was Topic I Don't Want to Talk About Number Two.

"So this is your plan," says Kendra. "Pretend to be our guardian during the day?"

"Pretty much," she says. She taps her binder with a long bony finger. "On the plus side, I made the entertainment manager think I was some twentysomething who worked here and talked my way into all sorts of cool freebies. Free snorkeling coupons, passes to a beachside barbecue, the whole thing. For now, let's just play this like we're actually on vacation and see how it goes."

"Awesome," says Ian. He gives the mountain witch

another once-over and shakes his head. "Wow, O'Dea. *Shorts.* You really went all out."

"Better believe it," she says. "Shaved my legs and everything."

A hand touches my shoulder, and before I know it, I'm up, snorting, throwing my back up against the headboard.

Side effect of surviving zombie peril: you become a light sleeper.

"Hey, man," says Ian, smiling. He's in his trunks and a tank top. "Calm down, it's just me."

I wipe the sleep from my eyes and glance at the window—barely light. "What time is it?"

"Keep your voice down," he whispers, pointing to Kyra in the next bed. "It's early. Kendra has some crazy morning activity planned for us. Get dressed."

For the first time this trip, I comply without argument, pulling on my trunks and grabbing my camera. The previous night flashes back in my mind—swimming in the cool blue ocean, tossing a Frisbee on the beach with Ian, devouring huge plates of plantains and barbecued pork—and for a moment, I wonder if maybe, just maybe, we might be okay here.

Kendra and O'Dea meet us out on the beach a ways down from our resort, standing next to a Puerto Rican man in board shorts. He salutes as we approach him.

"This is Esteban," says Kendra. "He'll be taking us out on the water this morning."

"What are we doing?" I ask.

She grins. "Well," she says, "*I've* never seen a whale before."

Ian and I coo at once. Without thinking, I begin stroking my camera. A whale tail breaking through the ocean is the ultimate footage for a nature photographer.

"I'm still not sure this is a great idea," says O'Dea, and my spirits start sinking.

"O'Dea, you've sensed no negative karma in this area so far, have you?" asks Kendra. O'Dea grumbles an agreement. "We'll be safe. This is a publicly visited section of ocean, anyway—there are four more tours within the hour."

We climb into Esteban's old wooden motorboat. He yanks the cord, the outboard rumbles to life, and we cut out into the ocean, skipping along the surface as we depart from land. Soon, the beach and the resort are just dots in the distance. In the early morning light, the sky is a full blue with thick scrambled-egg yellow creeping over the green hills of the horizon. The water, clear and serene blue out by the beach, turns a darker navy-green. Tiny dots of smaller islands pass us, strips of white beach topped with great frizzy outcroppings of palm trees and underbrush.

As we bounce along the water, I look at everyone's

faces, and they're all smiles—all except O'Dea's. Her bony hands clutch at her stomach, and between her lips, I see her gritted teeth. Is she seasick?

Suddenly, the boat takes a sharp left, and Esteban leans on the gas, sending us flying through the air and then landing loudly back in the boat. In the distance, a patch of silhouettes grows into an island, its tops separating into bushy trees. As we close in on it, Esteban cuts the motor, and we drift slowly toward the island, its shores leading to a great hilly uprising covered in lush green jungle. The only clouds I've seen all day, misty and gray, float over its bushy ridges, faintly touching them.

"What is this?" asks Kendra worriedly. "What's going on here?"

There's something floating on the water ahead of us, bobbing up and down in the surf—a buoy, maybe, but not your typical white-and-red affair. This is black, made of old weathered wood. As we come around it, I notice a face carved into it, like you see on old Hawaiian tikis, with gaping hollow eyes and a mouth full of fearsome blocky teeth.

"A place of legend," says Esteban, tossing a looped rope around the buoy. "The locals say . . . it's cursed."

O'Dea grunts, practically doubling over in pain. "We shouldn't be here—" Suddenly, her eyes go wide, full of genuine fear. "They're down there," she says in a voice as inky and deep as the ocean. "We need to leave."

"Not yet!" says Esteban, holding up his hand and grinning. "My employer told me to bring you here. He says that you must visit him on Isla Hambrienta."

"Isla Hambrienta," repeats Kendra softly. "The hungry island."

Ian and I look at each other, jaws dropping. The blood drains out of my face in the matter of seconds.

I hate being right.

And then we hear it—a sharp hissing sound, like the fuse of a firework, cuts through the air.

We all turn to the island, where something rises from the trees—a ball of light, twinkling like a star, followed by a tail of white smoke. It curves and then flies straight toward us. Suddenly, the boat is a mass of wrestling voices, and I have my camcorder only halfway raised before the projectile swoops down, hits the tiki, and explodes in a ball of fire.

CHAPTER FOUR

Ian

At first, it's just a boom, and then air sweeps past me like I'm in midlayup, or like I've jumped off the high-dive at the public pool, a blast of force in every direction all over the place, and when I hit the water, I barely feel it. But suddenly I'm deep, way deep, and I don't know which way is up and I can't see anything. There's that fuzzy slushing sound of other stuff hitting the water, and my eyes burn as I open them for a second and take in something weird and heavy and gray moving past me, and the lens cap fluttering after it like a tail makes me realize it's PJ's camera, drifting down into the ocean toward the murky black bottom—

Wait, I gotta focus. Gotta find air. Gotta figure out what the in *heck just happened.* Then light shimmers on my face, and I see a bit of sky through the water, so I pump my arms and make my way toward it.

The first breath I take is the sweetest thing I've ever tasted, but the minute it's over, the sweetness stops. The surface is a disaster area, total destruction, pieces of burning driftwood and gears from the motor everywhere, big salty waves hitting me in the face, that huge wooden statue looking like an exploded cigar butt bobbing around the water, and no sign of people, nothing, no one.

This last part takes a few seconds to hit me as I paddle around the surface, but man, when it does—

"PJ!" I scream. "KENDRA! O'DEA!"

Nothing. No answer. My pulse does double time and my hands go numb. This can't be happening.

Half of our boat, now just a big splintered slab of wood, drifts past me, and I grab onto it, my legs already hurting from treading water, pushing myself up. I look around the oily disaster area of the water, but there's only debris, no people.

Then the water explodes next to me, and this thing pops out, a mass of black tangles and a gaping mouth sucking in air, and every impulse in my body screams *"ZOMBIE!"* but then I realize that the weird stringy coating on the face is hair that I've only ever seen defying gravity in a big stupid poof.

"Here!" I shout, and Kendra's hands follow my voice and connect with the driftwood. Once she's breathed for a few seconds and wiped the hair out of her face, I ask, "PJ? Have you seen PJ?"

"What—oh God. Oh no." Kendra desperately scans the water, eyes blazing and mouth open, then points and shrieks, "*THERE!*"

PJ's floating with a bunch of debris around him, facedown, not moving.

It's like someone fires a starting gun—I'm off the driftwood, pounding through the water, grabbing PJ, turning him over, dragging him backward so that we can see his face. He's pale and salt water drips out of his mouth. He looks like a dead fish—no, that's not it, come on, I know what he looks like; he looks like one of the things we spent hours running from on the mountain. He looks like death warmed over, which opens up this pit in my stomach where all my blood and guts just flush into like a toilet, my feet stop kicking, I can't move or hear or breathe, just stare at his pale gross face—

A hand clenches hard around my chin and Kendra yanks my face toward hers, looking hard in my eyes. "I said, let's get to shore, okay?" she screams, and something deep inside of me unfreezes. I nod, and we start to kick. We call for O'Dea the whole time we paddle to shore while pushing this hunk of boat and my oldest friend in front of us, but there's no sign of her.

The minute I feel sand under my feet, I drag PJ off the boat and onto the shore and start shaking him. Normally, when he's conscious, his weird, worrisome personality makes him seem as big as me, but limp in my arms, I can feel how tiny he is, how scrawny, like a doll or something, and my throat hurts as I shake his body and yell, "WAKE UP WAKE UP WAKE UP—"

"Move over," snaps Kendra, shoving me away and laying PJ out. She pinches his nose, puts her mouth to his, and gives him CPR. His chest inflates for a second, then falls. Then she puts her hands together and pumps on his chest, one two three.

"You've got to wake him up!" I scream. "You've got to bring him back! I can't—he won't—*Kendra!*"

"Calm down!" she shrieks at me, then goes back down to PJ. The third time she pumps his chest, I figure that's it, he's done for, that we survived that mountain full of living corpses for nothing, because now he's dead thanks to a ball of fire and some seawater—

PJ's eyes fly open and his body shakes like he's being electrically shocked. A jet of water flies out of his mouth, and he rolls onto his side, coughing and hacking. Kendra exhales hard, lets her hands fall slack at her side, and flops back on the sand, staring skyward, but I'm already at PJ's side, putting a hand on his shoulder.

"You okay?" I ask him. "Can you hear me?"

After about a minute of coughing, including this deep wet gurgle that results in a bunch of gross white foam coming out of his mouth, he shrugs off my hand. "I'm okay," he rasps. "What, what happened? Where are we?"

"The island," I tell him. "Isla Whatever. Kendra and I swam you to shore."

He finally sits up and looks at us both, and I watch the situation sink into his mind slowly. "Are you two okay?"

It's the first really nice thing he's said to us since we got to Puerto Rico. "We're good, I think. Kendra?"

From the ground next to us, Kendra whispers a shuddering "Yes."

The sight of red on the sand next to her jacks my heart rate back up. "No you're not! You're bleeding!"

"A scratch . . . a nail in the driftwood . . ." She gulps. "I'll be fine."

"Let me take a look at it." I go to check out her scratch, but she pulls away.

"I said I'm fine," she says. "Please just give me a second, Ian."

Am I the only person here who realizes what we just went through? Yeah, PJ's yakking up half the ocean and Kendra's feeling all wasted from having to bring him back to life, but it's like I'm some salty pain in the butt here, not their *friend* trying to give them some *help*!

What, no thanks for directing Kendra to the driftwood that saved our lives—

PJ sits up, his eyes fixed hard on the horizon. "Where's O'Dea?"

The three of us scan every inch of the water, but there's no sign of O'Dea or Esteban, no frizzy white hair, no cheesy Hawaiian shirt, no nothing. Kendra and I swam farther than I thought, 'cause the last pieces of that floating wooden head are a dot in the distance. Even the bits of the boat and stuff have started to sink— every few seconds, some big piece of wood upends in the water, and then there's a hiss and a burble as it goes down, down, sunk. The ocean seemed blue and inviting before, and now looks inky and mean, like it was only pretending to be my friend.

And I just . . . don't know what to do. I call out her name, wade out into the surf and back, I even try drawing one of O'Dea's weird sigil things (spooky magical markings involving circles and crosses that make you think of a henna tattoo and a crop circle all at once) in the sand with my finger in the hopes of, I don't know, Gravedigger-summoning her or something. Nothing. The whole time. My head's a blank; my hands and feet feel big and dumb and useless; in fact my whole body, *I*, am useless.

"We should walk the beach," says Kendra finally. "They may have washed up a ways down from us."

Makes sense. A few pieces of wood from the boat have drifted ashore, so I take one and jam it into the sand—"So we'll know where we started," I say, and Kendra nods approvingly—and we get moving.

"Keep your eyes out for my camera," mumbles PJ, rubbing his hands together. "I mean, obviously, O'Dea's the important thing, but if you see it . . ."

The island is bigger than it looked from out in the water, and the whole way down the beach, it's the same thing—a stretch of just beautiful white beach, and then a wall of palm trees and shadows that trails off into forever. One ear gets crashing waves, the other gets buzzing insects.

When I stare into the jungle, I won't lie, it gets to me. There, a few yards of sand away from us, is vegetation like I've never seen, a wall of the greenest trees with the gnarliest trunks in the world, and then just darkness behind it, broken up by the occasional low-hanging vine and furry trailing moss. With no human beings coming by a little island like this often, nature has just gotten overgrown, and we're greeted with a mass of leaves the size of surfboards, piles of dead plants knee deep, all of it so colorful and bright against the neon blue sky that it feels like it's screaming at me.

And the sounds, man. I don't freak out about animals the way PJ does—to be honest, I was dying to see me some whale action—but the clicking and shrieking and humming and slithering and hooting that comes spilling out between the cracks of this huge maze of plant life isn't like the sounds of any animal I've ever seen crawl and fly; it's like the sounds of everything going crazy. So maybe that's where we are, with the heat pounding down on our face and nothing but miles of water in every direction—we're in Mother Nature's insane asylum, where all the crazy stuff goes to get big and run free.

On another trip, I think, a *normal* trip, the sand would feel soft and fun beneath my feet, and the ocean would be soothing and warm. Instead, it's a rock and a hard place, and I'm stepping on coals.

After five minutes of marching with no sign of O'Dea, I have to ask: "Anyone have a clue what happened out there?"

"It looked like someone shot that tiki with a missile, and it took out our boat with it," says PJ, shuddering.

"*Tikis* are the totemic statues of the Pacific cultures like the Maori," recites Kendra. "This was more of a *zemi*."

"Right, but who?" I ask. "Do you think they were trying to hit us?"

"Probably," says Kendra, her voice cold and dead. She wrings out her hair, and then whoosh, it all stands right back up.

"What do we think?" I ask her. "Was that magic?

Like, black magic? If this island's cursed, could it actually shoot some kind of magic missile at us?"

"Maybe," she says. "I didn't get a good look at it before it hit that buoy, or whatever it was. But it could just as easily been, I don't know, pirates, using this island as a base, or some kind of political guerilla regime. The Caribbean has a long history of unseemly characters using desert islands as their private bases of operations."

"What was that Esteban said about his employer?" I say. "Who was that, do you think?"

"I figured he meant the hotel," said Kendra with a shrug. "I went down to the information desk with a whale-watching brochure last night, and he was waiting there for me."

"I see something," says PJ, and he goes trotting off. Kendra and I catch the dark patch in the water too, and we follow him.

Esteban's shirt is all one flat piece now, ripped in half down the back, and its edges are torn, full of holes. Part of it is stained with some kind of dark fluid, and as I pull it out of the surf, the water that drips off it is kind of cloudy and smelly.

Feeling it heavy in my hand, seeing it all torn up, that just seals it. All the feelings I felt on the mountain—that gaping emptiness with a pinch of nausea, that leap in my heart rate that's the opposite of cardio, that nagging feeling that nothing's all right and the jungle behind us actually *hates us*—come blasting back into me. One glance at PJ and Kendra tells me they're feeling the exact same thing, that horrible punch to the guts. Without thinking, I let the shirt drop out of my hand and wonder where Esteban went.

"Well," I say, trying to choke down the lump in my throat, "let's start discussing our options—"

"*O'DEA!*" screams PJ, doubling over. "*O'DEA, THIS ISN'T FUNNY, SAY SOMETHING! PLEASE DON'T LEAVE US HERE!*" But his screams sound tiny on this open beach, with the waves crashing and the jungle buzzing and hissing and the blue glittering surface of the sea stretching out for what seems like forever.

He screams her name a few more times before Kendra resignedly says, "PJ, please stop. You'll go hoarse, and it doesn't appear to be helping."

He goes quiet, face pale, hands clutched at his chest, mouth open in a scream that flops into a frown. "That's it then," he says. "What'd I say back at the resort? We're done for. We barely survived without O'Dea the *last* time we did something like this."

"PJ, dude, she's got a point," I say, putting a hand on his shoulder. "We don't have time for moping right now—"

"Get offa me!" he shouts, wheeling around and standing at once, flinging my hand off his shoulder and getting right up in my face. "I'm not *moping*! I'm *mourning*! Our friend just disappeared and *we're next!*" He grabs my shirt hard enough for it to be a shove, and I feel my patience running on fumes, so I give him a nice little shove right back and he goes stumbling backward. There's a second there when he looks real ticked, like he wants to launch at me, but I can feel myself setting solidly—legs apart, arms up at my sides. He must see it too, because it's like the angry just spreads out through him, and he wraps his arms around himself and glares into the sand.

This is what I'm talking about—since when does PJ ever *consider* fighting me? Not that'd he'd lose, necessarily (I might be sick, missing one hand, and drugged), but that's not him! He's a nice guy, not a fighter, the kind of guy you can talk to without being worried that he's going to do something dumb like shove you for no reason! I mean, if anything, that's supposed to be *me*— but here I am, trying to be cool to my friends while he gets to go berserk.

"Calm down," says Kendra calmly. "Both of you."

I try. I try so hard to push down the energy like everyone says I should. But I can't. The heat and the sand and the fireball nearly killing us, all that I could stand, but PJ shoving me just doesn't compute. It's like there's something bad going on here, something gross in the air that makes all my muscles tense up and my arms and legs tingle with this sharp prickly feeling. There's something here that's out of place. I can taste it in the seawater and smell it in the breeze and hear it somewhere in the sound of the waves, like the roar you hear when you hold a big shell to your ear.

When the thought crosses my mind, it hits me like a sack of bricks: I can hear *myself*, because it's quiet. When we got here, all I could hear were birds and insects, buzzing and shrieking and doing their jungle thing. Now, silence, except for the crash of the waves and the rustle of the trees—

And then the drums kick in.

It's a steady, pounding beat, like someone slowed down a drum roll, played on some kind of basic hand drum, like some serious bongos, coming from deep within the jungle. At first I figure, great, there's someone nearby, we're saved. And then I think, no, we're doomed, because the drumbeat fills my ears, vibrates down the sides of my neck and into my bones, and Kendra and PJ are covering their ears, so I know I'm not just having some kind of salt water–inspired seizure or whatever.

I turn away from the jungle, feeling this kind of dizziness spread through my body, and when I look into the ocean, my eyes catch a dark shape way off in the water, swirling with movement. At first, I figure it's some seaweed or a fish, but then . . .

Then I watch the dark shape move toward the shore and split into a bunch of little pieces, swaying shapes like moving shadows that seem to creep their way through the water, closer and closer to the shore, little pieces of the shadow turning into things I recognize, parts of people, clouds of rags. The farther forward they come, the lower the water gets over them, the better I can pick out shapes, colors—

Eyes.

And yeah, that's when I straight-up lose it.

"Let's get moving!" I yell, pointing to the water. "They'll be here any second."

Kendra frowns. "What?"

"Don't you remember O'Dea right before our boat got blown up?" I shout. "She was all in pain, and she said, 'They're below us' or something like that. What else would she be talking about?"

Kendra blinks, then closes her eyes and says, "Oh no."

As if on cue, the first one breaks the surface of the water.

He was once an older man, but now he's something else, something disgusting. His eyes are milky and white, and the skin on his jowls is all bloated and flaky. His skull has a hole on its left side, out of which crawls a hermit crab. His tie-dyed shirt and cargo shorts are stained in black fluid and seaweed, the pockets bulging with seawater. In fact, seawater pours out of every part of him, his mouth and eyes and ears, all colored funny by rotting black blood that dribbles with it in sandy currents. His eyes, fat white circles like cocktail onions, settle on us. He opens his mouth, and out comes a moan, not like the dry raspy moaning that came out of the ones we found on the mountain, but a deep, gurgling sound, pushed up out of his guts. As he moans, a huge clump of seaweed falls out of his mouth.

Finally, I know what to do. As he walks slimily onto the beach, hands outstretched and throat bulging, the horror of seeing this creature is like the key turning in me, and then we have ignition, and I go running full speed at the horrible rubbery corpse and rear back a haymaker that's going to send him spinning, and—

"IAN!" shrieks Kendra.

And just as I raise my fist, the surf is totally full of them. One by one, the tops of their heads break the water, and they slime their way up onto the sand, their skin bloated gray and sagging like deflated balloons, their clothes all tourist outfits—bikinis, swim trunks, white captain's shirts. They all spew seawater and hang with kelp, their bodies moving in weird, lazy swings of arms and legs—unlike the stiff, dried-up mountain zombies, these creatures look like they've got joints made of rubber, their hips moving from side to side, their heads rolling around on their shoulders, their knees bending low and popping. There are men, women . . . and kids.

Oh God, there are tons of kids, little boys with broken legs as they drag cracked plastic buckets, little girls without noses in neon-colored onesies. And there are more of them than we've ever seen, man. By the looks of the dark shapes in the water, they go on forever, off into the ocean and all along the shore.

Zombies, as far as the eye can see.

Just like that, the rushing powerful energy that's been surging in my blood freezes, goes solid, leaving me with a rigid feeling inside. The whole army of floaters shuts me down, so that even my shaking hands and chattering teeth just *stop*, leaving me stuck there in the surf, fist pulled back, looking at this pale dripping dead man who's leading an entire army of bloated corpses toward me.

There's this loud, wet yelling sound, and then PJ darts forward and lands a sharp backhand on the first zombie, whose head snaps to the side with a moan before he stumbles back into the ocean with a loud splash.

"That felt good," huffs PJ, and I wonder if that punch was meant for me.

"Not now!" shrieks Kendra. She slaps my shoulder a few times and yells my name, but I'm still stuck, barely blinking. "Something's wrong. PJ, please help me." She and PJ grab my shoulders just as I stumble backward, the approaching army of snot-fleshed monsters only a few yards away, snapping their teeth and slowly extending their corroded claws. Already, the male zombie PJ punched is rising out of the surf, his jaw dangling off on one side with a big knob of bone popping out of it that makes my stomach tremble.

"Oh geez," moans PJ, "what do we do with him?"

Through the haze, I can almost hear Kendra think.

"We head into the jungle," she says. "Anything in there has to be better than . . . them."

For a moment, the dead are all about to snatch me up and tear me to pieces, just like I always imagined only with more floral-print clothing—and then everything changes as Kendra and PJ drag me, Ian Buckley of one-time basketball fame, into a vibrant tunnel of green.

CHAPTER FIVE

Kendra

A Researcher's Introduction to the Zombie, by Kendra Wright

A zombie (from the Haitian zumbi, *Kikongo for "fetish," which in this context means "an inanimate object with magical powers"), also known widely as a ghoul, revenant, or the living dead, is a soulless corpse reanimated by curses and witchcraft. Slow-moving and essentially brain-dead, these fleshy automatons return to the physical world upon dying in an area of the world damned by some form of historical bloodshed. These creatures seem to have only one goal in* their undead state—to devour living flesh, be it human or animal. Moreover, their very beings are toxic, and one bite or scratch from a zombie will cause the victim to die and become reborn as a zombie themselves. (The mechanics of this transformation are as yet unknown—whether the bite kills and the curse revives, or whether the zombie's saliva or flesh actually causes both death and reanimation.)

But what they lack in mental faculties or supernatural abilities, zombies possess in blind strength, the inability to feel pain of any kind, and an almost complete lack of mortality— indeed, it appears that the only way to destroy one of these creatures is through complete bodily dismemberment, until there is simply nothing left to attack you. Moreover, zombies tend to travel in numbers, as lone individuals do not often traverse the cursed regions in which they are found. Rather, it is usually exploratory groups that unwittingly find themselves doomed to life after death.

In this researcher's initial experiences, these creatures were found on a mountain in Montana, and were therefore decently mummified by the dry air and overexposure experienced in such an environment. As such, while a mix of human

ingenuity and their own stupidity dispatched
the bulk of the hostiles, it was found that such
creatures could be liquefied by applying hot water
to their desiccated flesh.

Which is why this researcher finds herself at an impasse.

These monsters that rise from the water—an army of undead tourists, designer beach clothes hanging from their swollen forms, brine-soaked romance novels clutched in their inhuman hands—are not only unaffected by hydration, but it looks like they're mostly made of seawater: these aren't the dried, leathery creatures we encountered on the mountain, but pale, gelatinous gobs of meat that look like mucus in human form.

Their wounds, open and oozing, are stringy and waterlogged, and instead of flies crawling on them, they have the vermin of the sea: crabs and barnacles and small fish. One woman's rotten face has a small octopus quivering its way up the side. A little boy's arm stump is crawling with sea urchins. An anemone, pink and limp in the open air, bulges out of a tall man's eye socket. This only goes to show that we were somewhat lucky with our last interaction with the undead, as those creatures existed in a relatively cool environment, and were encountered before the summer months, when vermin would pose a problem. These creatures are made only more abominable by their environment, draped and drenched with bottom-feeders and scavengers, representing every nightmare one has ever pictured when considering the sea.

And now, Kendra, all the rules you think were in place are gone. Water as a weapon doesn't work here, no matter what your previous experience tells you. But even worse than that, your fellow Gravediggers aren't playing by the rules anymore. Here's little earnest film geek PJ Wilson, shoulder to shoulder with you and cursing through tears and terror while you two drag Ian Buckley, the fearless jock with the iron stomach, as he stares wide-eyed at the oncoming horde of living dead, a shoelace of vomit hanging from the corner of his mouth.

All because you wanted to witness whales in their natural beauty. Congratulations.

Most of my time leading up to this moment has been spent researching the Caribbean environment and the witchcraft religion Santeria, but now that we're in the jungle itself, I realize how out of my league I am. Glossy green palm leaves and low-hanging branches slap into us as we bound and jump through the jungle, a hilly mesh of vines, roots, and strange trees that seem to grow at non-Euclidian angles. All three of us are good about snaking through narrow openings between trunks and leaping over large foot-snagging rocks beneath us (it helps that PJ isn't hobbled by a twisted ankle, as he was in our last adventure). All the while, the foliage around us shudders with the sound of animals fleeing from us, and the air, practically water itself with the humidity, suffocates us.

A pang of disappointment pierces my panic as sweat pours down my scalp and every square centimeter of my skin seems to itch in tandem. My research was rushed, my preparation worthless. I never even imagined I could be somewhere as wild as this.

"Did you see them?" yelps Ian as we make our way deeper and deeper into the jungle. He finally stands up and shakes off our grip, staring back to where, off in the distance, the crashing and moaning of the walking dead grow. "That's, like, *waaaay* more than last time! And the way they looked, all bloated and gross from being under water for however long?" He makes a throat noise and expectorates into the underbrush. "Oh man, how long you think they've been down there? How are there *that many* zombies under the water around here? You think *they're* what got O'Dea and Esteban?"

"Yeah," mumbles PJ, "probably." His eyes clench shut, and he swears under his breath.

They're already coming apart, Kendra—Ian's freezing act, PJ's irritation. Take control of this situation.

"We need to keep moving," I tell them. "At least until we find whoever was playing those drums." The two of them look unimpressed. "Guys, this is not our first . . . zombie rodeo. If we survived the mountain, we can survive this."

That seems to revive their spirits at least slightly: Ian squares his shoulders, bounces on his ankles, and says, "Right on." PJ blinks the fears out of his eyes, takes a slow deep breath, and nods stoically.

The jungle we wade through is thick and heavy with life—as we crunch through massive ferns and tall grass, the ground writhes with insects, reptiles, frogs, and tiny mammals. My mind, overwhelmed by this place and the putrid beings following us, begs for distraction, screams at me to try and rattle off their Latin names and notable qualities. The air is thick and muggy with humid tropical heat, but rather than cool us down with deep shade, the heavy blanket of branches and leaves overhead seems to keep the heat sealed in like an oven, causing sweat to course down my face and soak into my shirt. What little sunlight does make it through the canopy cuts through the scenery here and there in quivering spots and dust-illuminated shards, making the jungle disorienting, dreamlike. Finally, my body feels the ache of the recent past—the pain in my joints from swimming, the twist of my stomach at the sight of the corroded dead stumbling their way ashore—and I cannot help but groan in my throat, exhausted.

But thankfully, the zombies don't appear to have made it far since we've started our trek. The trees ring with gurgling moans, but they're distant. Sadly, the drums have also died off, so any chance we had at following them is now lost. However, we cannot give up hope that their very existence means there are people around, good or bad. One hopes that, no matter how hardened or skeptical they are, the person or persons playing those drums would not let three sixth graders get eaten by the undead.

Okay, Kendra, you've found yourself in dire, life-threatening situations before. So take stock. Last time, you had an arrogant jock, a hobbled sensitive film geek, some ramen noodles, and a diary, all in a rocky deciduous forest. What are you working with this time around?

Sadly, my tools this time around are not only out of their element, they're genuinely broken. Ian, my face-forward strong-willed rascal and zombie bait, is pacing the jungle floor, mumbling to himself about being cool, maintaining composure, thinking like a wolf. PJ, our big-hearted artistic zombie expert, broods inconsolably, a grimace of pure hatred playing across his quivering lips. Most likely the curse on this place that brought the dead back to life is tampering with their resolve. But it's not them alone—even I, all-knowing Queen Brain, wasn't able to see this terrible place coming until that skull-face buoy floated right into my field of vision. The thought makes my skin crawl: how easily I overlooked the possible danger in the name of animal watching and field research. It's as though this time around, we should be more prepared for the undead horrors that approach us, and instead we're disoriented and dumbstruck by it. All that plus terrain we've never dealt with before—the jungle, the ocean—is spelling out defeat.

For a moment, I'm enraged at O'Dea—four months and she didn't think that perhaps we'd need some tips on being Gravediggers?—and then I immediately loathe myself for it. Our friend and savior is gone, and already I'm cursing her name.

It's not her fault you're shutting down, Kendra. Training or not, O'Dea's gone. She can't help you—no. No dwelling on that now. No crying, Kendra. She would want you to survive. She would believe in you, no matter how overwhelmed and useless you may currently feel.

"Let's pull ourselves together," I say loudly, trying to calm down my friends. "We've got to think about the next couple of hours."

"Right, right!" shouts Ian, darting to my side. "Go for it, Kendra. You're the genius, the brainiac. Lay it on us."

Part of me is stunned and dare I say a little creeped out by Ian's manic and immediate agreement with my statement, but I choose not to mention it. As long as he's listening to me, we'll be okay.

"Unlike last time," I posit, letting the loose thoughts in my head collect into what could be called a concept, "our families are relatively close to us, and since the locals believe this island to be cursed, they are all probably well aware of its location. So if we were to send up a flare, for instance, we have a great chance of rescue."

"Where are we going to get a flare?" asks PJ glumly.

"Well . . . maybe not a flare," I say. "Maybe we need to start a large fire."

"Isn't it incredibly dangerous to set a fire in a jungle?" asks PJ.

"Well . . . yes," I say. "But if we took precautionary measures—"

"Maybe we're just doomed," says PJ. "Ever consider that?"

"Come on, man," Ian pleads. "Aren't there any zombie movies that take place on islands? How do they—"

PJ laughs a cold, mirthless laugh that sounds like binary code, sterile and somewhat hostile. "Listen to you two," he says. "You both think it's like O'Dea says, like we're destined to beat the zombies and save the day, just like we did last time. Well, it's *not* like last time. There are oceans on all sides, there are more zombies than I've ever seen in a movie *or* in real life, and our Warden is probably *dead*."

"Dude, your knowledge of zombie movies was a big help the last time!" says Ian.

"It doesn't seem like it helped O'Dea," he says through gritted teeth.

"I know, PJ," I say, trying to fight back the lump in my throat. "She was our friend. But she . . . she would want us to keep going. To find a way to beat them. Ian's right, your knowledge of zombies films helped us last time—it might help us now."

PJ screws up his mouth. "You want to know? Fine. The answer's yes. At least a *third* of the great zombie movies of all time take place on islands or in jungles, Ian! *Shock Waves, White Zombie, I Walked with a Zombie,* even the movie *Zombie.* You'd know this if you'd ever watched one of them after we were attacked by *actual zombies.* But what you should also know is that in about ninety-nine percent of these movies, everyone dies at the end. At best, there's maybe one survivor." He looks into my eyes, his face so resigned and slack, it looks old. "Stop thinking there's a strategy here, or that you've somehow got some kind of abilities. Our goal for the next few hours, and the hours after that, and the ones after *that,* is to survive, by any means possible."

Words fail me. My mouth feels made of stone; in fact, my whole body feels rooted to the spot. This is a PJ I've seen glimpses of for the past few months, but have never seen entirely. Here, though, in the shadows of the jungle, there is a tension in that small bony form and a fire in those wide, deep-set eyes that's truly frightening.

He snorts, turns, and walks away. Ian watches him

go, then slaps me lightly on the shoulder. "Go easy on him," he says, "I think he's just freaked out about O'Dea."

"So am I," I say, shocked at Ian's response. "We . . . we all are. I'm terrified, Ian. This is new to me too."

He glances at me with an eyebrow raised, then says, "He's scared, is all. It's just a different way of saying it. We're all dealing with things a little strangely. I mean, like when I froze up back there at the beach—what was *that* about?" He gives me a loud, forced laugh and a glassy-eyed grin that lets me know he's actually incredibly upset about it. His demeanor only worsens the clammy sensation inside of me.

"Ian," I say softly, looking into his big eyes and scraggly blond hair for support, "we're going to be okay, right?"

The smile drops. For a moment, he's silent, and then he shrugs. "I . . . really hope so," he mumbles, and bounds after PJ, leaving me to follow behind him through a thriving green hell.

The heat is infernal, and soon all our clothes undergo a gross, fragrant metamorphosis, the salt water drying to make the cotton brittle and salt encrusted, only to grow heavy and slick again with sweat. Beads of perspiration hang from my face, trickling their way down my neck and collarbone with my every step, only to be replaced by new droplets.

A flash of memory—the resort, where my father is no doubt getting a massage and a pedicure as I trudge through the Puerto Rican wilderness—makes me grind my teeth. Instinctually, I reach for my smartphone to text some of my online buddies and see if they have any advice for finding fresh water in the jungle, but then I remember that I left my phone at the hotel, worried it might fall into the ocean.

The island goes quickly from thick and luscious to jagged and hilly, its bright green fauna pushing its way up between craggy countryside that slowly ascends. We climb two huge vine-trellised rocks and come to the edge of a giant pit descending into the jungle floor, deep enough that its bottom is obscured by a grove of small trees. Dead vegetation clings to the walls, dotted with the colorful plumes of tiny birds and sending up the deep, cool, sedimentary smell of wet earth and rotten vegetation. Every surface below seems to shiver and sway with crawling animal life. This place would be a researcher's dream, if only we had a helicopter and a shark tank.

"Might be tunnels down there," says Ian. "O'Dea had tunnels all through her mountain, remember? Maybe she got to shore before we did, hid underground?"

"Probably not," I tell him. "There aren't really deep enough spaces on an island of this size."

"It's a lot bigger than it looks from the dinghy," says

Ian. "Aren't desert islands always just, like, little bits of sand with a couple of palm trees?"

Get the brain working, Kendra. "This part of the world is littered with islands," I explain. "Some of them are huge. This one seems midsize. It could be up to two hundred square miles, two-twenty-five."

"Wonderful," grumbles PJ. "We're surrounded by zombies in a swarming jungle the size of Chicago."

Another spike of irritation makes me turn to PJ, finger raised and brow furrowed, but Ian jumps in, trying to save the day in his new manic and upsetting manner. "But, okay," he gibbers, "if there are other people around here—especially people playing drums that we can hear nearby—that's not that far, is it, Kendra?"

He's feeding it to you, Kendra, but what other option do you have? Bite. "No," I said, "it's not awful." *Great, Kendra, but keep going. You've got a couple of simple facts—the floating object in the water, the army of zombies—so put them together to draw a conclusion.*

"Given our estimate of the island's size and the range of sound a typical set of drums might have, I think one might guess that this person even wanted us to hear them. Perhaps it's a Warden, guiding us to her location given that the zombies have begun attacking the island."

"But those are just two of a hundred possibilities," says PJ pitifully. "Was it this Warden who tried to hit us with that missile on the water? Was it a Warden listening in to our conversation in the graveyard back home?

"Well, ostensibly—"

"Those drums could be some recording left here ages ago," he goes on. "Or maybe they're being used to *summon* the zombies!"

PJ's hopeless voice and his accusing stare make my hands form into claws, but they also bring a slight sting to the backs of my eyes. I'm fully aware that PJ is simply in one of his bad moods and is stewing in it vocally, but I can't help feeling betrayed, wondering where my friend of the past four months has gone. What did I do to deserve this treatment from someone with whom I fit so perfectly?

"I'm just trying to help," I say between clenched teeth. "If you have any meaningful suggestions, I'd love to—"

"We've got company," says Ian intensely.

His eyes are fixed out in the jungle. I follow their gaze to see the shape of a man, stomping blindly through the trees, reveal itself. His skin is a light coffee brown, and his beach shorts are unmistakably the ones we saw waiting on the beach for us this morning. A humming-bird tattoo on the left forearm seals the deal, though his face remains turned away from us.

"It's Esteban," I say. "Maybe he knows his way around this place." I cup my hands over my mouth and call out: "ESTEBAN! OVER HERE!"

Our guide stops and slowly turns his head to face us. My heart misses at least two beats and then struggles to exit my body from between my pectoral ribs.

It's not Esteban. Not anymore.

The eyes retain a bit of their color, but the pupils have dimmed to an upsetting cloudy blue; they show no signs of movement, even when leaves and vines slap his passing face. His jaw hangs agape, a row of teeth visible like turrets in a line above the darkening lower lip. Two fist-sized chunks of meat are missing from one of his biceps, and while a smear of blood or two is still visible on his skin, the wounds have crusted over black, and a spiderweb of dark necrotized veins spreads out from the wounds.

"Oh no," says PJ, backing slowly into the jungle.

"Easy," I tell him. "Remember, they're slow-moving. We can easily outrun him if—"

Esteban moans sadly, then begins *careening* (I'll go ahead and say it's five) toward us with slow but heavy steps, twisting his way around trees without so much as a stumble.

Keep this in mind, Kendra—when they're fresh, they have most of their muscle and ligament from everyday life. They can still move nimbly.

"Okay," I mumble, "we should probably start moving."

Ian and PJ both eye Esteban with very different

types of fear—Ian's spastic and uncontrolled, PJ's angry and unsurprised—but they nod and turn with me to go.

But unlike Esteban, it seems, the long-dead ones rising from the festering seas are similar to the ones up on the mountain—very slow, but so silent they almost blend in with your surroundings, until they're right on top of you.

I turn to leave and come face to face with every dream I've had for the past four months.

His face is half eaten by fish, the white sagging skin chipped away in little nibbles that come together into gaping stomas around his cheeks and chin. A pale barnacle-dotted potbelly juts out before him like a bloated gray egg. Beneath his blue swim trunks, one leg is missing meat down to the shinbone, while the other twists forward at a funny angle and oozes black fluid. One of his eyes remains, fleshy and white; the other is gone, revealing a gaping black hole.

For a moment, the whole world is sucked of sound, of temperature, of sensation as a whole, and there is only me, mouth open, facing the horror, and the horror stares back with slow-dawning hunger.

Then our mouths open simultaneously, and while I scream as loud as possible, he snarls and launches his remaining yellow teeth toward my face. My hand goes up, and his cold, clammy hand snatches it out of the air, and I try to wrench him to my side and toss him to the ground. I take a step to my left—

My foot finds no purchase behind me.

For a split second, I'm suspended in air, my arms whirling out at my sides, the zombie still trying to reach me and devour me even as we fall together, and in that blink I see Ian's panic and PJ's rancor vanish, and they both go reaching out for me at once, their eyes wide with the fear of losing me.

But it's too late. The zombie and I slip over the edge of the pit, and we fall.

My name is screamed one last time—by Ian or PJ, I can't tell which—as I fall into the earthen crevice below.

CHAPTER SIX

PJ

One minute, Kendra is there, her mouth wide open in a silent scream as she dangles from the edge of the pit, her hand around a large green weed, and my instincts buzz like hornets telling me to grab her. Then she screams and falls, tumbling with a crash into the underbrush below.

"KENDRA!" I shout, scrambling for the edge of the pit, and I just watch her and a living corpse go tumbling down the slope into the trees before they're gone.

"PJ, they're getting closer!" shouts Ian, tugging at my shirt. Already, the gurgling moans of the zombie horde around us have gotten louder and louder, with zombie Esteban's hoarse snarling taking the lead.

The shock of watching her fall mixes with the guilt curdling in my heart. If I could've only shaken this feeling of anger, of outrage, maybe she wouldn't have fallen. All I could do was be a jerk to her for trying to be the grown-up among us, caught up in the horror of this place, and now she's fallen into a murky pit with a flesh-eating monster. My insides feel burned by shock, but clammy with despair.

No, no, please no. This isn't what I meant to have happen. This is just so confusing, so overwhelming, that I let myself become that guy. If this were a movie, I'd *hate* me right now.

"We need to slide down into the pit and find her!" I shout at him.

But Ian's barely there. "What?" he breathes, his body tensing up, his eyes glazing over. It's as though someone is shocking him with a stun gun—he's turned stiff and silent as a board.

In the trees around us they appear, shuddering blue faces with fat milky eyes, bloated mouths flopping open and closed with hunger. Their extended arms quiver with each putrid step. The moaning is deafening; they must still be coming out of the water, given how loud their moaning is getting. Something about their outfits really unsettles me. The last time we dealt with zombies, it was a crew of dead modern dance students on a hiking trip, all wearing either flannel or spandex. These zombies, though, are even worse—*tourists*. It's as if an entire airport's worth of travelers, easily the most irritable group of people in the world, turned on us and decided to eat us. They drag fanny packs and cameras, reaching out hands with motion sickness bracelets around the wrists. One man we run into, short and fat and missing a huge section of his scalp, wears a soggy T-shirt that reads KISS ME—I'M WASTED!

The sight of the shambling undead hordes, the fact that we've just lost Kendra, the sweltering heat: it all pours gasoline on the fire raging in my head. For a moment, I don't know what to do; then in a blur of red I charge forward and kick zombie Esteban in the knee as hard as my foot will allow me. His leg snaps backward with a sickening crack, and for a moment he stumbles, a perplexed look on his face, but then he lurches at me again, dragging his brutalized leg behind him. My hands seem to work on their own, desperately burning extra energy in the form of rage, and I punch him over and over in the chest, which isn't very different from punching a wall.

His hands grab onto my shoulders, and when I try to pull away, his steely fingers don't let me. For a moment, feeling his cold hands pulling me close, I just give up. O'Dea's gone, Kendra's gone, Ian's freaking out . . . there's no way I'm making it out of here alive. I'm no

Gravedigger, whatever that may be. Why fight it?

There's a flash of gray as Ian appears at my side, a huge rock in hand, and cracks zombie Esteban in the forehead; he gurgles and tumbles backward, his bruising grip unlatching from my shoulders. A few feet behind him, a zombie in a black bowling shirt, his stomach cavity open and excavated by sea life, groans at us with extended fingers, and Ian hefts the rock into the guy's gaping belly, which drags him down to the forest floor with a sickening *plop*.

After shaking all over and dry heaving twice, Ian looks at me. "There's no time," he pants, tugging at my arm. "We need to get moving."

"But *Kendra*—"

"I'm fine!" echoes a voice from the bottom of the ditch. "Listen to Ian!"

"Kendra, you can't mean that!" I scream. "Hold on, we'll come down and—"

"If you come down here, they'll follow you over the edge!" she calls back. "I'm FINE! RUN!"

"We'll come back for you!" I yell down the mountain as Ian tugs me away.

"That . . . seems pretty unlikely," she cries. "Just keep Ian from doing anything stupid. . . ."

The scenery goes by me in a blur as I try to keep my vision straight and my throat from closing up. Even after hearing her voice, I can't shake the image from my mind—her falling over that edge—where it plays in a constant loop of guilt and panic. As we run, everything is absolute chaos, a sweaty collage of green foliage, yellow sun, black shadow, and fear, heart-wrenching fear.

"I can't believe you would do that!" shouts Ian as we run.

"ME?!" I scream.

"You don't think I saw it, but I did!" He skids to a halt, so I hang back, and he jabs his index finger at my face. "You just gave up! You could've fought harder, could've gotten away from him, but you didn't! You almost let yourself get bitten!"

Caught, red-handed. Ashamed at myself, bitter at Ian, I feel myself ball up inside, livid with rage. "You would've left Kendra there!" I exclaim. "All you care about is yourself!"

"*My*self?!" he bellows. "PJ, if you get bitten, I'm alone here! You can't do that to me, man! If I'm going to look out for you, you have to look out for yourself!"

"Yeah, 'cause you're so good at that," I snap. "Good job choking back there! How long did that zombie have a hold on me before you thought to pick up a rock? For a jock, you're a pretty lousy hero!"

Ian takes a step back, stunned, and honestly, so do I. The words seem to hang in the air like the awful jungle humidity around us. Because I knew, I've known for weeks—without his school sports, Ian's been feeling like he's been falling down on the job. Kendra barely noticed, too caught up in her feelings over her parents' divorce (I noticed that too), but I've watched Ian chomp at the bit for months. And now that we're here, he's choking, freaking out in the face of danger. But I went ahead and called him on it, because . . . because I'm scared, still, and angry. Because O'Dea has been out of touch for months, never answering my letters or training us in what roles we're supposed to play here, and now she's gone and we're alone. Because my world got expanded into a place full of monsters and magic and real friends, and here I am, same old shrimpy little PJ, and the people who used to be there for me are gone.

This isn't right. It's the curse, the heat, the zombies, something. But I'm better than this.

"Ian—" But he's marching off into the jungle before my apology can find form, and I scramble to keep up with him.

"Fine," he stammers. "Lousy hero, huh. Have fun letting the zombies devour you alive. If I'm such a crappy friend and a bad Gravedigger, then you won't need me hanging around bothering you anymore—"

The underbrush in front of Ian collapses downward. His arms go flailing out at his sides, and I only have a split second to grab the collar of his shirt and yank him back. We both tumble to the ground, Ian crab-walking frantically away.

The pit is a good eight to nine feet down. The bottom

is a mass of sharpened wooden stakes jutting up into the air, their points sharp and blackened. The vine-covered tarp disguising it dangles down the edge of the ditch, then slides its way in.

"You okay?" I gasp.

"Yeah," he says, rubbing his eyes. "Just fine. Maybe I could use a minute, but, uh, I should be good."

While Ian catches his breath, I stare over the edge of the pit of death. Something in the hole full of spikes catches the light and glints at me. Slowly, I crawl forward and see a shape, boxy and black with silver buttons, dangling from a stake down in the shadows—

Behind us, there's the cracking of twigs underfoot and the scurry of animals, followed by a gurgling low moan. We shuffle quickly back to our feet and dart behind a nearby tree, our eyes following the noise. After a few minutes, zombie Esteban lumbers into view. He hasn't been a walking corpse for long, but already he looks more dead than alive—ashen skin, stiff movements, blackened residue on his wound, gore-caked teeth bared. His busted shin and large gaping head gash ooze black syrupy gore. He limps forward on his busted leg with his eyes in the air like he's following a pretty bug or a soap bubble, like he's being led on by something he can't see.

"We should run," Ian whispers. "He's faster than the rest of them, but they're probably not that far behind."

"Wait," I whisper. "There's something down in the

pit. It might be a clue as to what's going on here."

"Then how do we get past him?" he asks.

It's a good question. If we so much as peek out from behind the tree, the zombie (I think I can stop calling him Esteban by now—*That's not the woman you loved*, as the movies say) will be on us in a second.

But watching this meat marionette lurch through the jungle, I feel my loathing well back up like some bitter acidic aftertaste. It's the same sensation that made me break Esteban's leg, the feeling that I want, more than anything, for this awful dead presence to stop following me and leave me be. I look back into the spiked pit, and it dawns on me in a single brilliant moment.

Who says we need to get past him?

"I've got an idea," I say to Ian. "On three, I'm going to run between the zombie and the pit. You come up behind him and shove him."

Ian stares blankly at me for a second, and then it all clicks. "I got it now. Perfect, I'm an *awesome* shover."

I somehow manage to not say, *I remember from the beach.* "Okay. On three."

"Okay, one—"

Zombie Esteban turns his head to us with a sickening pop of dead joints. A low, phlegmy moan escapes his mouth.

"GO GO GO GO!"

I dart out between the zombie and the pit and begin

waving my arms as hard as possible. "Hey, zombie! Come and get it! Hot and tasty, just like Mom used to make it!"

The zombie slow-staggers over to me, his arms thrust out into grotesque claws in front of him. When he's three steps away from me, when I can smell the salt water on his breath and the tangy roadkill scent of his wounds, I drop to the ground and hope that Ian's done his job . . . but when I look up, I see Ian frozen, his back to the tree, chewing his lip.

No, no, please Ian, now is not the time to lose your nerve.

Thankfully, the zombie's not too smart and lunges anyway. His foot catches my side as he stumbles over me and goes tumbling into the pit. There's a moan, followed by a harsh wet *SHINK*, like the first stab into a pumpkin on Halloween.

Ian rushes over me, panting. Sweat pours down his brow, and something between a smile and grimace lines his face.

"Got him!" he says, punching the air. "See, and I, I didn't even need to push him! Nice crouching, PJ!" Ian offers a hand to lift me to my feet, but I wave him away and get up myself. At least this bit of heroism has left him feeling confident.

Once I'm on my feet, I peer over the lip of the ditch. It's . . . not pleasant. The zombie hangs in midair, speared five times through the torso and suspended over the bottom of the cave, his head dangling loosely. And he's . . . oozing. The zombies we fought on the mountain were mostly dust, scabs, and maggots. But Esteban was pretty fresh, and this climate is incredibly humid, so there's a lot more . . . goo than we're used to.

The smell hits me, and I reel back, coughing and waving a hand in front of my face. Ian steps forward, sniffs the air, and gags. At least we can't see his face.

"Rotting meat isn't my favorite scent," I tell him.

"Yeah, I know." He coughs, then leans for a second time over the lip of the ditch.

"You're going in for another whiff?"

"I can see the thing you were talking about," he says. He points, and I dash up next to Ian, holding my shirt collar to my face to keep out the smell. Sure enough, a foot below and a few inches to the left of the zombie is a walkie-talkie, dangling from a stake point by a wrist strap.

The moaning in the distance grows louder, and swaying shapes begin stepping out of the jungle behind us, the huge shading layers of leaves and foliage spewing up gray, stiff figures, as though the thriving body of Mother Nature were popping pimples.

"We need to get it," I tell him. "There's no time to waste."

"Is *need* really the right word?" says Ian. "What happened to just surviving, like you were telling Kendra?"

Guilt creeps back into my heart, cold and heavy. Kendra might still be with us, and she'd have a quick answer for Ian. Here I am, mouth flapping. "This might be necessary to our survival," I tell him, and then, because I'm lost here, "Kendra would probably agree. It's a clue, a piece of the puzzle."

Ian nods. "She is a sucker for clues. . . . It's just pretty far down, so it's going to be dangerous to get to. How do you want to do this?"

There's only one real way for us to get it, an idea that makes the knot in my throat clench even tighter, but there are hungry corpses on our tail—too many of them, by the looks of the jungle landscape.

"Hold me by the feet and lower me down," I tell him. "I'll grab it."

"You sure?" he says, his eyes wide and incredulous. "I've got these long basketball arms. It might make more sense for you to lower me."

"I don't think I'm strong enough to hold you," I tell him, hoping to stroke his ego. "I'm lighter than you are."

He heaves a sigh and wipes a sweaty mat of hair off his forehead. "Well, let's get to it," he says.

We figure it out as we go—I lie flat on my belly, and Ian wraps his hands around my ankles and digs his heels in. Slowly, we scoot our way forward until I'm hanging over the edge of this ditch, easing my way down into the shadows. The air is cool and damp down here, even if I'm positive the air around me is just swimming with zombie bacteria and repulsive lichen spores. If my mother could see me now, she'd throw up.

Slowly, by inches, I pass the point of the nearest stake and inch toward the walkie-talkie, its spine of buttons appearing in the darkness. My hand stretches out, and my fingers feel the woven polyester of its strap, and—

There's a noise like clapping steak, and an icy hand closes on my wrist, forcing a scream out of my throat. My head turns till I see zombie Esteban's face focused on mine, his mouth gnashing in hunger, his cloudy eyes wide beneath a furrowed brow.

"PJ, what's going on?" calls Ian frantically.

"He's still alive!" I scream.

"Hold on, I'm pulling you up," he yells, and I feel his hands tighten on my ankles.

"Not yet!" I scream. With all my might, I push my hand forward, straining at the dangling box while trying to resist the zombie's grasp. The dead are strong, though, and hard as I try, I can't stop him from slowly bringing my fingers to his mouth.

But then my hand closes around the strap of the walkie-talkie, and the word "PULL!" comes out of me louder than I've ever heard. Ian yanks me upward, my arm slipping out of the zombie's grip with the help of some horrible black viscous fluid.

Once I'm back on ground and the blood has flowed out of my head, I snatch a palm leaf and begin frantically wiping off my arm. Earlier, I blew off the movies and their rules, but in this instant, as the danger becomes all too real, they come flooding back into my head like a swarm of hornets. First rule of zombie movies: the zombie infection is spread through fluids, saliva, blood, and the like. If this stuff sinks into my pores, I'm a goner.

"PJ?" pants Ian. "You okay?"

"I think I got the blood off in time," I tell him, but as I say it, I know something's wrong. My hand shakes around the walkie-talkie; I'm so happy to feel the plastic square in my hand that I squeeze too hard, and the materials creak. A feeling like electricity charges through my teeth, making them rattle in my skull. My head swims, the memory of Esteban's, no, the *zombie's* hand closing on my wrist, losing O'Dea and Kendra, heat, boy, is it hot. . . .

Everything turns rubbery, and the next thing I feel are Ian's arms, one around my waist, one on my shoulder, lowering me to the ground.

"PJ!" bellows Ian, shaking me.

My mouth, all gummy, manages to wheeze out the words, "I'm . . . fainting, aren't I?"

"PJ, stay with me!" shouts Ian. The moaning seems to grow around us, and behind him, I see deep empty sockets and white moldy eyes appear, the bloated soft-fleshed forms around them slumping into view. They seem to be everywhere.

"A glass of water . . . would be so nice right now," I hear myself sigh.

Ian begins trying to carry me, hugging me around the waist and pulling me in great grunting drags, but it's obvious I'm just a little too heavy for him, no matter how fast he can run or how high he can jump. He seems to be moving at roughly the same speed as a zombie now, but in my semiconscious daze I can't even really tell.

Half passed out, I still understand what a dead weight I am, and if it weren't for the angry speech he gave me earlier, I'd even tell Ian to put me down, head into the jungle, save himself, and let me take the heat off him. But even then, it wouldn't matter. Because as much as I miss her, O'Dea really burned us here. If she'd known we might end up in this situation again, with monsters closing in on all sides and the dark forces of nature trying to do us in, she could've said something about what being a Gravedigger means. A few instructions, some history, anything. Instead, we wandered in here unprepared, all three of us. Even if Ian were to let me go or use me as a zombie stopper, he doesn't have a much better idea of what he's doing than I do. This was a disaster from the moment we landed here.

That's the feeling deep in my gut, the hatred that

feels both searing hot and damply cold at the same time. It's the knowledge that no matter hard I fight, how often I win or lose, I'm the weak one, who holds everyone back, who does nothing but get hurt and almost kill those around him: my friends, my sister, O'Dea, everyone. My purpose in life seems to be to let them all down.

There's a noise, somewhere above us, a shriek that sounds like some kind of horrible giant bird or insect, but from where I'm slumped in Ian's arms, I can't see anything. Ian glances up, and then he winces and lowers his head. Suddenly, a volley of objects—stones, bones, coconuts, and something that can't be as disgusting as it looks—goes flying past us, smashing into the first wave of oncoming zombies, who gasp and groan as they go stumbling off their feet and falling into the underbrush around us, their slow-witted brethren trampling and tripping over them.

A sensation like a hundred small hands touches my back, and suddenly to Ian's wide-eyed surprise, I leave his arms, my limp form carried upward and into the trees. Ian stares after me as I float into the air, carried off my feet and upward by the phantom hands, out of the reach of the oncoming horde.

I'm almost positive this means I've died of heat-stroke in Ian's arms. While I wish he looked a bit more broken up about it, I can't help but feel grateful that at least I'm being pulled up instead of down.

CHAPTER SEVEN

Ian

They may be saving PJ, but these monkeys don't look happy about it. As they haul him up into the tree, their little hands gripping his arms and cradling his head, they stare at me with these huge dark eyes peering out of their pink faces, bodies hunched over so that it looks like they're glaring down at me, as if to say, *All right, Buckley, you've tried your best and hey, look, even if you did choke like some fourth grader when those zombies came out of the water, you had a couple of cool moments hitting Esteban with that rock, but you might want to back off for a second. This here's monkey business.*

For a second, I'm scared that they're going to drag

him off somewhere to eat him, because really, what do I know about Puerto Rican monkeys? But a crew of them are still taking out of the front line of zombies with every projectile they can find, including some they, well, make themselves (funky), and the shuddering waterlogged dead tourists—at least the first line of them—stumble to the ground and try to ooze their way back onto their feet as more and more of their slimy friends come shambling into view, torn mouths opening in foamy hisses and hands clawing clumsily at the air.

"Please!" I shout at the monkeys, because in my current state I can't do much but pray they'll understand me. "Please, don't take him from me—"

There's a tugging at my hand, and I look down to see a monkey, its fur dirty-blond and coarse and its face rage-pink, gripping my hand and yanking at it. Up in the canopy of trees overhead, PJ's silhouette moves, dragged by some few dozen bounding forms. What else can I do? I chase after it, following the monkeys on their crazy path over the jungle floor. Over my shoulder, I see a few of the remaining projectile launchers on the ground now, darting nimbly between the zombie tourists who limp after the monkeys, gurgling all the while.

The monkeys in the trees manage to hold on to PJ well enough, though once or twice a hand or foot dangles loose and I feel my defensive reflex fly off the charts, my hands going up in the air in case I have to catch PJ off the backboard for the rebound, but they seem to have their little monkey paws securely fastened to him. My job doesn't get much easier, though; the one monkey who grabbed my hand shrieks as he leads me through the forest, but doesn't once consider the terrain, and I find myself squeezing between trees he can bounce through, scaling massive moss-covered downed trunks he can leap over, and squelching my feet in fly-covered puddles of muck that he can swing past.

With every step deeper into it, the jungle grows more insane, like something straight out of *Tarzan* on steroids. Huge thick-trunked trees hang with icicles of moss so green it looks radioactive, their roots twisting up out of the moist soft ground like human arms. Rope-thick vines dangle down from the sun-blocking canopy overhead. Massive palm leaves, long-fingered ferns, and the occasional bushy patch of flowers unlike anything I've ever seen sprout all around me, blazing pink-red and made up of petals half an inch thick. The bugs swarm in a nonstop cloud around my face anytime I slow down for even a second, mosquitoes and horseflies biting my neck and scalp, and I can see the back ends of small creatures running off into the underbrush, just a tail or a bit of a leg or even just grass bending back into place and swaying like it's laughing at me, like I have no idea what *actually* lives around here.

It's a mixed blessing, 'cause on the one hand, yeah, this is incredible, this is exactly the type of place where a Gravedigger should have a crazy zombie hunt, but on the other hand, the bugs are eating me alive, the heat is stuffing itself down my throat, two of my friends might be dead and one's being dragged through the trees by monkeys, and I have no idea what might be living around us, how to deal with what this terrain can throw at me. The woods on the mountain were what we're used to in the American West, you know, sturdy and gray and hard. This, this is something else.

In the distance, I hear rushing water, and as I break through a curtain of vines in an attempt to remain under the dark blotch that's PJ being dragged through the trees by monkeys, I come out in front of a small pool beneath a wall of rocks, the pool fed by a tiny waterfall pouring down the rocks. All around it, the cold damp stone and white crashing water seem to emit a cool temperature, and the water in the pool is so clear that I could count the pebbles at the bottom.

Before I can think twice or go over any of the tips I read in Kendra's survival books last week about checking for purity and blah blah dee blahblah, I'm on my knees cupping handful after handful of water directly into my face, feeling it trace a perfect line of *cool* from my mouth to my stomach, and sure, it tastes the teeniest bit like dirt, but other than that it's probably the best mouthful of water I've ever drunk.

I hear a shrieking behind me, and turn to see the monkeys holding PJ out over a tree branch, staring at me. When I dart back, they toss him into my arms, and I drag his limp body over to the pool. He's not *quite* unconscious, but his eyes are opening and closing at different rates, and all he can do is make this hissing noise like an inner tube deflating that makes my stomach bunch up in knots.

At the edge of the pool, I cup a handful of water into his mouth and shake him a little. "PJ. PJ, man, wake up." No response, so I feed him another handful. The water dribbles out of his mouth. "PJ, I'm not doing this twice in one day." Still nothing. It makes me think of him letting himself go limp in that zombie's hands, and I actually feel myself grimace at him, and suddenly I'm throttling him as hard as I can, and then I put my hand in the pool and splash cold water across his face, screaming, "PJ, GET UP!"

That does it—he sits up spluttering, his eyes blinking hard, and after he gives a quick glance around, he plunges his face to the water, taking long, deep gulps until he's out of breath and comes up gasping.

"Thanks, Ian," he whispers, wiping at his mouth. "You saved my life again."

Suddenly, I feel guilty—for shaking him, for getting angry at him, but mostly because I couldn't help him, because he had to be saved by our new animal friends. It's so lame, so not tough, that honestly, I can't even lie about it. I feel like there's a phantom Coach Leider here giving me the death stare, saying, *Don't act like you're the real hero here, Buckley. Thank the monkeys.*

"It wasn't me," I grumble, turning away from the waterfall, "it was—*GYAH!*"

The jungle surrounding our little oasis is packed with these golden brown monkeys. They perch on every tree branch, sit in clusters around every trunk, and they aren't moving or leaping about or screeching or grooming each other, they're just watching us. The bright green of the jungle is dotted everywhere we look with their pink faces, huge shiny eyes, and quiet unmoving expressions.

"Those things saved me?" says PJ.

"They led us here," I whisper. I'm scared that if I speak too loudly, they're going to go nuts, and we'll have a monkey riot on our hands. "Dragged you most of the way."

"Bet I'm riddled with parasites now," says PJ, going heavy on the disgust.

"I don't know," I say. "Monkeys are pretty good groomers, right? I bet they pick each other clean."

"You never know with exotic animals, though," he insists, and then, after a moment, adds, "and they normally don't like humans."

"Now that *is* true," I say, nodding my head toward the thickest batch of faces, where two tiny baby monkey faces peer out from between a large mother monkey's arms. "I mean, look at them, just sitting there. I feel like monkeys don't do that, you know? Why are they just staring at us?"

They respect you.

My hair stands on end, and I take a step back from PJ. He reaches frantically into his pocket and pulls out the boxy black shape he dragged from the spiked pit—a walkie-talkie, black and heavy, equipped with a tiny screen, lanyard, and some kind of logo, a red *DM* in this intense scary font I feel like I've seen before.

PJ just stares at it with his mouth open, so I yank the walkie-talkie away from him and hit the Speak button. "Hello? Is anyone out there?"

There's a pause, then a crackle of static, and then the voice comes on, deep and soft, practiced in its calm.

It has always been that way, says the fuzzy voice, smooth and oily. *The beasts of the earth respond to those chosen by the energies behind the veil of our reality, just as they are repelled by those vessels of the dark side. The Wardens must learn to talk to the animals through practice and enchantment, but Gravediggers are chosen, not taught. The creatures of the land, air, and ocean will always respect you—all but the fly and its brethren, for they are cold and strange and their very existences thrive on decay and death.*

"Please," I say, "please, if you're out there, my name is Ian Buckley, I'm lost—"

You're not lost, coos the voice.

"Trust me, pal," I shout, feeling drowned in anger, monkey eyes pressing on me, "I'm pretty lost here!"

But you've been doing so well, hums the voice. *You fought off the horde, at least for a bit. You got that nice punch in, and your friend his leg-breaking kick. Then you followed the beasts. It was a smart thing to do, given your options. They've distracted the horde for long enough for you to regain your breath, it seems. It's all working out.*

"Is he watching us?" asks PJ in a hushed tone, but I can barely hear him, angry at the voice for thinking it knows more about how I've screwed this all up than I do.

"But I . . . I lost Kendra!" I shout. "And O'Dea! I couldn't even save my friend—some animals did it for me—"

Ian, your time will come.

PJ's eyes go wide and meet mine. The sound of my own name makes me feel like I'm swallowing a mouthful of lead. "How do you know who I am?"

Don't worry about that now, it crackles. *You're hopelessly outnumbered. Forget being the hero and simply go where the situation leads you. Gravediggers think on their feet.*

PJ grabs the walkie-talkie out of my hand. "Sir," he

shouts into it, "you say we're hopelessly outnumbered—what kind of numbers are you talking about?"

There's a pause, and then a crackle as our mystery guest actually sighs into his mouthpiece. *I won't lie to you, PJ. It's a lot.*

"A lot like thirty?" he says. "A hundred?"

About fifty years ago, a cruise ship called the Alabaster *anchored a ways out from Isla Hambrienta,* intones the voice. *It was small, for a cruise ship, but still couldn't come anywhere near the island. And one night, a group of thieves trying to escape a heist at a textile plant on the mainland boated out to it. The* Alabaster *was having a big Fourth of July party, and the fireworks they set off attracted the thieves. They boarded the ship and took it hostage, began slaughtering anyone on board who spoke out against them.*

Slaughtering—man, what an awful word. "No one tried to stop them?" I ask, feeling angry, wishing I could've done something to help these poor tourists.

Oh, some of the guests managed to escape their clutches, and the thieves chased them through the ship. Eventually, a fight ensued between the intruders and the crew. One of the bandits, not to be defeated, pulled the pin on a grenade he had been saving in case things got hairy, and he blasted a hole in the ship. Many died at the thieves' hands, and many went down with the Alabaster, *and some even leaped into the water in hopes of swimming to the island . . . but by morning, all three hundred and fifty guests, the seventy crew members, and the thirteen thieves were all dead and gone.*

The bottom of my stomach vanishes, and it's like my guts are sucked into a whirlpool. Slowly, 'cause math is honestly not really my game, I count off the numbers in my head—three fifty plus seventy plus thirteen equals . . . *equals* . . .

"Four hundred and thirty-three," says PJ, just *seconds* before I was about to spit out the exact same thing.

My mind throws an image in front of my eyes—ten dead bodies, on their feet, mouths open, hands outstretched, and then I put ten more lines of ten behind them, then four of *that* plus another third or so . . . and suddenly, I'm looking at an endless crowd, a field of upright corpses that stretches off into the distance, and while I'm imagining staring at them, they all look at me at once with those empty white eyes, and one of them moans, and then a moan goes through the whole crowd—

"We are definitely out of our league," I say softly.

No, the voice on the other end of the walkie-talkie announces. *Do not think like that. The undead's greatest power is their numbers and their resilience, but they are a slow and stupid terror, easily distracted by animals and loud noises. Stay ahead of the larger herds, and you will be able to fend them off. Your Warden would have you believe that you need training, weapons, but you* are *the weapon, you* are *the fight.*

"Our Warden was our friend," snaps PJ, his eyes narrowing at the buzzing black box. "She helped us."

Really? asks the voice. *And now that she brought you here and left you . . . how much did she really help?*

"What do you know about O'Dea?" I shout into the walkie-talkie.

Then static, for a long time, so long that PJ takes the walkie-talkie away and starts shaking it, messing with every knob and button on its face while I stand there, letting those last words sink into me. Nothing, just more white noise. Our adviser, whoever he was, has totally split on us.

I ask PJ, "What do you think?"

He slowly shakes his head, an expression of confusion crossing his face. "Honestly, Ian? I have absolutely no idea."

"He was right, though," I tell him. "O'Dea didn't give us many guidelines on what to do here."

PJ tightens up his mouth and gives the walkie-talkie a death stare. "She . . . she probably thought we did so well on the mountain that we'd be okay here."

"But that guy sounded pretty sure of himself," I say. It feels like my heart's being torn out, but I have to break it to PJ: "If he knows so much about us, then he could know things we haven't even thought about, PJ."

"I can't believe O'Dea would do anything that might

hurt us," he cries, throwing his hands wide, but I can tell it's gotten to him; he's doubting her too. "She's not going to save our lives once only to lead us to some desert island full of zombies."

"Then how's that person know—"

"Because . . . maybe he's watching us," says PJ, but I can tell he's grasping at straws, the way his eyes wander around and crinkle up. "There might be cameras around here."

"PJ, he knew our *names*," I say. "Look, I don't like this either, but we need to consider *every* option."

"Maybe he's . . . a ghost," says PJ. "Of one of the people who died on the ship."

"So, what, there are zombies *and* ghosts now?"

Wait a second. If there are zombies, if this land is cursed . . .

"If this place has zombies, shouldn't there be a Warden containing them?" I say, and can see by the way he flinches that he knows I'm right. "What about that floating wood head in the water—who blew that up? We've seen O'Dea do some crazy stuff, man—who's to say she couldn't use magic to blow up that—what'd Kendra call it, zemi?"

"She would've told us *something* if that were the case," he gasps, like he's trying to convince himself more than anything.

"PJ, you know I'm right—"

Suddenly, a monkey's shriek cuts through the air,

and all heads, ours and the observing monkeys', turn up to the air. Then we hear more shrieks and see a group of monkeys go flying through the trees overhead. Then the gurgling comes in soft, along with the buzzing of bugs, and the smell, holy geez, it's like fish eggs and bad oysters served out of a septic tank, cutting through the air. The rest of the monkeys all break out of their hypnotic stare and go running and leaping up the edge of the waterfall, tugging on our clothes and shrieking at us to follow.

"Forget it," I say, though I'm dying to drive it home, to have him look me in the eyes and agree with me. "We move for now. Keep your eyes peeled for other people and more tech like this one. And *ghosts*, I guess," I throw in, because you know what, someone's gotta say it.

The rock wall next to the waterfall isn't very steep—more of a small hill than a real cliff—but it's slippery, and I make sure to place my foot carefully every time I move. As I get to the grassy top, I turn to see PJ still only a third of the way up, his footing sloppy and his sneakers sliding around anytime he wants to put weight on them. For a second, I want to go to help him, but something whitehot and mean in the back of my head stops me.

He won't look at me as he climbs, panting, to the top of the hill. Behind him, I can see the underbrush rustling slowly as shapes between the leaves come staggering into view.

As we turn to head deeper into the jungle, I let my hand drag across a tree trunk, feeling the grassy moss and soft rubbery vines pass beneath my fingers. Focus on the jungle. Gotta get my head together. Gotta think about what Coach Leider would do, what my dad would do, what *Kendra* would do. That's it, think like Kendra. You and she worked so well together last time, right? She'd probably say something like, like—

Like, *Vines aren't rubbery, Ian.*

"Wait," I mumble, freezing, then taking two steps back and staring at the tree I just brushed against. It's like the many other huge trees in the jungle here, brown-gray trunk streaked with cream of spinach green, bottom a tangle of tentacly roots, top a massive branch network. But it has a single vine traveling from up in the canopy down into the ground, twisting around the tree in a way that I don't feel like vines do, sporting a skin too perfect and smooth for a vine. As my hand wraps around it, I know it's rubber, not a vine.

Holding on to the rubber vine, I run circles around the tree, unwrapping it from the trunk until I can see where it disappears up in the leaves. I jump in the air, grab the cord as high as I can, and yank hard. There's this loud woody splitting noise, and then a black shape comes dropping out of the sky toward us, hitting the jungle floor with a bushy crash as we take a step back. After a few seconds, I yank it up by the cord and hold it dangling for PJ and me to see—a black cube about the size of a box of matches with a single black eye bulging out of one side. A security camera.

"There you go," snaps PJ. "Hate to say I told you so, but—"

Before he can finish his sentence, my anger wells up and breaks the chains holding it back, and the heat, the stupid voice on the walkie-talkie, PJ being so mean *and* being right, it all explodes inside of me, and I whip the camera over my head like a mace, pitching it over the edge of the waterfall. The zombie tourists have wandered out into the open—numerous, loud now that they've spotted us—and the camera smashes, *bull's-eye*, into the face of a zombie rocking dreadlocks and red Bermuda shorts, destroying half of his skull with a satisfying glass shatter and *crunch*. He falls to the ground, but even knocked on his butt, he wheels his arms in the air.

When I look back at PJ, he's got this stunned, upset look in his eyes that makes me angry. Was that too real for him? 'Cause if so, I don't know what to tell him. Just because I freeze up sometimes when dealing with the living dead, just because, fine, I'm *scared* of them, doesn't mean I've lost my touch. Right?

As we storm off into the jungle, I wonder about Kendra. I wish she were here—Kendra's the perfect partner for this kind of thing. She's probably already built a ham radio out of two coconuts and a rock.

CHAPTER EIGHT

Kendra

On the one hand, Kendra, it is impossible to express how lucky you are.

The zombie let go of your hand during the fall, and you landed in a tree rather than right on the rocky forest floor. Your only wounds are relatively superficial—nothing is broken, only a little battered and scratched. Technically, what you told the boys right after you fell was correct— you are fine. For all intents and purposes, karma has smiled on you.

But even you have to admit—it doesn't get more horrific than this.

Around me rise the shadowy, mossy rock walls of the

ravine, a smattering of trees obscuring me in smoky blue shadows. The tree I landed in is short, but strong and shady, a nice place to relax on a warm summer day. And at its base, in the muddy forest floor below me, clambers half of a zombie, gurgling and moaning as he tries, and fails, to claw his way up the trunk and get to me.

A few yards away, I can see his board shorts–clad lower pelvis and legs lying next to a large rock, coated in a chunky sheen of black slime; when the zombie hit the rock, it split him in two, but since he's a magically undead monster, his torso decided to come crawling after me, leaving the black trail of human sap I see extending from his long tail of necrotized flesh and spine to his lifeless legs. Now, we're here, me relaxing in the cool humidity of the tree, the zombie moaning desperately at me as he scrapes his discolored dead hands against the tree trunk, a perpetually terrible situation—caused by slipping into a pit—that leaves me relieved, repulsed, and resigned all at once.

When we first landed, me in the tree and the zombie on a rock, I was simply relieved to be alive. When the upper half of the zombie began its greedy crawl toward the tree, I felt a spike of panicked adrenaline seize my heart and had to slap a hand across my mouth to keep from screaming. But I've been in this tree for at least twenty minutes now, and he is nothing more than a consistent horror, up close and personal for me to pore over at will. When I finally bring myself to look him dead on (har, har), my gag reflex spasms. There he is, in all his glory—his vacant eyes, his open black mouth, his fish-chewed ears and nose, the black scabby goo trailing out from behind him.

The eyes and face are the most jarring. Though he moves and makes noise ceaselessly, there is no life beneath that quivering gelatinous meat, just some kind of awful primal earth instinct, a dominating desire to kill and devour. He cannot fathom the hours I've researched his presence in folklore and schlock cinema, the count-less nights I've studied and practiced to make my brain the sharpened tool it is.

If that weren't enough, there's a cut on my elbow, small and harmless but nonetheless bleeding. Every so often, I feel a droplet slip between my fingers and watch in horror as the glob of red falls as though in slow motion, spattering on the tree's trunk. This only excites the zombie, who lunges at the red-stained wood as though to bite off a hunk of flesh; when his teeth splinter on the trunk, I watch as he slowly extends a swollen black tongue and laps up the blood, sending my stomach into a new round of acrobatics and a hot wet feeling behind my eyes. With each taste he gets, he becomes agitated, his hunger reinforced. His eyes roll in his skull, his jaws snap together in loud clicks, and his train of guts and vertebrae twitches and wags like a tail.

In my travels, I've seen zombies do unspeakable things—tear each other to pieces, wander around missing most of their bodies—but something about watching this revenant slurp at a tree trunk to get a drop of my blood seems to touch me deep down within my gastrointestinal tract, balling my fear and exhausting and loathing into a solid sphere that fights its way up.

My head turns, and suddenly a considerable amount of seawater goes gushing out of my mouth. My body spasms with a round of dry heaves, but soon a cold sweat settles in, and I take a moment to wipe my mouth, close my eyes, and let it pass.

Though I am generally independent as a young person, this is the first time I've ever thrown up without a parent present to help me. For a moment, their faces flash into my mind, and tears pour down my face. My heart feels as though it might rip in half. It's so immature, but I can't help it: I miss my parents. I wish they were here, to pat my back, hand me a glass of water, tell me everything's going to be all right.

Steady, Kendra. Sometimes adventurers throw up. Christopher Columbus probably retched all the time. Don't get too upset—it will make you hopeless. Think. What can do you next?

As hard as it is for me to tear my watery eyes away from the grotesque spectacle below, I look up at the sunlit canopy of green leaves over me, block out the moaning, and try to figure out my location.

Perfect. Right now, you're in more of an overgrown pit than a valley of any sort. You can't have fallen more than, what, forty feet? If that. Accordingly, this area has either a) stone walls around it on all sides, or b) an exit point, where the ditch edge gives way to some sort of larger area.

Right? Right, Kendra? Stop crying.

Now, if it's the latter, then you have a good chance of outrunning the half creature beneath you and gaining new ground, be it in some kind of secondary pit or an area where the hillside descends into ground as low as this. If it's the former, your plan is going to have to get elaborate. You may need to design some sort of rope and pulley system out of palm trees and vines. Shouldn't take you more than, say, a year or two.

There's a throbbing pain behind my eyes, and I have to close them and pinch my brow to dull it. This isn't good. Suffice it to say I'm still in trouble.

Part of me wishes the boys had come rappelling down to save me, but deep in my mind, I'm aware that it was the right thing to send them off. They need all the help they can get, and to be honest, a solid slab of fear still rests in my gut that they were too slow and got surrounded—and they would've only led the other corpses down toward me. We learned that the last time—if they hear me, they'll come marching over the edge to try and get at me. Still, the thought of Ian and PJ running around a desert island without a brain frightens me . . . though not as much as the idea of more zombies descending into this pit. Yet deep down, a shard of hope—that they'll come rescue me—remains.

From above me, at the top of the hill, I can hear the faint tramping of slow footsteps, the occasional sea water–choked moan. The zombies have overrun the island, and judging by the constant heavy treads and hungry moans, it sounds like there are quite a lot more of them up there than we've ever dealt with before. One false cry and I'll be up to my waist in psychotic torsos trying to inch their way up my tree.

Next to me, there's a chittering squeak, like silverware on a plate.

It appears I'm not as alone as I think.

A gang of rhesus monkeys (Latin name *Macaca mulatta*, if I remember correctly—introduced, not indigenous, to Puerto Rico and its surrounding islands) fills the tree next to me, hunched over and watching intently as the zombie licks my blood out of the dirt. Their slumped brown bodies hang in the branches, the occasional pink face glancing at me before looking away with a chirp and a scratch. Their presence hits me with a wave of relief, which puts a smile on my face. It's not simply me and the dead after all.

The more I focus around me, the more I can see

all sorts of animals in the branches within this ditch—mostly monkeys, but the occasional banana quit and lizard, all perched silently in the trees and staring intently at the shambling half man clawing at the trunk below me. Each one makes me feel less helpless, more like part of the actual order here. I'm not the one out of place, the zombie is.

One of the rhesus monkeys climbs over to a branch near me and perches there, seeming to face me. When I reach a hand out to it, it ducks its head away once, but then it lets me run my fingers down the back of its skull, its fur grainy and tough.

"You're not afraid of me, are you?" I whisper to it.

The monkey says nothing (*Brilliant deduction, Kendra*) but still doesn't move.

"Is it because of what I am? A zombie exterminator?" I ask. The sound of my voice sends the half zombie into new *paroxysms* (a vocabulary word from December of last year, classic) of hunger. "No one's talking to you," I snap at him, as though he could possibly understand me. Instead, my voice continues to excite him, making his moans come out like throaty panting that rises with each extension of his arm, *hungh, hungh, hungh*, until I find myself infuriated and screaming, "ENOUGH WITH THE MOANING!"

The monkeys at my side begin hopping and screeching as I get agitated, racing from one branch to another.

One of them bounces out of sight and returns with a coconut that it pitches at the zombie, knocking a gash in the bloated gray meat of his face. A few of its fellows follow suit, bouncing into the trees on either side of me and returning with coconuts that they use to batter the zombie. As they fire one projectile after another with violent force, doing their best to cause as much damage to the shambling creature as possible, I can't help but feel proud and excited to be defended, if even so meagerly. Without knowing why, I begin to laugh at their feeble attacks, and as I do so, their shrieks go quiet and they cease their barrage. I laugh for a while, letting big, crazy whoops out into the air, and soon the monkeys start whooping along in their weird falsettos.

If I wasn't more skeptical, I would suggest the idea that my emotional response to the zombie below me triggered the rhesus monkeys' sudden behavior shift. But I'm a woman of reason and not inclined to make wild guesses at what could be explainable animal psychology.

Just because the dead walk doesn't mean we should give up hope on facts.

One of the monkeys begins gesturing with its paws and screaming.

My eyes follow its movements and focus on the zombie's legs a few yards off, earlier a tangled mess of gray fleshy right angles, now squirming with . . . freckles?

That's what it appears to be, a mass of writhing red dots that have spontaneously popped up on the zombie's useless lower extremities—

The freckles move across the zombie's shorts and onto the ground.

Ants, Kendra. A massive swarm of fire ants.

Whatever good karma was left on this island just ran out.

"Oh no," I hear myself mumble as the wave of squirming ruby dots comes over the zombie's legs, causing them to twitch and shake as the ants devour the meat off the bones. At first, I hope they are satisfied eating away at the waterlogged flesh of the zombie's useless lower half, but soon some of the crimson invertebrates pass over the lower extremities and begin inching forward, scattering the few small animals brave enough to share the forest floor with the zombie.

The ants find the trail of gore between the monster's top and bottom portions and begin feasting on what little meat is there. The rest follow it toward the zombie's torso as he claws at my tree.

Remember your research, Kendra. These are most likely RIFA, red imported fire ant, Solenopsis invicta. Come in nests of up to five hundred thousand. They usually eat other insects, but are known to survive on most anything, including carrion, which, one expects, includes zombie flesh. (Note to self: While other predators won't devour zombified humans, insects and fish have no problem with it. This phenomenon must be examined.) They are not known for killing humans but do sting in concert with each other, and will generally attack without provocation.

Meaning that if they get up in this tree with you, things are about to get extremely uncomfortable. So get thinking. What would Jane Goodall do, or Dr. Livingston, or—

Forget them, Kendra: what did O'Dea do? She was always the best at getting you out of these situations. What would be her first step? How did she take control of her terrain? She made tunnels, set up magical barriers—

Talked to animals.

My new primate companions furiously shake the tree next to mine, chittering and squeaking at me as though to invite me over. The limbs closest to my neighboring tree are weak, definitely not strong enough to climb on, but maybe to hang or swing from. If I could get over to that other tree, it might give me enough lead time on the ants and half zombie to outrun them and try to find a way out of here.

Below me, the fire ants reach the zombie torso, flooding over it. The undead creature feels no pain, so he pays no mind to the tiny red insects swarming over his shredded waist, onto his back, and up to his face, crawling over his dead eyes and ears. Bit by bit, they nibble away at his graying flesh and turn to red mush as they crawl into his snapping mouth. (The sight reminds me of when Ian and I resorted to eating termites during our last zombie encounter, and I gag.)

The swarm seems to stop at the zombie, and for a moment I consider myself saved—

"YOW!"

A single fire ant bites my arm and jabs his sting into my skin with a feeling not unlike being hit with a hot ember. I flick it off with a cry, only to feel panic grip me as I spy more and more making their way toward me. That's how they operate—one sting releases a phero-mone that invites others to attack; then they latch on with their teeth and continue fiercely stinging.

No time to lose, Kendra. Get moving.

I scoot as far along one branch as possible, until I can feel the leaves from the other tree touching my finger-tips. The rhesus monkeys squeal and gibber, seemingly agitated at the prospect of me being devoured alive by a swarm of ants. They reach their hands out, clenching fingers over and over as if ready to grab me when I leap.

One hard push, Kendra. One small leap, and you can grab that branch, swing into that tree, make it to safety.

My legs shove against my tree's trunk, and for a moment, I am suspended in air. Then my hand closes around the branch in front of me, and my body swings out of one tree and—

—narrowly misses the second one.

"Oh, just *great*—"

Another split second of antigravity, and then I land posterior first onto the jungle floor, my tailbone crying out in a jolt of pain. Above me, the monkeys in the tree begin shrieking wildly. There's only a moment for me to hold my rear and hiss through my incisors, and then the half zombie is crawling forward at me, gasping hungrily as it claws the ground in the hopes of gaining on me, its rotten snaggle-toothed, insect-covered face filling my field of vision, reminding me of every haunting dream I've had since the mountain.

A scream escapes my lips as I try to scoot back from the ant-riddled corpse as he groans and slavers his way across the jungle floor, somehow gaining on me even with his complete lack of legs. At first, I am positive I can get to my feet and run from him, but then my back presses against the cold, jagged wall of stone around the pit, and realize I've run out of places to go.

And now you die, Kendra. That's all there is to it. You had a good life—loved your parents, made amazing friends with magical powers. I'm sorry we couldn't think you out of this one. Hopefully he'll get you in the throat, make it quick, so you don't have fire ant stings as your last sensation. Maybe you'll come back as an owl.

The zombie moans through a mouthful of squirming red ants and reaches out a hand, covered with stinging ruby dots, toward my face.

Then, sounds, sounds unlike anything I've ever

heard, roaring thunder right next to my face. It sends me wriggling in terror. The zombie's skull explodes, and then he bursts all along his back, sending a shower of petrified flesh, black scabby goo, and twitching red ants flying across the jungle, painting the trees with thick dark blood. A stripe of it hits my shirt, and I bite my lip so hard it hurts, trying not to cry out again.

For a moment, there is deafening silence, and then a loud hissing noise and a cold feeling on my shoulder and chest.

"There we go."

My eyes swing over and take in a man crouched in front of me, muscular and huge, his mouth twisted beneath a handlebar mustache. He is dressed in military gear—shiny black combat boots, brown leather gloves, black shirt, black fatigues, and a black soldier's cap. A wreath of nylon rope hangs over one shoulder, a smoking assault rifle over the other. He looks powerful and muscular, but his face is that of an old soul, creased with lines and tightened into practiced concentration.

In his hand is a tiny aerosol can from which he sprays some kind of freezing agent on the splatter of zombie blood on my shirt. When he finishes, he gives the shirt a shake, and the black fluid falls off in crystallized pieces.

"Can't have any of that getting into your skin," he says in a gruff baritone voice. "Wouldn't want you getting infected."

"Who—who are you?" I manage to say.

He smiles. "A friend. Your saving grace. Dario. Whatever you like." He stares at me with a confused, dreamy smile. "Wow, look at you. You're just some sweet little girl. It's amazing, who is chosen."

"Excuse me?!"

"Never mind. Sorry to have taken so long in retrieving you, I just—OW!" He slaps his neck, stares at the crushed fire ant, and swears. "Damn ants. Come on, let's get out of here before they swarm us—"

Before he can finish his sentence, there's a blur followed by a hideous splattering noise. Across the pit from us, an undead vacationer has come over the edge, landing in a mangled pile of still-twitching hunks of bone. Looking up, I see more of their shambling forms eagerly heading toward the edge.

"The gunshots must have drawn them," he says, sighing. "Follow me."

He lifts me to my feet, then turns to leave just as another zombie hits the ground in a vivid crunch. Though this man's military gear makes me feel anything but safe, following him seems to be better than the alternative. As we leave, the crunching splats behind us pick up in number.

We stalk through a narrow swath of jungle, the stone walls of the cliff closing in on the sides, the ground growing muddy and loose beneath my feet. My guide's burly frame takes the lead, a machete in his hand, one massive ham hock of an arm slicing through the tangle of pricker bushes, barbed wire, and brown dinner-plate-sized mushrooms growing around us.

"Where am I?" I ask him.

"We actually call this little area of the island the Ant Pit," he says. "You can see why. We've been looking all over for you until we realized that we didn't have a camera down there. My boss was scared we lost you."

"Your boss?" I ask him.

"The current owner of Isla Hambrienta," he says, using his huge blade to spin up and toss away a massive cobweb like it was cotton candy. "He has surveillance technology set up all over the island. Don't worry—your friends are all right."

The rush of relief that comes with the man's statement seems to be timed perfectly with our emergence from the trench of the Ant Pit. With a few expert chops of his machete, my companion and I come out from between the two rock walls and into a vast valley filled with luscious green jungle that swarms up in a great glossy canopy toward the sky, surrounded on all sides by sloping verdant hills. In the middle of it all, however, is something that sets off countless alarms in my brain, it's so unexpected—a huge gray concrete wall at least twenty feet tall, pushing up through the jungle and standing out garishly among the living green all around it. I can hear noises inside—people shouting, motors starting, earth crunching under wheels. My suspicion of such an artificial creation amidst nature's splendor is easily overdone by the pure, soothing relief that seems to fill my every vein and artery.

Civilization. A chance at survival.

"What is this?" I ask him.

"Headquarters," replies my guide. "The boss has very specific needs—"

A crackling, tinny voice interrupts him: *"Dario? Dario, are you there?"*

My guide holds up a finger—*One second*—and pulls a walkie-talkie from his belt. "This is Dario, sir."

"Did you find her?" crackles the voice. *"Is she safe?"*

"She's with me now, sir. We're about a quarter mile from the compound."

"Get her here ASAP," says the speaker. *"The horde should reach us in less than ten minutes, and her friends are on their way."*

From behind the concrete walls, the sound of drums, deep and menacing, fills the air.

My guide—Dario—puts his walkie-talkie back in its belt clip and nods toward the walled compound. "We have to get inside quickly," he explains. "They're almost here." He nods up at the nearest hill. My eyes follow his finger to the trees atop the hills, which rustle and shake with an endless parade of slow-moving shapes that lumber and slouch downhill. A hideous gurgling moan finds its way to my ears, and a shudder creeps through my body.

"I see," I answer. "Let's get going, then."

We march through the jungle toward the compound, my eyes never leaving the rustling shapes in the bush around us. Perhaps—hopefully—two of those silhouettes are Ian and PJ.

CHAPTER NINE

PJ

The air smells like the tail end of a garbage truck as we charge through the jungle, following the green rubber wires as they snake across the forest floor, joined by ever more cables snaking down from their own carefully placed security cameras overhead. I can feel every breath in my mouth, my hair, my chest. Sweat beads up all over my body, but the humidity keeps it from going anywhere, leaving it to hang on my face and soak into my clothes. My entire being feels disgusting, covered in a thin film of itchy grossness. My T-shirt weighs about twenty pounds.

But that's the least of our problems.

The hillside is full of zombies, slow and statuelike as they moan and grunt their way down into the valley, leaving trails of seawater and seaweed behind them. Every rock we hop down from, every tree we come around, reveals to us a new crew of four or five undead, their pale gray flesh crawling with blue veins and snails. And when we come into view, it's always the same—the hands go up, the mouths open with a gush of salt water and the occasional sea creature, and then they begin gurgling their way toward us.

The terrain is strange and foreign to me. The trees here seem misshapen, the local creatures worryingly bright and fast. Huge plants rise out of the ground beside us, vine-covered palms and towering cacti, and there is the sound of animals, birds, and lizards, and maybe some kind of jungle mouse or something, all scurrying away from us and the line of dead on our tails.

Except the bugs. Along with the moaning and the slow, plodding footsteps, the zombies carry with them now a constant hum of insects, flies, and beetles fluttering over and basking in the reek of the walking dead. The zombies don't seem to notice, moving forward despite the stingers in their skin and the feet on their eyes. My whole body shakes every time I hear the wall of buzzing get louder. One more step they've gained on us.

When the burning in my chest beats the fear in my heart, I ask Ian to stop, and the two of us take a second to lean on a tree and catch our breath, even though we can see the shambling corpses approaching us in the distance. We must have gotten good at gauging chase time since our last encounter. The idea almost makes me smile: *If a zombie leaves Philadelphia going .025 miles an hour, and you're running from it at . . .*

"Where do you think the wires lead?" I ask through my heavy breathing.

"We just have to keep running and find out," pants Ian. "Hopefully, there's a Warden at the end of the trail, wherever it leads."

"Maybe," I tell him. "But aren't security cameras a little modern for a Warden? O'Dea was using those old Indian stone walls for barriers, and we saw that big wooden zemi head in the water."

Ian nods. "I just keep waiting for some sign of a Warden, you know? The mountain was covered with sigils and stuff, and all we've seen here is a floating head."

"Good point," I tell him. "Maybe you were right all along—maybe the Warden here just went crazy and torched her seal."

"Why would anyone do that, though?" he asks, squinting.

A sickening thought occurs to me. "Maybe she saw us coming and wants to hurt us," I say. "Maybe this is her way of getting back at the Gravediggers." I shake my head, trying to think. We really do need Kendra right now—if someone *was* trying to attack us, splitting us up is a good way to do it. Maybe there's still time to go back for her, before the zombies overrun the pit she fell in.

As if on cue, two little kids about Kyra's age, one boy and one girl, lurch out of the underbrush, their eyes sunken and their mouths full of black water. The little boy sees me, drops his filth-filled plastic bucket, and begins shuffling in our direction, his throat shivering in a young, high-pitched moan.

Look at them—no older than Kyra. The idea sends a shiver down my spine and a wave of nausea through my stomach.

"Let's keep going," says Ian, a shadow of disgust clouding his face.

My legs, my lungs, everything screams in protest. "Ian, I don't know how much farther I can run," I tell him.

The little zombies reach us, and once again, Ian freezes up, hands at his side, mouth hanging open. I've never seen him like this, so unable to move and act, and it makes my mouth go dry. In my irritation, I shove the little zombie tourists away, watching them stumble to the ground, and then I grab Ian by the arm and lead him away.

Through the haze, I try to remember the one thing I was ever really good at—knowing about movies. All the classic island-of-zombies films flutter through my mind, but they're a confused blur and almost always end in tragedy. Unless you're the virtuous farm girl or the single powerful survivor, you never make it out alive.

But wait. What did O'Dea say—*Gravediggers are chosen when they're needed*? Maybe that's the answer. Maybe those tough, powerful lone-survivor types in all the scary movies were picked by the universe to make it out alive.

"Maybe we need to fight them," I tell him.

Ian's eyes fly wildly around the closing ring of zombies shambling toward us. "PJ, that's crazy. There are over four hundred of them here, and two of us. Besides, we don't have any weapons. Come on, running *always* works."

No. I'm sick of running.

"If O'Dea says we're Gravediggers, it means we're supposed to fight them," I tell him. "Running isn't helping. We need to find some way to combat them."

"And what are you going to do?" shouts Ian. "Just take 'em on hand to hand? Hope that weapons are just going to fall out of the sky?"

Now there's an idea.

In a crouch, I pick up one of the green wires on the jungle floor, pulling up dirt where it's been partially buried to keep it out of view. My eyes follow it up into a tree branch directly over the oncoming horde. With a flashback of Ian's camera mace, I yank hard on the cord, until there's a snap and a security camera comes toppling out of the tree, cracking an overweight zombie tourist in her leathery skull and sending her sprawling, her girth sloshing around in her one-piece bathing suit.

"I get it," says Ian, picking another wire off the ground. Another sharp yank, another zombie down, this one a skinny teenager with no eyes and his ribs poking out from beneath his gray-blue skin.

From behind a nearby tree, a tall zombie, his white polo shirt stained reddish-black and his rotten black mouth torn up one side, comes shambling toward us, no more than ten feet away, and a new idea crosses my mind. For a moment, Ian looks petrified with fear, but when I call his name and toss him the other end of the cable, he gulps and nods knowingly.

"Three, two, one, *NOW*." We go sprinting at the zombie, the wire pulled as tight as possible, and clothes-line the zombie, dragging him backward with a wheezing groan. For a moment, I'm stunned by how ingenious our plan is—

There's a bloodcurdling crunch, and the wire sinks into the zombie's waist. He groans, clawed hands wheeling in the air, and his stomach, head, and shoulders fall forward with a horrible ripping sound. The upper torso lands facedown on the jungle floor with a crash, blackened innards and shreds of meat and barnacles flying everywhere. The creature's legs take two steps back, then fall to the ground. The smell that rises out of the open halves of this guy cannot be described in polite terms.

"*Awesome,*" says Ian, dropping our gore-covered camera wire.

"That was a good idea, though," I tell him. "What if every ten yards, we tie these between two trees, create a tripwire for them? They're probably too stupid to walk around them."

Ian nods furiously, inching farther back from the zombie's upper torso, which continues to moan and claw at the dirty wire. "As long as leaving here is involved," he says.

He's right—*keep moving* is another zombie movie law. With how little I've been watching horror films and shooting my own movies lately—a bit too much like art imitating life these days—I've grown rusty.

We tromp farther into the jungle. Soon, Ian and I are back to panting, desperately trying to catch our breaths. The humidity is terrible—it's like drowning out here, with hot water replacing air in our lungs. My chest has an ember inside it, and every breath is like the push of a bellows.

But my plan works—every few feet, we stop, yank a length of camera cord up from the dirt, and string it tightly between two trees at waist level. As we get farther along, we see our plan take effect, with zombies bunching up into crowds as a front line of staggering, waterlogged corpses push desperately at the wire holding them back. These simple barriers won't hold long—from behind the zombies we can see, there's the sound of hundreds more making their way toward us—but the wires will at least buy us some time, and hopefully will split the legs off one or two more of them.

As we go about tying our fifth zombie clothesline up, my hands feel strange grooves in the trunk of the tree, and I take a step back to observe the bark. What I see sends prickles of cold up and down the back of my neck. I call for Ian, and when he finishes tying his end of the wire and circling around, the bright look in his eyes tells me we're on the same page.

Embedded in the trunk are carefully carved sigils, flourished with dots, lines, and witchy curlicues. I know them from our previous adventure—symbols of power for the Wardens of a cursed place, used to channel magic and contain dark forces. These have great gashes carved through them, like they've been crossed out with a knife.

"Look," says Ian, pointing to the ground. At the tree's base are the pieces of a tribal mask split in two, its once-whole face a grisly grinning skull. In fact, the more my eyes change focus to the background, the more

I start seeing multiple trees, all covered with slashed-up sigils and little bits and pieces of other totems that resemble the zemi we found sticking out of the water—grinning skulls, screaming ghost faces, menacing ogrish mouths—strewn about us. Every magic-looking item in the jungle has been defaced.

"What do you think it means?" asks Ian.

"I don't know" is all I can muster. "It looks like someone really wants those zombies on this island, though."

"Guess your theory is right," says Ian. "Warden goes insane, decides to kill us with zombies."

No, wait, that's not it. Something else is going on here. My mind focuses on the slashes in the trees, the splits in the masks. I study them like a shot in a movie—the artistry, the execution, the steadiness of the hand, the intent. You learn early on in film that nothing's unintentional. There was a designer responsible for every little detail, from the buttons on the romantic lead's dress to the mountains in the distance.

And if you've seen enough movies, as I have, you can tell when a director switched designers midway through.

"No," I tell him. "Look at the slashes through the sigils—done with great strength and little care. And the masks look like they've been broken over someone's knee. This was somebody else, not the person who carved these little designs and built these masks."

Ian squints and blinks. "I don't know, man," he mumbles. "That's a lot of guessing."

"Look at the detail," I tell him. "Anyone with hands small enough to carve these symbols probably couldn't even lift the knife that would be needed to—"

"Forget it," said Ian, pointing to a thick black shape in the leaves at our feet: a wire, snaking off into the distance. "Let's get to wherever all these wires are leading. Once we're there, we can figure this out."

"If whoever put up those cameras is the same person who destroyed these sigils, this might mean trouble," I tell him. All the plot possibilities start running through my head—crazy Warden? Guerilla warriors? Intelligent zombies trying to get more zombies on board? "We can't just go barreling off into the jungle, hoping everything's going to be okay."

"Sure we can!" he says, pointing behind us, toward the moaning and shuffling in the jungle. "You were right before—we've got to survive, and we need to fight them! So far, that's been working out pretty well. Come on, man, we've done this before. Let's keep setting these booby traps and hope we keep them back for long enough."

Honestly, this is nothing like last time; the mountain was a stroll in the park compared to this. It's like Ian *wants* this to be round two of the same story, the sequel, even though *he* isn't behaving like he did last time. Neither of us is. But somewhere deep in my heart, in the part of me that still yearns to watch movies and take care of my sister and be a good person, I feel something pushing me, telling me to agree with him.

"Fine," I tell him. "We keep moving. But if we get taken hostage by hard-core child soldiers with guns, don't say I didn't warn you."

"Duly noted," says Ian, rolling his eyes.

We push on ahead, spiny plants and palm leaves raking our skin (who knew the edges of palm leaves could be so sharp?). All around us, the jungle is alive with the sounds of animals chattering and whooping as they escape the mindless attackers approaching us. Finally, as I stub my toe on a low-lying vine and figure that I can go no further, my eyes follow the wires on the ground until they stop—at a wall. Not a wall like the one on the mountain, all cobbled together, but gray solid concrete wall, like the kind you see on the side of the highway.

Slowly, my eyes look past the endless undergrowth of the jungle and take in more and more of it—about twenty feet high and connecting with some other wall to make some kind of fort or shelter. I tap Ian's shoulder, and he looks up with his eyes glazed, trying to figure out what it is we're looking at. When he does, he drops the wire he's attempting to tie around a tree trunk, and we go barreling for the wall until we smack against it, the concrete cool and pebbly beneath my hand.

"Now what?" asks Ian after a moment.

"There's got to be some kind of door or something," I say. "Maybe if we run around the edge—"

Behind us, there's a snap, followed by a crescendo of moaning. Two more snaps follow, and the sound of the gurgling undead grows deafening.

"I think our clotheslines have just broken," I say softly.

A few yards away, the underbrush crunches beneath unstoppable dead feet, and we see the inevitable. A beach zombie in a bikini sways into view, her one empty eye socket squirming with flies and beetles. Behind her, two more zombie tourists, a stout hairy man in a Speedo and a teenage kid in swim trunks with a huge piece of his cheek missing that reveals a sparkling set of braces, come shuffling into view. They tromp toward us, arms rising, mouths open in rasping growls that drip black brackish blood, heads surrounded in halos of winged insects. And behind *them*, swaying like bruise-colored grass in the breeze, is an endless crowd of *them*, making their inevitable way through every obstacle toward us.

The next thing I know, Ian and I are pounding on the concrete wall, shouting "LET US IN!" until our voices go high and crack. Ian even backs up and throws a shoulder into the wall, like *that* will do anything.

A whirring noise above me pulls me out of our desperate pounding, and my eyes rise up to find a security camera mounted on the wall above us. As I stare at it, its lens refocuses.

"Ian, look!" I say, and then begin waving my arms at the camera. "HEY!" I shout. "HEY! DOWN HERE! COME ON, YOU FOUND-FOOTAGE-LOVING JERKWADS, LET US IN!"

The camera pans over away from us and to the zombies (who are crowding their way closer and closer as we speak). As much as we scream and shout, it stays pinned on the oncoming horde, not on us.

"Okay, plan B," says Ian. He points to a huge tree only a few feet away from the wall, its trunk leaning in a slant along the concrete barrier. "We climb that and try to climb over the wall."

"If they're not going to save us when we wave at their camera, they're going to be upset if we climb over their wall," I say. "And they might not be the kind of people who—" The bikini zombie comes lunging for me, mouth gaping wide in a hungry gasp, and in a bolt of pure panic I grab a stick from off the ground and jab it in her eye socket with a wet crunching sound and a bustle of flies. I shove her back into Speedo and Braces, who all shuffle backward for barely a second before coming back at us.

"You were saying?" says Ian.

"Never mind," I say.

Ian gets on his feet, hunched over to keep himself balanced as he shimmies up the trunk like one of the monkeys we just befriended. When I wrap my body around the tree, the bark bites into my cheek and legs with its ridged edges, but somehow I manage to inch my way bit by bit up the tree until I'm a good ten feet off the ground, and can see the top of the concrete wall backed by brilliant blue sky.

Beneath us, the horde converges, a mass of putrid pale gray skin and torn, stained swim gear. Their hands reach up like the tentacles of some big sea anemone, fingers twitching and swaying as they attempt to claw us out of the air. The stench is unbearable, drifting up to us in big soggy clouds and burning our nostrils. My eyes water, and I can't help but gag, feeling all the fresh monkey water threatening to come back on me. Ian whistles, scrunching up his nose.

That familiar old voice, the one in my heart that's pushing me on, speaks to me about how I would shoot this great death scene, and I have to clench my eyes shut hard to force it out. Not the time, not now . . . but it's no use, I can't get it out of my head. For a moment, I raise one hand, making an L of it so as to corner a frame, and take in the view from where I am—a bit of palm tree in the foreground, a bit of foliage in the background, and the zombie tourists, a horrible crowd of walking drowned death, all clawing up at us like they're trying to fly. If only I could put a yellow filter on it, make it look older and more—

My balance slips for a moment. I cling tight to the tree, but it's no use—I go sliding over the edge, my body hanging down from the underside of the trunk like some kind of tree sloth. Ian calls out my name, panicked. Beneath us, the zombies get excited, beginning a new round of hissing and growling.

"Hold on, PJ!" screams Ian. "I'm going to come get you—hey, what the—" Then he's gone, yanked over the edge of the concrete wall.

"Ian!" I scream. "Are you okay?"

A man dressed in muted green army fatigues leans over the edge of the wall, extending a hand down to me.

"Who are you?" I ask.

"Does it matter?" he booms. "Come on, take my hand."

Oh God. On the one hand, this is my only chance at survival. On the other, if I let go, there's a great chance I'm going to fall right into the zombie horde.

"Do it!" shouts the guy.

"One," I count. "Two . . . THREE!" With every muscle in my body, I swing hard toward the wall, throwing out my hand, and I feel the soldier's huge, rough palm wrap around my wrist just as I lose my grip and go dangling. In no time, he's got me yanked over the wall and into safety. Behind me, the white noise of gurgling dead throats and humming insects fades to a manageable level.

We descend a metal ladder to the floor, where Ian stands next to a different man in the same outfit with a rifle strapped around his neck. Ian's chest rises and falls, and I hop down next to him.

"You all right, man?" he says.

"I think so," I tell him, and then, taking in the rest of our surroundings, "Where are we?"

Within the barrier is some sort of facility, sprawling out in all directions. Half of it is occupied by what look like thatched huts of various sizes and lengths, and the other is full of massive silver trailers like the kind used on Hollywood sets, except these are done in a military motif, metal siding riveted throughout. The ground beneath us is pounded dirt strewn with sawdust. Through the compound runs a huge rubber walkway splitting the miniature city in two, half huts, half trailers. Along it course wires, cables, and pipes, all manner of modern technology and plumbing.

People in military fatigues, some of them carrying huge guns, walk around with aggressive frowns, every so often climbing one of the ladders dotting the inside of the wall. A few scattered men and women in lab coats scuttle here and there, their hands full of papers and iPads. In the distance, a helicopter stands, a big red *DM* logo stenciled on its side in intense red letters—in fact, the *DM* seems to be on everything around us: the trailers, the huts, even the walkway beneath us.

"You're safe now, guys," says one of the soldiers.

For a moment, we're just stunned, and then Ian and I are hugging hard, cackling at the top of our lungs at the idea of "safe," of not having to run or hide or rely on the charity of monkeys from here on out. But there's still one problem: "We have a friend out in the jungle, who fell down a deep pit—"

"The little girl with all the hair?" says the soldier who grabbed me, sending my heart into backflips. "Yeah, she's here. They're waiting for you."

"They?" I ask as we follow behind him.

"Your friend," he says, "and your host."

We walk through the compound, following the soft padding of the soldier's feet on the rubber walkway. The whole time, the people we pass give us an eye, as though they've been expecting us. There's an eerie feeling around, making the place feel very quiet even though motors rev and wires hum and zombies moan in the background.

"One of these soldiers must have been the guy talking to us on the walkie-talkie," I whisper to Ian.

"Definitely," he says. "It had this weird *DM* logo on it too. Man, I could *swear* I know that logo from someplace. . . ."

Finally, we reach one large thatched hut near the far wall, humming electrically, with a single door that says DM. Our soldier knocks twice on the door, and a voice spits out of an intercom speaker: "*Yeah, bring them in.*"

He opens the door and ushers us into . . .

. . . air-conditioning. Glorious, crisp, livable air-conditioning. And the faint smell of pine.

The thatched hut is a lot less island rustic on the inside than it appeared from outside. The thatch and reeds are just a covering—within, there are white walls and a ceiling like a steel cage. Every available piece of space on one wall is filled with television screens displaying different parts of the island, most of them featuring the lumbering silhouettes of the zombie horde. Speakers mounted on one wall softly play punk rock.

Across the hut, Kendra smiles up at us from a puffy beanbag chair. "Fancy meeting you here," she says.

In seconds, Ian and I are across the room, our arms around her, screaming in joy. She laughs and blushes dark brown, but hugs us back, joining in our laughter. For the first time today, all is right with me.

"How'd you get here?" I ask her.

"He sent someone to get me," she says, pointing across the room, where a skinny boy with long hair and dark glasses smiles at us from behind a desk. He's taller than us, but not by much—maybe he's around sixteen years old?

"Who the heck is he?" asks Ian.

The boy laughs. "Believe it or not, Ian, I'm your biggest fan."

CHAPTER TEN

Ian

It's already kind of weird and random, this teenage kid having some kind of ultra-tech-savvy home base out in the middle of the island of the zombies, but him knowing my name is just too much, so I back up a few steps.

"Who are you?" I ask.

"Danny," he says, putting out a hand.

My hand itches to shake his, but I just can't quite do it, 'cause somewhere in the back of my head, I hear my mom's voice from when I was little, saying, *Don't talk to strangers*, and given the circumstances—the fortress on the island and the wall of zombie-filled monitors—this guy is as strange as it gets.

"Ian, relax," says Kendra. "Danny's a friend. He saved our lives." She turns to him looking all sorry. "He's just nervous. He doesn't know you."

"It's all good," he says, waving her off. "These guys have had a raw day."

For a minute, I'm superconfused—annoyed at Kendra for talking about me like I'm some little boy, freaked out by the flickering images of zombies on screens all around me, worried about this skinny teenager who somehow knows my name. And then I see the poster on the wall behind him, a framed picture of a giant radioactive mutant with green slime pouring out of its mouth and barbed wire over its fists wielding chainsaw nunchakus in front of a crowd of demonically possessed Wall Street businessmen who come pouring out of a half-destroyed city in the background. It's a picture I know from the pages of magazines and the side of a cartridge that's stacked on my desk at home. And suddenly, the *DM* logo stings me like a hornet, and I realize that I *do* know it, that I see it *everywhere*, because this guy, Danny . . .

"Wait . . . are you Danny Melee?" I say, more out of surprise than anything.

He grins. "Bingo dingo."

"You created *Total Wasteland*!" I say, pointing at the poster overhead.

He nods. "And *Pulverizer*, and *Blood Bucket*, and

EctoNauts 2 through 6, and the *Diabolicum* series. Yup, that's me. Here, let's try this again. . . ."

He extends his hand again, and this time I snatch it and shake it hard while he and Kendra laugh, because Danny Melee, wow, man, a household name for anyone who likes to spend their rainy days blowing away zombies (fake zombies, digital zombies) and beating demons at puzzles. He's the child-king of the video game industry, the boy who made his first first-person-shooter when he was eight years old (*Chum*, which totally changed the lesson plan for every game maker out there), who earned his first million at age ten and used it to start an international gaming empire.

The legend himself, in the flesh before me, shaking my hand and laughing with me and my friends. Suddenly, all my worry about getting here turns into this big stupid golf-ball-sized lump in my throat and this tight feeling in my temples, and I'm nodding and grinning, and aw geez, I should let go of his hand—he probably thinks I'm a psychopath.

"I'm a huge fan of your games," I tell him, and then, I don't know why I spill it, but, "All except *Diabolicum II*." I feel my face go off like a light bulb. "Blah, sorry, no offense, it's just—"

He nods. "Too hard."

"Way too hard."

"You're not the first, Ian," he says. "Total tragedy

too, *Shakespearean* tragedy." That line gets a giggle and lip bite from Kendra. "After level three, some really gruesome stuff goes down, but no one could get to it." A disappointed frown crosses his narrow face, dragging the tip of his pointed nose down. It makes him look like a pimply scarecrow, all scrawny branch-limbs and greasy long hair in his face. Then he looks behind me and his eyes light up with a crazy kind of glow. "Speaking of gruesome! PJ, sir, you and I have *words*."

I almost forgot about PJ, and when I turn around I wish that I had. He's standing there, arms wrapped around himself, forehead all bunched up into a Droopy-style wrinkle. "Do we."

"*Horror movies*, my man," says *Danny freakin' Melee*. "Have you heard of this Japanese flick, *Shadow Maiden Village*? So gory. I'm talking Herschell Gordon Lewis gory—"

"Do you have a phone?" snaps PJ, being totally rude. "Sorry, but . . . horror movies can wait. Our parents are at a resort on the mainland, and they're—"

"Done and done, comrades," says Danny.

"What?"

"I called them when I got here," says Kendra, beaming. "I told them that our whale-watching guide took us to an exclusive resort on one of the outlying islands. I figured that would be better than telling them the truth." She shoots a mischievous glance at Danny. "I even had the resort's 'host' speak to them."

Danny clears his throat and says, in a flawless deep French accent, "Absolutely, Monsieur Wright. Your children will be treated as royalty today." This gets Kendra giggling, and Danny takes a little bow, and now I'm giggling, because hey, he's a genius *and* does a perfect French accent; that's not too shabby—

"Did you tell them that O'Dea is missing and probably dead out there?" says PJ in a hard, loud voice that makes us all go silent. "Because that's pretty important."

Kendra turns toward Danny, mouth open and hands held up in an apology, but Melee is cool as a cucumber about it. He picks up a walkie-talkie and puts it to his face. "Dario, any word on that older woman from the recon teams? Over."

A buzz of noise, and then, "None yet, sir. Just some clothing, but it could belong to the hostiles. We assume that since she's a Warden, she'll be able to handle herself. Over." *Hostiles.* That's badass—not zombies or ghouls or whatever, just *hostiles*, the enemy.

"There you go," says Melee. "I've got people all over the island looking for your friend. If she's still around." He shakes his head. "Though with how these Wardens behave, you can never tell."

Kendra and I share a different glance, like, *What does that mean?*

"How do you know about the Wardens?" asks Kendra.

"What are you even *doing* here?" I ask him.

As Danny opens his mouth, there's beeping noise. He pulls a smartphone out of his pocket—the Melee Industries MonoLithium 4.7—smiles, and stands up. "Let's talk about that," he says, "over lunch."

Oh my GOD, CHEESEBURGER.

It's crispy on the outside, perfectly pink and juicy on the inside, dripping, *DRIPPING* with cheddar, ketchup, and a little mayo. The lettuce and tomato are so fresh, it's like they were cut right at the table. The bun is fluffy, more of a potato roll than a burger bun. And if my burger-experienced tongue reads it correctly, there's, what, half a pickle, maybe with a little pickled onion? Danny Melee's chef must be a psychic, because this, man, this is my perfect burger.

We're in a different hut, one done up like a booth at an old-school 1950s diner. Red leather seats, squeezable condiment bottles, the works. We each have specially made lunches—my burger, Kendra's sushi, PJ's croak misser (I think it's called), and Melee's bagel with locks, which I guess are a kind of fish. From what I'm guessing, all these huts and trailers look the same on the outside, but each has its own super high-tech interior, probably all designed by Melee himself. It's like a dream, but this guy, this nerd-turned-multi-millionaire, he seems totally cool with it, like Willy Wonka's skater cousin who gave up the candy biz so he could focus on video games where you dis-member mutants and fire off guns the size of your torso.

After a few minutes of straight-up mindless devouring, I pick up where Kendra left off. "So, Danny," I ask him, "what brings you here?"

"Research, my friend," says Danny, a big smile spreading across his face, like what's it called, the Cheshire cat. "I've got a new game in the works, the likes of which people've never seen, and I've got to do the proper research."

PJ and I share a confused glance; Kendra nods excitedly, cupping her chin. "I don't understand," I come back with. "Is it a . . . a zombie game?"

"Not just any zombie game," says Danny, all excited. "The greatest zombie game of all time. These days, people want a dose of reality in games. Like those army games designed by actual Marines. So I thought why not study *real* zombies, and the *real* people who deal with them? I tossed around a few bucks, did a ton of research, and learned about this place." His smile gets even larger, and he slaps the table with a laugh. "I can tell by the looks on your faces, right? *How'd he find out?!* Wasn't easy, that's the God's-honest. Basically, I'm in New York talking to this Haitian *mambo*—"

"That's a voodoo priestess," says Kendra, in this tone of voice like Danny's teaching a class and we need to pay attention.

"Right, and she's telling me about zombies, the kind they used in Haiti, which were just people all cracked out on mind-altering blowfish powder."

"Fugu," says Kendra excitedly.

"Bingo dingo, Ringo. But I find this one book at her place called *The Warden's Handbook*, and unlike the other stuff she's got lying around, this one's in perfect, readable English, or, well, French, 'cause she's *Haitian*, but you get the idea, it's just *not* in glyphs and sigils and all that. So I page through it, and lo and behold, it's basically the truth about zombies." He's got his big bony hands out in front of him, sort of like PJ framing a shot, only it's like he wants us to get ready, like this is the greatest story ever told. It's sort of a happy version of what PJ does. "So I start digging deeper, asking experts more and more involved in the occult . . . and finally I heard about this place. A secluded 'hungry island' where the locals claim you can see the dead souls of this sunken cruise ship, the *Alabaster*, just sitting at the bottom of the ocean. Only resident? An old woman with 'strange ways' that seem very similar to those in this book I've just come across. And I realize, bam, this is the most *perfect* zombie observation area the world has ever known. This is where my game is going to get made." He frowns, shakes his head, sips his coffee. "But then all the Warden trouble started."

"Oh no, what happened?" says Kendra, leaning

forward and speaking in this faint tone of voice I don't think I've ever heard before.

"It's a bizarre story," he says. "I go ahead and buy this island. Is that a crazy thing to do? Yes. I admit it. But! I'm a little crazy, and I'm invested in giving my fans the most realistic zombie game they've ever seen. Right after I buy it, I take a helicopter in and I meet her, Jeniveve, old woman, *obviously* the island's Warden. At first, she's kind and sweet, gives my team some talismans to ward off any evil karma, and I'm thinking, great, amazing. But then she goes crazy. Starts saying I owe her huge sums of money, threatening to unleash the zombies in the water. I try to talk with her, but it's no use. Then, one day, I find the whole island sabotaged. The sacred masks broken, the symbols on the trees crossed out."

"We saw those on the way here," I say through a big mouthful of beef and bun. "We talked about the Warden going crazy. And then that voice on—"

"Wait," says PJ, cutting me off, his face all pinched and sour. "Was it her who destroyed that buoy head floating out on the water? Or do the zombies just come and go as they please?"

"You got it, PJ," says Danny. "The zemi was incredibly powerful, keeping them down there, apparently. She shot some kind of jungle missle out into the air, blew it up."

PJ squints at him, not buying it. "A *jungle missile?*"

"Oh yeah," says Danny. "She straight-up Hadoukened it into the sky. Tells us we want to see zombies, she'll show us zombies. And then today, we see two things on our security cameras: the island's crawling with zombies, and there are these three kids running around trying to escape them." He smiles at me. "And then we start picking up your chatter on the microphones. And I start to realize what you are. Just like the book said—three of you. And you can commune with the animals—they *love* you! And of course, you're kicking zombie butt left and right. You're Gravediggers, aren't you? You're the fate-chosen zombie fighters."

"We didn't kick *that* much butt," says Kendra, looking away and shrugging.

"Oh, stop the modesty!" says Danny. "You were amazing! Ian, that rock throw! PJ, that leg-shattering kick—"

"All those cameras, and you didn't see what happened to O'Dea?" asks PJ, who, honestly, is getting on my nerves. Why can't he just hang with this cool dude who saved our lives?

"PJ, trust me," says Danny. "My main guy, Dario, is out there looking for her. He was a poacher in Kenya for ages, so he can take on a slew of walking corpses. Though I have to admit, my cameras would be more helpful if you didn't tear twenty-seven of them down to use as maces and tripwires."

"Sorry," I say, feeling heat creep into my face. "It was all we had."

Danny holds up a hand. "No worries. It was totally awesome, so I'm going to let it slide. However, from what I overheard of your conversations out on the island, it sounds like you've done this before. Is that right?"

I'm about to look at PJ and Kendra, try and gauge whether or not we should tell him about Homeroom Earth, our school trip that revealed that walking dead people exist, but Kendra just launches right into it before I can. "We fought a bunch of zombies on a mountain in Montana, where we met O'Dea," she blurts.

"Really," says Danny.

"Well . . . we just found them, by accident," says Kendra. "We didn't know what we were doing. And the zombies were different. It's a long story."

"What do you mean, different?" asks Danny, perking up. "Faster? More powerful?"

"Well, they were mountain zombies," I say. "Dried up by the altitude, dusty and old. These are underwater zombies, all gooey and bloated."

Danny leans toward me, rubbing his chin. "Keep going. Tell me everything."

After dessert—sundaes all around—we move to Melee's third hut, which is done up like an old-school video arcade to a *T*, man, right down to the change dispenser, the soda machine, even the vintage stickers on the sides of the consoles, with all of Danny's games remodeled as stand-up arcade consoles, joysticks and all. The minute we're inside, Danny's putting a roll of quarters into my hands, and I'm hooked up to one of these consoles. It's a little tough, figuring out the controls for *Pulverizer* on three buttons and a joystick when I'm used to my Xbox controller, but my thumbs are quick learners, and I'm whupping street gangs and devil worshippers like nobody's business. At least with these pixilated monsters, I can actually kick butt rather than puking my guts out or having to drag a half-conscious PJ.

The whole time, Danny asks us about zombies, checking in with Dario on his walkie-talkie every time O'Dea gets brought up. He obviously wants this game to be ultrarealistic, because he really quizzes us on every detail. Things I'd never even thought about before.

"Which smelled worse, the mountain zombies or the water ones?"

"Definitely water ones. The mountain ones were like dusty beef jerky, man."

"When they tore each other apart, was there any human stuff left inside, or was it just mush?"

"Oh, there were plenty of . . . human remains from which O'Dea could gather her wares."

"How fast do they get at their fastest?"

"A hard stumble, but not a run. They'd make lousy ball players."

"Do animals eat them?"

"Only insects, it appears. And fish, apparently, judging these most recent revenants."

"Do they lunge with their hands or their mouths?"

"Hands, usually. Sometimes both. Whatever's closest, I guess."

"PJ, were they anything like the ones in the Romero movies?"

"No."

Every time I try to bring up the voice on the walkie-talkie, PJ cuts me off with a complaint—"It's too chilly in here" or "And you're sure those walls are strong enough?" After a while, I catch a dirty stare from him and decide to stop asking.

"You seem to want to know quite a bit about zombies," says Kendra.

"*Everything*," says Danny. "Down to the color of their toenails. This game has to be one-hundred-percent watertight factually. Besides, I'm such a research nerd. All the fact-finding side of game making is my jam."

"I know the feeling," sighs Kendra, her eyes softening.

"You're the geek of the group, huh?" says Danny, smiling. "You know, I have a full-on laboratory set up here, if you want to see some of the stuff we're working on."

"Absolutely!" yelps Kendra, then reels it back in. "If that's all right."

"Totally!" he says. "You have to sign a privacy waiver, but then, yeah, I'd love to get your opinion on my work so far." As he moves toward the door, he shouts back, "You maniacs going to be all right here?"

"We're good," I say as I behead a knife-wielding lowlife and grab a sweet five-hit combo bonus.

"There's an intercom by the door," he says. "If you need anything, you just press the button and speak into it. Feel free to ask for snacks or whatever."

"We got it," says PJ.

Melee and Kendra head back out into the brutal tropical heat and sun, chattering away about scientific progress and lab conditions on the island. It's weird, how different she's acting—it's like there's something always in her eyes, and she keeps shaking her head and smiling at Danny. I don't get it—was there some inside joke between them before we showed up?

After they close the door behind them, the room is silent except for the crashes and smashes of Hank Butcher of *Pulverizer* obliterating a meth warehouse, and it's pretty obvious that PJ is dying to say something, because he's never this quiet when it's just us. "How long are you going to play that?" PJ asks from behind me.

Did I call it or what? "Probably for a while," I say. "I still have a ton of lives. There's a Player Two stick if you're down. . . ." He's quiet again, so I say what he's been driving at since we entered Danny's compound. "I get it, man. You don't like it here."

"And you do?"

"There's air-conditioning, there's video games, there's food . . . PJ, the guy's probably going to give you a new camera if you ask. What's not to like?" The screen goes blank in a flash, and the sound of fist meeting face dies out with a moan. Stepping back, I see PJ holding the cord, its three prongs dangling at the end of his hand. "Hey, I was playing that!"

"This doesn't stink to you?" he asks. "A crazy rich guy on an island full of zombies? The fact that he's been watching you on security cameras, but we didn't get rescued until I was dangling from a branch over a pit of monsters?"

Huh. Hearing him say that sends a wave of cold through my chest and stomach . . . but still, it doesn't make sense. "But he saved our lives," I say to him. "He let Kendra call our parents! He even got on his walkie-talkie and told us—"

"Ian, that wasn't him!" whispers PJ, his eyes going wide. "Listen to that kid—he's a teenager who probably pounds Mountain Dew all day. His voice is all scratchy and phlegmy. That man on the walkie-talkie was someone else. Something's going on here—" He shudders and hugs himself. "And the *zombies*. Isn't it weird that's he's so interested in them?"

"*You* know everything about zombies!" I say,

looking for an excuse to not have to worry, or rage, or cry, to just hang out and play some video games, even though I'm beginning to think he's right.

"I like zombie *movies*," he says. "But since I learned they're real, I've been less interested. This guy thinks they're just amazing. It's like he's happy they're here. This is a guy who's read the Warden's handbook, a book we've never seen, but he's asking *us* all about zombies? He probably knows more about being a Gravedigger than we do! Something's not right here."

I try to tell myself he's overreacting, but it's no use—he's got me. The more PJ talks, the worse my stomach feels, and the more this whole place, this fancy jungle compound, seems over-the-top and unnecessary. Everyone else—Danny Melee and all his fancy employees—knows what's going on here, but we three, the kids who just narrowly escaped being eaten alive, have no clue. He's right about the voice too—that was an adult on that walkie-talkie, someone who knew exactly what he was saying. Just like that, the cheeseburger, the arcade games, they're all *wrong*.

Man, I don't want to keep this up. My whole body aches, and I was really happy thinking that this, this was it, our problems were over. But nope.

"What are you thinking?" I ask him.

"I think he definitely blew up the zemi in the water," he says, and *ugh*, what if he's right? Now that PJ has me started, things are beginning to look worse and worse. It also means there's no relaxing, there's no downtime, this is fourth-quarter, twenty-eight-seconds-left serious, and we have to get moving. And I don't really want to. My lungs kind of hurt and the idea of seeing another zombie just brings me down hard.

"We don't know if that's true—"

"Ian, there are so many guns around," he says, looking me dead in the eyes. "With this kind of firepower, he could easily have a grenade launcher." He sneers. "But you're right—it was a *jungle missile.*"

Fine, there it is, sound logic. "What are you thinking we should do?"

"Now that we're safe from the zombies, we need to figure out what's really going on here," says PJ, chewing his lip. "We need someone who knows how to get to the bottom of this. We need . . . we need . . ."

"We need Kendra," I tell him, as much as it pains me to admit it. For the real detective work, we need our Queen Brain. "Let's go get her, then."

"I'm not sure it's going to be that easy," says PJ. "She seems pretty enamored of this guy already."

"She's been here two hours, tops!" I tell him. "Come on, how in love with the guy could she be—"

"He's taking her to his *lab*, Ian. *Kendra,* to his desert island zombie research lab."

Holy jeez. Hearing him put it into words shakes me

with a hard reality check to the side. Kendra's a spazzed-out genius nerd who doesn't know how to be human, but she's definitely a spazzed-out genius nerd who knows how to be a *girl*.

His lab. Oh man, we might have already lost her.

CHAPTER ELEVEN

Kendra

"And there's my Harvard degree," says Danny.

Speechless. Truly . . . speechless.

We stand in the metal trailer, the inside of which has been converted into a laboratory. Top-of-the-line computer monitors and flat screens glow black, asleep. Chemistry equipment looms all around us—burners, beakers, pipettes, glass stirrers, microscopes, even the occasional centrifuge, all clean and professional and bursting with possibility. On one wall is a huge projector screen, and along the other hang the degrees of all the research staff that Danny has working for him on the island, biologists and botanists here to study the zombies as a race—and there, among their diplomas, is Danny Melee's, from, dare I say its name, *Harvard*.

When Danny first explained to me who he was—I am not a gamer, web-oriented person though I may be—I assumed this island retreat would be comprised mainly of umbrella drinks and hammocks. How wrong I was. He is not a sniveling pimply know-it-all, he's brilliant, and talented, and he's confident, and . . . dark complexioned. And rather tall.

Has dashing *been a vocabulary word yet, Kendra?*

"But you're so young," I stammer, taking in the gothic script that awards Danny a BA in Computer Science with a minor in Graphic Design.

"Yeah, I did it in a couple of years starting when I was thirteen, right after *Chum 2* blew up," he says. "It was actually pretty hard, but I just worked nonstop. It was tough, 'cause I was designing *Diabolicum III* while I was there." He grins sheepishly. "Programming demonic assassins while you're running late to class. Weird life, right?"

Overwhelmed by his short collegiate stint and the feeling that he is literally radiating some kind of heat that I can feel behind my face, I turn to the rest of the lab, a garden of research materials in epic bloom.

"I'm impressed by how . . . extensive your set-up is," I say, trying to find words over my *bafflement* (two? Is that even a word this week? He has nice eyes). "It must

174

have been very expensive."

"Yeah, but I have tons of money," he says. "This kind of research is worth it. You have to understand, Kendra, we came here to make a video game, and we might be revolutionizing science as we know it."

"How so?" I ask.

"Well, here." He sits down at a computer monitor and pats the chair next to him. Slowly, I lower myself into the seat, forcing myself to pin my eyes to the monitor so I stop staring at him. And the devil-may-care way he tucks his hair behind his ear.

He taps the enter key, and the computer wakes up. After the hourglass spins a few times, a black screen with a white line across it fills the square in front of me, throwing dramatic shadows over Danny's smiling face.

"Vocal recognition," coos a woman's voice, causing the line to spike and quiver.

"Danny Danny Bo-Banny," says Danny. He winks at me, and I can't help but giggle.

"Hello, Mr. Melee," hums the computer. "What can I do for you?"

"Ms. Redfield, meet Kendra Wright," he says. He looks at me with an adorably matter-of-fact shrug. "I thought it'd be cool if we named her when we coded her. I like my programs to have personalities, you know?"

"Brilliant," I say.

Easy, Kendra. What will he think, you getting all sidled

up to him? For once in your overeducated life, be cool.

"Do me a favor, say something to her?" He motions to a microphone attached to the computer.

"Uh . . . great to be here?"

"Did you get that, Ms. Redfield?"

"Certainly, Mr. Melee," hums the room. "Ms. Wright's password is now in my vocal databanks. Would you like me to create an account for her?"

"Word, thanks," he says, then gestures nonchalantly at the computer. "Go ahead, ask her a question about our research. Anything you want to know?"

And here I am, my mouth dry, my mind blank. Here is a voice-respondent computer program loaded with information about the walking undead corpses that have so swallowed your free time and brain cell activity for the past four months, and I can think of nothing to say, caught in the headlights of this teenage genius millionaire's eyes.

"Um . . . how . . . are you, Ms. Redfield?"

Immediately, I am embarrassed beyond belief as my mind scours over and over the idiotic nervousness-soaked question that just escaped my lips. This young man's entire digital research library at my fingertips, and I ask the computer how it is?

"I'm fine, Ms. Wright," says the computer in a monotone. "A bit hot today."

Danny gives me a smile that I can only describe as

sweet, as though he's humoring me for my stupid question. My shoulders rise around my ears, and a worm of shame creeps into my stomach.

This is unacceptable. This boy did not bring you to your lab because he wanted to entertain you, Kendra. He saw something in you, too. Those bright, clever eyes recognized a fellow genius, a companion, a friend. You are confronted with a computer here, your favorite of all tools. Do what you're best at doing.

"Ms. Redfield, bring up a full diagnostic of an average zombie specimen with all updated information of the last month highlighted and notated," I said, trying to sound half as brilliant as Danny.

"Now we're talking!" he says with a grin that makes my fingertips tingle.

"Current or game model, Mr. Melee?" hums Ms. Redfield.

"Current, please," Danny says suddenly, waving a hand at the computer. A bloom of heat comes to his cheeks. "My game model isn't fully written yet," he explains. "Work in progress, needs updating. You'll be the first to see it when it's done."

"I can't wait," I tell him.

A screen on the far wall flickers to life, and up comes a digital three-dimensional model of a zombie, rotating as a list of data begins appearing next to it. The rotating digital creature isn't an exact replica of one of the half-melting cadavers banging at the walls outside, just a basic skeleton of one—the bony outstretched arms, the sunken eyes, the slack jaw, the slouched posture. The boxes of written data and sticky notes onscreen sprout lines that point to various color-coded areas of the zombie's body, streaming off endless paragraphs of description.

"This is all the basic stuff we need to know about the zombies," he says. "As you can see, they have a constantly fluctuating body heat depending on their surroundings, blood that clots almost instantly, and a constant but significantly slowed decay process. The fungus that reanimates them is very aggressive—"

"Fungus?" I ask, turning to face him.

"Oh yeah," says Danny. "I guess this is all new to you guys. Ms. Redfield, can we get a close-up on the Melee spore in action next to our digital zombie up there?"

The zombie model moves to the side, and up comes a round microscopic view video of a series of small maggot-shaped blurs shuddering their way along, their outer membranes an oily black color and lined with what look like tiny quivering hairs. The very sight of them twitching and writhing that close up makes the hairs on the nape of my own neck bristle, almost in recognition. It's as though this unseen fungal particle and I are strangely acquainted.

"Meet the Melee spore," he says. "It's a parasitic fungus that actually emulates the behavior of a virus. Watch . . ."

A few red blood cells float onto the screen. The black-lined spore cell drifts over to one, and a single tiny black hair brushes against it, making the blood cell shudder as though stung. The red cell floats away, but already it's beginning to turn a deep inky black. "It's a mean sucker, too," says Danny with a whistle. "That's just the beginning. It actually turns white blood cells into *other* Melee spores, so that the healing process of the zombie's bite is what eventually kills you. By the time you die and reanimate, your brain has basically turned into a large, jelly-like mushroom."

"Is that why head shots don't kill them?" I ask, hoping to use what little practical zombie knowledge I have to my advantage.

"Close!" he says excitedly, slapping me lightly on the arm and sending a wave of excited dizziness through me. "Ms. Redfield, highlight clusters of fungal infestation in the specimen."

Onscreen, the zombie's body takes center stage again and flickers. Blue lines not unlike a human nervous system spread throughout the digital model, making the digital creature look like it's full of lightning. They all meet along the creature's back, where they form a hard, thick line that is flecked with knobs and nodules—a spinal cord.

"Head shots don't work because their brains migrate to their spines," says Danny. "During our tests on some of the zombies we used to drag up from the ocean, before they took over the island, we found that the spore is symbiotic with the nerves. While the brain goes quick—it basically becomes gristle and channels all the corrupted blood—the spine is all nerves, all motor functions. That's what the fungus craves, so that's what the spore controls. You have to crush their spines to re-kill them, so dismemberment, crushing, even *really* advanced decay, these are the ways to destroy them."

"Fascinating," I mumble to no one in particular, taking in the diagram and feeling my own mind nearly drool at the staggering amount of data flashing across the screen.

This is what you've missed while you've been so caught up in making friends and attempting to be normal these past months, Kendra. This is what your mind craves: discovery, progress, as much raw information as humanly possible. When's the last time you pulled up a digital diagram of an animal or peered into a microscope?

"It's pretty disgusting," he says, laughing. "Something like this actually occurs among carpenter ants in Thailand."

"I read about that on *National Geographic*'s website!" I exclaim, my voice echoing throughout the trailer.

He gives a start, but my elation at knowing something he's talking about far outweighs any embarrassment I feel for crying out so loudly. "It's called *Ophiocordyceps*! The fungus splits out of their brains in tuning fork–shaped growths! It makes them behave strangely to increase the spread of the spores!"

"Exactly!" he exclaims. "Wow, this is great. Finally, someone who understands! Who's done her homework!"

A warm feeling, not unlike how I feel when one of my web friends "Likes" one of my posts, spreads through me.

You know that feeling, Kendra. When your fascination becomes something bigger than research, when the facts aren't simply research any longer but something personal, something that inspires you to knowledge? The boys are great—they're your friends, your fellow Gravediggers— but he is a fellow scholar, a fellow thinker. This, Kendra, this is someone just like you. And he's looking at you with those eyes, like he's finally seeing something that meets his approval, and there's a smile on those lips, you could just—

Wait a second.

"Wait a second," I say, trying to shake the blush out of my face and get my mind in order. The niggling worm of doubt won't leave my head, and though Danny's been to Harvard and runs an empire and has smooth skin and smells incredible, some part of his explanation sits poorly with me. "What about the Wardens?"

He snorts. "What about them? A bunch of crazy old witches."

"Exactly, though," I say, holding out my hands. "You're saying this is just a fungus, but what about their magic? How is the fungus related to the curse on the earth?"

His smile half falls—it downgrades from charmed to amused—and he shakes his head. "Come on, Kendra, you're not actually swallowing all this curse mumbo-jumbo, are you?"

My skin crawls with the way he looks at me, as though he's thoroughly disappointed. Immediately, I wonder whether I should have opened my overly curious mouth. Without knowing why, I say, "I'm sorry," but then I can't stop myself. "But . . . you've seen it yourself. The sigils, the, the magic fireball—"

"I mean, I'm not saying the Wardens aren't powerful," says Danny, rolling his eyes. "But *magic* is a big word that gets tossed around a lot. People used to say medicine and lightning and, I don't know, *poetry* were magic. The minute I realized these 'cursed' zombies were caused by a perfectly analyzable fungus, I knew it was all a bunch of hocus-pocus. It's just like in Haiti—it's all drugs, botany, and chemical imbalances that bring the dead back to life."

"But Danny, I've felt it," I try to explain. "O'Dea has used the evil eye on me. I've seen severed hands open doors by being set on fire like candles."

"With all due respect, Kendra, you're being sold a video game," he says. "Even if it looks real, it's all a routine. Trust me, I know." The words sting me to my core, and I look down, trying to consider O'Dea a liar without shrinking into my chair. He goes on: "Maybe the Wardens have some kind of telekinesis, or have the ability to control the electrical currents around them. Maybe they've learned to cultivate the fungus, calm its spread, or increase its potency. And hey, maybe it's *scientifically* paranormal. Maybe there's some serious fringe science going on here, some interdimensional challenges. But I sorely doubt it."

"But . . . the zombies are caused by something terrible happening, aren't they? Bloodshed leaves the land cursed. You told me this island was cursed by a sunken cruise ship—"

"Again, that's all just a bunch of superstition," says Danny. "I think these places were infected with the fungus before that. The crew of the *Alabaster*—that's the ship that went down by here, the source of all the zombies— probably got infected by the fungus, then went crazy and sank the ship. Same with your mountain. But the idea that, just because a bunch of people died here, this evil fungus magically sprouts and starts bringing them back?" He shakes his head. "Sorry. I won't believe that. Not enough hard science. Just because we've been taught that the dead shouldn't walk doesn't mean I should believe every old wives' tale I'm being told by some crazy witches off in the wilderness. I mean, really, Kendra, grow up—" I must be projecting my emotions in my body language, because he stops and puts a hand on my shoulder, sending a shiver down my vertebrae. "Sorry, look, I didn't mean to sound like a jerk just then."

"No," I mumble, "you're merely expressing your scientific findings."

"Yeah, but I can't be going all patronizing on you," he says, rubbing his hand back and forth. When I finally look up into his eyes, they are sympathetic and kind. "I guess I got a little too excited, finally meeting someone else who might understand these concepts. Most of the time, I feel like I'm midway through *Moby-Dick* while everyone else is stuck on *Burly Bunny*. And I figured you'd see eye-to-eye with me."

A furnace seems to rage in my chest, sending a lovely warmth through my whole body. If he sees me as his intellectual equal, then there must be something to his theories—after all, I'm rather assured of my own beliefs on the subject. And honestly, he's right—so much "magic" has been explained away over the centuries. The Wardens exist in such a weird, insular society that perhaps they've grown to believe what they know is a lie. Has O'Dea ever shown me a microscope slide, or read me a page from this supposed handbook of hers? No, she merely brought me out here unknowingly, without her *magic* to guide her. Danny, meanwhile, is the person who saved my life and handed me evidence. Perhaps it's time to do some rethinking. . . .

"Ahem."

We both spin in our seats, startled. Dario, Danny's huge mustachioed right-hand man, stands behind us, hands clasped behind his back. He smiles at us with what I read to be kind restraint.

"What's up, Dario?" asks Danny.

"Ms. Wright's friends are looking for her," booms Dario.

"Of course," says Danny. "Let's meet up with them."

"We don't have to," I say, trying to force down my disappointment at our research time being cut off. "They'll be fine. Just put on a movie; that should entertain them."

"Nah, you should spend time with them," he says, rising from his chair. "New place, surrounded by zombies . . . they're probably a little freaked out. Speaking of which, how heavily infested are the walls?"

"Not too bad, but the numbers are growing," says Dario. "With your permission, sir, we might attempt to do a quick sweep and destroy a layer of them, just to keep down the crowds still coming from the wreck of the *Alabaster*."

"Go ahead," says Danny, flinging a hand, in charge

of a whole compound as though it's nothing. "Come on, let's go see your travel buddies."

Slowly, I get out of my chair and follow Danny out of the lab, Dario keeping a close tail on us as we stumble out into the damp heat and searing tropical sunlight.

Ian and PJ stand in the center of the compound, accompanied by a man in green fatigues with a rifle in hand. They appear uncomfortable, *jittery* as one might say. At first, I assume they've run out of entertainment, and then I follow their eyes to the wall around the compound, and my ears pick up on the sound rippling through the air so hard that it's almost deafening—moaning, gurgling, the shuffling sound of wet putrescent meat slapping against the wall, the steady drone of insects in the air.

"What's cooking, gents?" says Danny, holding out a closed fist for them to bump. It's cute how he slips into "boy speak" around them. Ian responds in kind. PJ, unsurprisingly, doesn't budge. "Ian, how'd you do on *Pulverizer*?"

"Uh, okay," he says, making a so-so gesture. "Got past the sewer level, but that one's so easy." He shrugs. "Well, you know. Of course you know."

"Word," says Danny. "PJ, you ready to hunker down and watch some horror movies soon?"

"Right, sure," says PJ. "Listen, we were hoping to talk to Kendra."

"Sure," says Danny.

After a brief moment of silence, PJ says, "Yeah, uh, alone, is the thing. Kind of . . . private Gravedigger stuff."

Danny holds up his hands. "Totally, sorry, here I am, hanging around. You guys talk, just let me know when you're done and we'll hang out."

"You don't have to leave!" I say, turning to the boys. "Ian, PJ, you should see Danny's research on the zombies. It's fascinating. Danny, tell them."

"You know what, I want to give you survivors your privacy to talk shop," says Danny, holding up his hands and taking in PJ's sour expression. "Dario, let's go take a look at those numbers." I wave to Danny as he and Dario saunter off, then turn back to my sweaty and agitated friends, frustrated that they've scared our savior and gracious host away.

"What is it?" I ask.

"He your boyfriend now or something?" asks Ian, nodding toward Danny.

Keep calm, Kendra. The last time you bashed Ian in the face was a number of months ago, and you've done well at not bashing him since. Besides, he'll never be able to understand someone as brilliant as Danny.

"He's a great mind and a priceless resource in our victory over these zombies surrounding the compound," I say, folding my arms. "But *thank you*, Ian. Even while we're faced with hundreds of living corpses, you find a way to be obnoxious."

"About that," says PJ. "Let's get out of here, okay?"

"What?"

"Let's leave," he says. "Go back to the resort."

"But . . . but this place!" I say, holding back my astonishment. How can PJ, so obsessed with the cinematic, not see the amazing qualities of this island research facility? "We can't just leave! We're guests of a millionaire genius who wants nothing more than to help us with our war against the undead!" *Go for his weak spot, Kendra.* "PJ, think of the footage! I'm sure Danny has a camera he can lend you, and you could become the official videographer of—"

PJ shakes his head. "Kendra, you're not considering this fully. Think of it this way: in the books you've read—"

"And are you really just going to abandon the search for O'Dea? How heartless."

"—*in the books you've read,*" he continues, his voice wracked with nerves, "do rich geniuses ever do good things on desert islands? No. They hunt humans for game or splice people into manimals or open dinosaur theme parks that go haywire. We need to get back home and get the authorities here."

"Where's your proof?" I ask him, incensed that he would immediately assume Danny is a maniac. "Was it that he saved our lives? Fed us? Allowed us to contact our parents?"

I observe his hardened expression faltering, the old PJ Wilson timidity flickering in his eye. Typical—he has no idea of what he's talking about. "I don't have any proof," he finally admits. "All I know is, this guy gives me the creeps."

"Everything gives you the creeps," I tell him. "Christmas presents would give you the creeps. We've been over this. You're a hypochondriac." I turn to Ian, who shifts from foot to foot as he eyes the buzzing insects that cover the top of the concrete walls. "Ian, can I get some support?"

Ian hisses through his teeth and shakes his head. "Gotta go with PJ here."

"What?" This is genuinely shocking to me—Ian is normally so adventure prone. "All the junk food and arcade games you could ever desire, and you want to abandon them?"

"None of this adds up," he says. "It's all so easy—we *happen* to get to this awesome compound where everything's cool, we *happen* to find out this guy is doing zombie research . . . and has he *really* been trying to find O'Dea? I mean, no one's running around, freaking out about all the walking corpses on the other side of these walls. This all seems like part of a plan."

These boys will never understand, Kendra. They see

someone as smart and rich and fascinating as Danny as a threat.

"This is ridiculous," I tell them. "Let's think about this logically. First, we're safe here—"

"No we're not!" cries PJ, throwing his arms up. "There are zombies everywhere, and we're at the whim of some teenage gamer."

"If you'd give him a chance, you'd see that Danny is more than just a gamer!"

"You're *not* thinking about this logically!" says PJ, jabbing a finger at me. "Just because you have a crush on someone doesn't mean they've got your best interests at heart!"

My cheeks blaze. My words catch in my throat, jagged and hard-edged. Ian whistles softly, looking at his feet. "*Excuse* me?"

"The Kendra I met on the mountain would've never fallen in so easily with this jerk," says PJ, already looking worried he's gone too far, which he most certainly has. "She would've analyzed every situation carefully and made an intelligent decision. Where's *that* Kendra when you need her?"

His words leave a deep emotional sting within me, given how much I've considered that idea of late. Ian rolls his eyes and says something about going easy on me, but the damage is done, and shame radiates out from my chest and into my cheeks, my fingertips, my teeth, the backs of my eyes.

"Maybe you never knew me," I try to say, but the last two words are swallowed up by a tightness in the back of my throat, and then I can't even look at him, so I turn and march off, anger blinding me.

"Kendra," Ian calls out after me, but I keep my head down and my teeth clenched for fear that I might cry, or punch PJ, or perhaps both.

As I approach Danny's laboratory trailer, I hear a voice call out, "Whoa, whoa, slow down," and I see Danny trotting up next to me. "You okay?" he says. "Wow, you look peeved."

"They're always such *children*," I say loudly, hoping they can hear. "They're incapable of being mature, or generous."

"Oh, come on," he says. "To be fair, you're, what, eleven?"

"*Twelve*," I insist, then feel like even more of a complete idiot. That's all I am to him, a brainy little girl who thinks she has any idea of what she's talking about. He's a teenage Harvard grad. I'm nothing compared to him. "Never mind. I probably sound like some puerile brat to you. I'm sure you have better things to do than talk to me right now."

"Aw, it's not like that!" he says, putting a hand on my shoulder and sending goose bumps down my arms. "Kendra, I don't care how old you are, you've got one doozy of a brain on you. You remind me of me at your age—and just like you, I had a lot of people in my life who were unable to understand how quickly I was maturing and coming into my own. You can't let them bring you down."

The corner of his mouth lifts sadly, and my shame seems to slough off in layers. His belief in me is like a jump start, bringing me out of my malaise.

"Thank you," I say to him. "I suppose I let it get to me a bit too much. It's just difficult, being part of this Gravedigger . . . trio. Like I'm supposed to fill my role and not ask questions."

Danny nods knowingly. "Look, I'm not trying to butt my way into anything," he says quietly, "but if you need a hand with those two, maybe I can help."

"What do you mean?"

"Well, it seems like you have two headstrong guys and one bright young mind," he says. "Maybe I can help . . . even the scales. Be a temporary Gravedigger—a supporting presence."

Doesn't that sound wonderful, Kendra? Another deductive intellect on board with us, taking things into consideration the way they should be considered, on the same mature, rational page as you, with the background and the resources to back up his claims. Someone with kind eyes, and a sweet smile, and a love of knowledge. Someone like you.

"I'd like that very much," I tell him.

"Great," he says, tugging me deeper into the compound. "Come on, this is too heavy a conversation for such a nice day, zombies permitting. Let me give you the grand tour. If you liked the lab, you'll love the library."

"Sounds great," I tell him. He hooks out an elbow, and I loop my arm with his. We walk off between the line of huts and trailers, technicians and security personnel stopping to let us pass and giving Danny a polite "Mr. Melee" as we go.

Someone like this could only help us. I'm positive. And I'm sure, once they've been given time to work out their ridiculous prejudices, that the boys will see what a wonderful asset he will be.

CHAPTER TWELVE

PJ

I couldn't trust this guy less.

It's not the money, or the island, or the video games. I took the time to run through those facts in my head, and none of them are what I totally hate about him and this place. That'd be easy—of course I don't love video game geniuses who seem more interested in us being Gravediggers than in our safety. That's a given.

It's that he's lying to us through his bleached teeth. Honestly, look how unfazed he is by us showing up, by the zombies getting loose on the island, by our friend O'Dea either getting lost on his private island or eaten alive by ravenous cadavers. If we'd come upon a shaken, forlorn, *scared* Danny Melee, I might have believed his nonsense about magic fireballs and traitorous Wardens ... but he's taking it all in stride, cool as a cucumber, as though we're all on vacation.

I've seen this movie a million times before—like I said to Ian, the island horror story is so classic, I can recite it in my sleep. And when the genius scientist or missionary or general that an intrepid crew discovers on the island isn't upset, when he's behaving as though everything is going according to plan, it's because it *is*. Because there *is* a plan. And either he came up with it or somebody else we haven't met yet is running the show here.

I think Ian's got it, though. When I pointed out that it wasn't Danny who talked to us on the walkie-talkie, it broke through Danny Melee's hold on him—and to be fair, yeah, this whole island compound with its high walls and high-tech faux thatch huts is pretty impressive—and now Ian's eyes, once distracted, are taking in how intense and strange this whole thing is. Every time we pass an armed guard or a WARNING: HIGH VOLTAGE sign, Ian's forehead wrinkles up, as though he's thinking, *Wait a second, that's not normal.*

Obviously, we're going to have to do this without Kendra for now. Everyone in a five-mile radius can see she's totally head over heels for Danny the whiz kid, and unlike how he won Ian over with junk food and good times, Melee's got his hooks in her emotionally. I admit, maybe I was too harsh, pointing out her crush and making that crack about the old her, but I know that's why she's so smitten with this guy—he's like her, the loner and the brain, the person who stays in charge by quick thinking. The fact that she didn't listen to me with a calm and mechanical mind is proof enough. Her heart's all mixed up in something outside the real issue here, and it's blinding her to what's really important, O'Dea and the undead and getting away from these zombies.

"We need to find out what's really going on," I whisper to Ian as we head back toward the game room, outside of which waits a guard in fatigues with a small pistol in his belt.

"What's your plan?" he whispers back.

Good question. It's time to think like Kendra: obviously our babysitter here is intended to keep us from participating in anything other than the regularly scheduled playtime and snackfest. First things first—we have to get rid of him, and then we're free to do a little snooping.

"Excuse me, sir," I say to our guard, "my friend and I were hoping to get something to eat."

"Rations are to be delivered to you," he says, his eyes hidden behind his shades, giving us a little nod. "Just use the intercom in the game room—"

"Actually, it seems like it's broken," I say. "Right, Ian?"

Ian blinks, dumbfounded. "Is it? I didn't notice."

I glare at Ian, hoping my scowl gets across the point of my words. "Yeah," I say. "We weren't able to get Kendra or Danny on it earlier. Remember?"

Ian rubs his chin, confused, and then, thank you sweet merciful heaven, his eyes widen and he nods hard and knowingly. *Riiight,* he says. "Yeah, it's totally busted. Can you, uh, just run to the kitchen . . . hut . . . and get us some food?"

The soldier glances off into the compound grimly, then back at us. "Kitchen's a trailer," he says. "Okay, sure, I'll go. But you two have to stay here, got it?"

"Oh, of course," says Ian, slapping him on the back and smiling convincingly. (Wow, Ian's a decent actor when he wants to be.) "Us wandering off? We wouldn't do that to you, man. We'd go ourselves, but I doubt you want us sneaking around here on our own, right?"

"What do you want?" he asks.

We need time to get away and really check out the compound. He has to be gone for longer than it takes to grab a bag of potato chips. "We need two salted caramel and hot fudge sundaes with whipped cream but no cherries," I tell him. "And probably a pizza, with mild peppers, sausage, and anchovies. I'm lactose intolerant, so the ice cream and cheese needs to be dairy free, and

Ian here has a gluten allergy, so the pizza dough needs to have no wheat flour in it. Okay?"

The guard stares at me like I'm a freak of nature but finally nods and marches off into the avenues of the compound.

"I think we're good," I tell Ian.

"You don't even know." He smiles as he holds up our guard's identification card, dangling at the end of a lanyard. "Should be able to get into most anywhere now."

"You're a genius," I tell him.

He laughs. "Yeah, okay. Come on, we don't have much time."

We creep off between the big blocky trailers, making sure to stay out of sight of anyone wearing green fatigues.

Ian's the front runner, quick on his feet and lanky enough to stretch his neck around corners and spy danger before it gets to us. At one point, I block out the totally absurd position we're in and look at him—all muscle, back against a steel wall, dirty blond hair sweaty in his face, surrounded by loaded guns and sweltering tropical heat. What's fascinating is how ready he seems now, surrounded by soldiers and machinery, and how quickly he freezes up when facing the zombies. Danger and adventure don't seem to bother him, but the living dead stop him in his tracks.

"Wait," he says as we creep around the corner of

another trailer. "Look." We watch as a group of men and women in bright white lab coats come out of a nearby gray trailer, stenciled with the words PRIVATE! AUTHORIZED PERSONNEL ONLY! Once they're gone, Ian waves his hand toward the trailer's entrance. On the frame is a small black card swiper, and when Ian runs the armed guard's ID through it, the door pops open with a click and we barge inside.

"Finally, they have arrived," says a voice like milk.

"'Bout time, if you ask me," says a voice like gravel.

The holding cells in the trailer aren't like jail cells, with bars and big key locks, but like pet aquariums. Everything is clear, made from the panes of shatterproof plastic with the holes punched in them that span from floor to ceiling to the small benches and reading lamp that sit within each one. In each is a television and a small cot covered in a bedspread. O'Dea sits in one cell, her left forearm bandaged up, while in the other sits a young girl, probably a few years older than us, with dark brown skin and black hair wearing a sleeveless T-shirt and shorts. O'Dea smiles meekly at us, but the other girl keeps her arms folded and her small, black eyes laser beaming at us.

The explosion of relief and happiness in my chest launches me forward, my hands slapping onto the plastic screens separating me and my friend. I'm sure I look like a fly flinging itself into the window, but I don't care.

"You're alive," I cry, taking in her hunched form and wrinkled face and trying as hard as humanly possible not to whoop so loudly that we get found out. "You're alive! They didn't hurt you!"

"Of course I'm alive," she snaps. "You think some video game nerd and his cronies are gonna take me out? Not likely."

"What happened to your arm?" asks Ian, looking happy but alarmed. "You didn't get . . ."

"Bit?" she shakes her head. "When that crazy nerd kid first tried to bring me in, I tried to fight 'em off. Twisted my wrist pretty bad. That's all."

"So Danny Melee's had you here the whole time?" I ask. "What's he been doing to you?"

"Begging, mainly," sneers the younger girl. She's a little shorter than O'Dea, but commands the same presence. "Threatening, otherwise. Where's your third? You three should be working together. Gravediggers always work best in threes."

"Danny Melee laid his million-dollar charm on her, so she's getting a tour of his compound," I tell her.

"Not good," says O'Dea, rubbing her chin. "No telling what that little creep has planned for you kids. With how agitated he was about zombies and Wardens and all that, he probably wants to be part of the game, have his own little zombie adventure. And outsiders messing with the balance is never a good thing."

"What's he been begging you for?" I ask.

"What else—*answers!*" She spits, a pretty gross action within a small plastic cell, but very O'Dea nonetheless. *"How do the drums work? How do the sigils work?* And the *cure!* If I had a nickel for every time some idiot asked about a *cure,* or talked about the *virus,* I'd be able to buy a zombie ranch! He keeps telling me that he *knows* there's a scientific explanation. When threatening to shoot me didn't work, he offered me a million dollars." She shakes her head. "Idiot. That dumb nerd's going to get us all killed."

"People of his kind think anything can be bought," mutters the pretty dark-skinned girl, her upper lip curling.

"Boys, this is Josefina," says O'Dea, motioning to her neighbor. "Josefina, the blond scrawny one's Ian; the little one with the shaky hands is PJ. Josefina's grandmother is the Warden of this island. She's training to take over the family business."

"How are you?" I say, smiling into the girl's dark eyes.

"Quite angry," she snaps back. "I have been kept in this cell for almost two weeks. I would like to leave immediately, if it's quite all right."

"Right, right!" We scramble around the edges of the terrarium walls looking for some kind of handle or lock, but our searches are fruitless. In fact, both of the cells look like they have no doors, like Danny had them built around O'Dea and this Josefina woman.

"Any idea how these things open?" I ask O'Dea.

"I'm afraid we're a little stuck here," she says, sighing and putting a callused hand flat against the plastic pane between us. "Nothing will budge. Everything's nailed or screwed to the ground. I'm afraid I just sat here and let them seal me up like a frog in a jar." Her eyes stay creased, but I can see them go a little soft, and my heart feels as though it's bleeding. "That little weasel told me he knew where you were. That he'd hurt you if I didn't follow his orders. Trust me, PJ, I wanted to go after you kids, but two muscle-bound chumps grabbed me the minute I washed ashore."

"Do you know what he's trying to do?" I ask her. "Shady stuff is going on all over this island."

"Beats me," says O'Dea. "But I bet it's not good. It never is, when normal people stick their noses into the darkness."

"He asked us many questions about the cursed," says Josefina. "Their persistence, appearance, strengths, weaknesses. But he won't listen to our answers. He thinks we are lying to him, and that we are actually scientists or mind-readers." She snorts. "He called me a *faith healer*. The *nerve*!"

Ian frowns. "But when he bought the island, did he—"

"Enough interrogation!" says O'Dea, rapping her

knuckle on the glass. "You need to find a way for us to get out of these plastic boxes! We may have air-conditioning and seven hundred channels, but I'd rather be out there with the dead than in here!"

"There isn't some kind of Warden magic you can use?" asks Ian. "You know, pull the old Hand of Glory trick and knock down the walls?"

"That's exactly the problem," growls O'Dea. "We need organic matter for magic—plants, dirt, bones, pieces of zombies, things like that. With all this high-tech cutting-edge equipment, there's not an organic thing in here. Everything's made of some sort of synthesized artificial material."

"But if we brought you the right materials, could you use them to get out of here?" I ask, the beginnings of a plan slowly coming together in my head. "What would you need to unscrew a panel or shake loose a seam?"

"Bring us part of one of the cursed," says Josefina. "That should be enough of a conduit."

"A zombie?" laughs Ian. "Do you want us to just stroll over to the neighbors and grab a cup of zombie parts?"

"I don't care *how* you find them," Josefina says. "Just bring us a large piece of a cursed body, a hand, a jaw, a heart or lung, and we may be able to use it to shake the walls of this prison."

Her tone sends me jumping, almost afraid. "Are

you sure?" I ask, the thought of abandoning O'Dea for a second time wrenching me apart with worry. "What if they torture you while we're gone? One of us should stay—"

"You've got Gravedigging to do," says O'Dea, waving me off. "You've got to find the right spot for yourself, and then sink your hook into it."

". . . O'Dea, *what does that mean*?" I say.

"It means you've got hands-on work ahead," she says with a grunt. "Go find us a piece of a zombie, PJ. We'll be fine until you return."

As we leave the air-conditioned and shadowy trailer, the outside of the compound assaults my every sense— the blazing hot sun blinds me, the sound of buzzing insects and moaning zombies from outside the wall burrows deep into my ears, and my nostrils burn and stomach heaves at the tangy stench of bad meat hanging in the air. As I watch lab techs and security guards stroll between the huts and trailers, a shudder goes down my spine, leaving me feeling cold and clammy inside even in the suffocating humid heat. Now that I know O'Dea has been a secret prisoner here this whole time, this walled-in encampment of Danny Melee's seems even more like a little county of hell made real. The fact that we now have to find a hunk of a reanimated corpse just adds to that.

"I wish I knew what she means whenever she says

that," mumbles Ian as we stroll along one of the rubber walkways that line the main paths between the trailers and huts. "All this Gravedigger talk. What are we supposed to do, exactly?"

He has a good point. The more O'Dea has talked about us being Gravediggers, the more I've felt confused about what that means. Over and over, she's told us to be on guard, to get ready for trouble coming our way, but there's been no training, no explanation of which way to turn from here on out. Maybe she was right in the graveyard back home—maybe Gravediggers are simply chosen, and we'll obtain our zombie-fighting skills out of nowhere—but this learning-by-doing routine is a bit much. I'm personally getting a little fed up with just walking into situations where I have absolutely no idea what my next move is. Usually, that ends with me getting really upset at my friends. Or fainting. Or both.

"Gentlemen!" We both whirl on our heels to see Dario standing over us with a gigantic smile set beneath his shaggy Scotland Yard mustache. A spatter of black viscous zombie blood dots his shirt, but he uses some kind of aerosol spray on it and brushes it off in a small cloud of frozen zombie blood (since we're in the middle of sleuthing, I'm trying not to find that *extremely* cool). "Everything all right? I didn't expect to find you wandering around the compound on your own." The smile heightens, full-blast, and I almost shudder. "Though you really couldn't go very far, could you?"

"I . . . guess not," I say. "We were just . . . looking for a bathroom."

Hrm. That certainly sounds weak to *me*. Dario nods knowingly, silently, and I figure we've blown it . . . but then he points his thumb over his shoulder.

"There's a lavatory trailer right across from the game room, where you were before," he rumbles in his deep baritone. "Oh, and by the way, I have some news you'll probably be interested in hearing—one of our rescue staff just told me he thinks he's found signs of your friend O'Dea wandering out in the woods. Says if his tracking is right, he'll have her here in no time."

My throat feels like it's covered in slime, and ice cold bird's feet tiptoe down my spine. A glance at Ian, and I see him looking pale and more than a little angry. Because now it's certain—they're all in on it. Dario's just lied right to our faces, telling us that O'Dea's somewhere out in the forest when we know for a fact that she's locked up in a trailer three down and one across, encased in some kind of plastic jar like a lightning bug.

Something about Dario, too, made me wonder if maybe I was wrong. Call it a hunch, but this man-mountain seems familiar to me, like someone I met once a long time ago, and my instincts on things like this—or my worries, more often—are usually good enough that I had hoped he would be the guy to help us. But if he's high up enough in this little compound to be Danny's right-hand man, then he must know. And he lied to us with a smile on his face.

"Great," I say, trying to sound deeply relieved. I even ham it up with a little slapstick—hand to the chest, exhale, wipe my brow. "Oh, wow. I was so worried for a while. Thank you, Dario, you're a lifesaver."

"Not a problem, boys," says Dario. He gives us one last quick nod and then marches past us, nearly knocking me over with his broad shoulders. The minute he turns in between two huts, Ian drops to his knees and begins angrily scanning the walkway.

"What are you doing?" I ask him.

"Trying to find a piece of that zombie blood he sprayed hard," says Ian. "Maybe O'Dea could use it to get out." He sneers. "Then she can hold that lying sack down and I can pull his mustache out hair by hair."

"That's brilliant," I say. My eyes fly to the ground, but unlike Ian, I'm not concentrating on just the place where Dario was standing. I'm seeing the whole walkway—and the faint black gooey boot prints leading from the door of a trailer a few feet down.

"Look," I whisper, pointing. Ian's eyes follow my finger and he nods, rising to his feet. Slowly, we approach the trailer, its door going with scary instead of official—the sign here simply says BIOHAZARD WARN-ING! AUTHORIZED PERSONNEL ONLY.

"That's not good," I say to Ian.

"Definitely," he says.

O'Dea's constant Gravedigger comments echo in my head as I take in the bloody boot print half under the door. "Look," I say, trying to swallow the lump in my throat, "if there's a zombie loose in there, or most of a zombie, we're going to have to act fast—got it?"

"Sure thing," says Ian, shaking out his joints. "Let's do it."

"You're positive?" I ask. It may mess with his confidence, but I have to bring it up: "Because back in the jungle, when you were seizing up like—"

"I'll be *fine*," he snaps, his cheeks flushing red. "I must have eaten something bad. Forget it ever happened." He quickly glances over our shoulders to make sure the coast is clear—one or two guards are hanging around, but their backs are turned to us—and then Ian swipes the key card and we rush into the cool, dark trailer. I take the time to whirl around and slam the door behind us before any prying eyes could catch our movements.

"Oh no," says Ian at my back.

"What?" I ask him. "Do you think we were spotted, or—" When I turn around, I see what Ian's talking about, and my mouth goes dry.

"I'm getting the feeling things here are a lot worse than we thought," whispers Ian.

"Me too," I tell him, my face bathed with eerie blue light and my stomach freezing over.

CHAPTER THIRTEEN

Ian

I'm beginning to think it was that last zombie, in the arts and crafts room, and I know that sounds straight-up no-questions *insane*, but it makes a weird kind of sense.

When we were last up against zombies, one kind of got away from us, and we had to chase it to the camp grounds where our classmates were staying, and it cornered PJ in the arts and crafts room of this camp, Homeroom Earth it was called, but before it could get to him, Kendra came barreling by and melted it with a bucket of hot water (it was a mountain zombie, like Kendra said, so it was all crunchy and dry from the altitude). Or so I've *heard*. Because, here's the thing:

I wasn't there; I didn't face off with this thing; I just warned our teachers and got there in time to find PJ in a puddle of melted zombie.

Now, I'd faced just as many zombies as Kendra and PJ back there, more, even, since I'm the fast athletic kid and get sent out as zombie bait on the regular, so it wasn't that I've never gotten up close and personal with the living dead before, but they really got some one-on-one full contact *Gravedigging* going on in there, you know? They killed that zombie dead, which is what it seems like Gravediggers are meant to do—I don't *know*, definitely, because O'Dea just tells us things that sound like a Gravedigger is either a secret agent or some kind of monk—so maybe that was sort of a scrimmage for them as Gravediggers. And where was I? Nowhere. They got to stare walking death in the face while I cried for teacher.

So maybe, I figure, maybe that lack of practice . . .

. . . is why I keep . . . feeling like this. When I see them. Why my lungs seize and hurt, *ache* in my chest. Why it feels like my whole body's got solid concrete at the center, why my tongue feels like it's actually a rope tied to my guts, and if I pulled it, everything would come out.

The silver metal trailer we're in looks like some dark hallway, but it's lit blue by these two glass cylinders back by the far wall, each one stretching from floor to ceiling and trailing big heaps of wires, cables, and plastic tubes. And in each one floats a zombie, suspended in some kind of blue liquid, thrashing around softly so that little bubbles pop from its mouth and hair and float upward like tiny ghosts. On the left is a man missing his lower lip and most of the skin around his one eye, his polo shirt and board shorts billowing around him in the liquid like he's flying or skydiving. On the right, we have a woman, a little fleshier than her neighbor, her pale dead body wrapped in a bikini and most of her right hand rotted away to a skeleton's claw. And once the door is closed, their pale dead eyes fix on us, and their mouths open but no sound comes out, and they raise their hands and sort of weakly claw at the barrier in front of them, trying and failing to break through it and eat us alive, and every time they slap their dead hands against the glass, there's this thump and this squeak of meat on glass—

My back goes cold, and I realize I'm pressing against the wall, that my body is as flat and straight as a board, and that I haven't taken a breath in, like, thirty seconds, but it's like I can't, like I'm frozen solid in pace.

"Oh no," says PJ in this whispered, hard voice, all deep in the pit of his stomach. "Ian, this is worse than I thought. These have to be some kind of hyperbaric chambers, I'm guessing. They use them all the time in sci-fi movies for collecting data. Probably using whatever fluid this is to read their weight, temperature, things like that. Like this," he says, pointing. Within each cylinder is some sort of drain that seems to be sucking out all the black, brackish blood that clouds off the zombies. My eyes follow the drain to a tube, and then the tube to a third small cylinder on the floor, which collects the black sludgy crud into a single concentrated tube. "This is bad, Ian. This looks a lot like what we call *mad science*." Finally, he looks back at me, and his worried expression goes all slack with shock. "Holy—Ian, are you okay?"

"W-why?" I ask.

"You're really pale and shivering," he says. He puts his hands on my shoulders. "Man, you're freaking out. You have to relax."

But it's like I can't, like everything's gone extra-solid and black and white, and now I am breathing, but too hard, and—

"Look at them, Ian," he says. "They're more afraid of *you* than you are of them. Trust me."

And just like that, I feel some heat prickle back into my cheeks. My muscles slowly loosen up one after another, and I can look at the sad-looking corpses in the jars without wanting to blow chunks.

"Sorry," I tell him. "No big deal. Just . . ."

He smiles. "Having a PJ moment."

It manages to squeeze a laugh out of me, though it's

more about relief than anything else. "Totally, man." Slowly, I approach the twin glass tubes and stare at the corpses, their white hands squeaking as they slap at the glass, weak and pathetic. Over and over again, I repeat in my head what PJ said to me—*They're more afraid of you, Ian, they're terrified of you, they have no idea what they're in for if they mess with you*—and bit by bit, my old self comes back. Without even planning to, I put a hand up and touch the glass. I expect it to be cold, but it's warm, vibrating. The zombie inside, pawing at its jail cell, almost looks like it's putting its hand out to say, *No, please, stay away, Ian Buckley. I have no problem with you.*

"So . . . ," says PJ. "How do we . . . do this?"

"Do what?"

"Get one of them out of the jar."

My hand snaps back from the glass, like it's been shocked. Suddenly, I'm not so sure this zombie is all that scared of me. "What?"

"It's just . . . O'Dea needs us to bring her back some part of a zombie," says PJ with this tired shrug. "I mean, we found them. We should get . . . some of them."

"How do you expect to do that?" I ask him, feeling my heart rate threatening to speed up again.

"Maybe there's some sort of control panel," he whispers.

Footsteps ring out outside the door, and voices rumble. PJ and I share a glance, and I whisper the first thing that zips into my head: "Behind the tubes."

It's a tight fit between the wall of the trailer and the blue cylinder, and I'm pretty sure that sitting on this mass of electrical wires and plastic tubes is going to give me some form of butt cancer, but it works—we manage to ball ourselves up out of sight just as the door clicks open and three people enter. Now I'm just here, feeling my legs cramp up, with a few inches of glass between me and starving zombie.

"Where'd you leave her?" rumbles Dario's voice.

"Ah, she's in the library with that antique illuminated *Hexenhammer*," says Danny. "She's having the time of her life. Real brainiac, that one." There's a pause, and then he sighs. "So. Fungal concentration map's still the same, huh?"

"To a T," says a new voice. "No alteration whatsoever."

I bite my lip, trying not to even breathe loudly. My insides feel like rocks. Fungus concentration map? What does that even *mean*? PJ's right—we're in some hot water here.

"It doesn't seem to want to take," rumbles the voice of Dario. "Perhaps we should go without your coveted *head shot*."

"Not gonna happen," says Melee. "That's lame. No one wants to kill a zombie by tearing out its spine. Too in depth, too dirty. The kids want the head shot. It's clean, it's classic."

Wait a second, "head shot"—they're trying to make the zombies more *killable*? Maybe Kendra *was* right. . . .

"It might also be impossible," says Dario.

"You know I don't like that word," snaps Melee. "If we're going to set these things loose"—Whoa, never mind—"they're going to die by head shot. Besides, no one's going to figure out the spine thing until it's too late. We'll lose our audience early on. It'll be *Diabolicum II* all over again. Trust me on this, I know sandbox gameplay. What about the blood?"

"It's the first thing the fungus attacks—"

"Duly *noted*, Sean, I did the research, but have we had any luck either reversing it or bypassing it?"

"Still no change in the slightest," sighs Sean, the third voice. "Because it's the first part of their bodies to go, it would require injecting the deceased during the exact moment of resurrection. The *Alabaster* sank over thirty years ago—these guys' blood was contaminated way back then."

"Still no good," he says. "No one bought *Doom* or *Mortal Combat* or *Total Wasteland* because it had black chunky stuff going everywhere. These things are just so *boring*." He sighs. "All right. Well. Let's double our efforts, guys. If these kids are some real Gravediggers, I'd like to have them working with the game model by tomorrow afternoon."

Tomorrow afternoon? How long's this creep planning on keeping us here? We've got to leave. There's no time to lose. PJ and I have to figure out a—

Uh-oh. Across from me, I see PJ behind his tube, gritting his teeth and grabbing his leg, and from the way he's spazzing out, yup, that's a charley horse. He jams his fist in his mouth, and I try to do some sort of pushing-down-my-palms *Be cool* motion, but it's no use. He starts shaking, rocking back and forth . . . and shaking the cylinder with him.

"What's happening?" says Dario, sounding perplexed.

The tube in front of PJ shakes harder and harder, swings back and forth—

And then tips over, smashing on the floor.

Melee, Dario, and a pudgy balding scientist guy in a lab coat all cry out as goo and glass go everywhere. PJ leaps to his feet with a loud yelp, grabbing at his calf and screaming. My pants go wet as blue zombie preservative liquid splashes around my butt. With PJ's tube gone, I can see Danny, and his eyes are huge, but then suddenly they narrow and get this real sharp kind of brightness to them that I really don't like.

"I can explain everything," PJ moans, holding up his palms to Danny.

Before Danny can respond, the zombie crawls out of the end of his tube and reaches out a festering hand

217

toward the group, spitting scientific goo-glop as he moans deep from his decayed chest.

"I'll handle it," says Dario, producing a huge bowie knife. In a single motion, he grabs the zombie by the neck, wheels around, and drags the moaning corpse outside.

"They . . . aren't killed by getting them in the head," PJ says. "We found that out—"

"I know," says Danny, sounding annoyed. "It's the spine." And then there's a sound like ripping paper and squished cookie dough, and the zombie's bubbling moan cuts short and my throat feels bloated and dead, and PJ rears his arms up like he's seen something terrible. After a few more disgusting sounds ring out in the air—Danny doesn't even flinch, just eyes PJ the whole time—Dario returns, spraying himself with more of that freeze mist.

"Everything good?" says Danny.

"Nothing to worry about," says Dario, brushing the dried zombie gunk off his outfit.

"He's . . . really good at killing those things, huh?" says PJ, taking a step backward.

"Of course he is," snaps Danny. "That's easy. That's not what we're trying to do."

"You're . . . you're not?" asks PJ, reading my mind.

Danny glares at PJ like he's counting in his head, like Kendra, only without a real person behind the eyes.

"PJ, you know you're not supposed to be in here," he mutters.

"You're right," stammers PJ. "I was . . . looking for a movie, and then I found this room, and thought, wow, zombies! And so—"

"PJ," he barks, "stop that. It's like you think I'm stupid."

Oh, man, this is going to get nasty quick. I can hear it in Danny's voice—he doesn't buy it. Honestly, neither do I. Looking for a movie? Come on, PJ.

And I know there's something I can do to help him. Because by the looks on Danny and Dario and Mr. Lab Coat's faces, PJ's going to get it. There's no way out of here, not anytime soon. And there's something I can do, but even thinking about it makes my blood go cold; man, it's a serious risk to us all.

"I'm not Ian," snaps Danny. "Maybe he falls for garbage like that, but I have a brain."

That makes this way, way easier.

Before I can think, I make myself do: feet planted on the back of the tube, butt grounded, hard shove. It works almost better than I plan—instead of tipping over, the cylinder goes flying across the room and slams into Sean the scientist. The two fall to floor, the glass smashing all over him.

"Bail time!" I scream at PJ, jumping to my feet. Danny looks furious, but when he and Dario swipe out their arms at us, they slip on the tube slime and go sliding everywhere. Somehow, PJ and I manage to hop across the liquefied zombie remains and Danny Melee's chest and make it to the other end of the trailer. I look back and see Dario fending off the zombie with a thick-goo-coated forearm, his knife drawn. He shoves her head to the side, and there's this wet popping sound like when you hook your finger in your cheek, and something comes rolling at us—

"Ian, what are you doing!" shrieks PJ as I dart back, snap a hand out, and just try not to think about the sticky soft grapelike ball in my hand, with little red strands coming off it like some tail, all hanging between my fingers. Just like that, my legs reverse, and PJ and I are bolting across the compound, gaining ground back to O'Dea's cell. There's no time. Somewhere behind me, I can hear Danny's voice screaming the words "Those kids!" but I don't care. Once again, it's like the energy overflowed the fear, and I'm just doing, moving.

Next thing I know, we're bursting back into the Warden prison trailer, and I'm trying not to think about the thing in my hand, which feels like an old grape covered in snot. When I slap it on the glass, O'Dea and Josefina rear back, making loud *blecch* noises.

"How'd you get *that*!" asks O'Dea. "Look, it's staring at me!"

"Just *do it*," I shout, holding the eyeball against the

plastic wall while trying not to squish it.

"We just uncovered some serious bad stuff going down," pants PJ, his shoulder to the door. "And we might have accidentally released some zombies inside the compound."

"Oh, *wonderful!*" shouts Josefina.

"Whatever you're going to do, do it fast," I say, "because any minute now, they'll be here looking for us—"

But it doesn't even take a minute, it takes seconds. O'Dea puts both hands against the pane of plastic that forms her cell, closes her eyes, and starts a low growl in her throat that builds and builds until it's a bloodcurdling scream that sounds like it'll tear her throat in half. But then the eyeball starts to hum and turns cold and kind of tingly in my hand, and when I let go of it and we step away from the pane, it hangs there against the wall shivering as though O'Dea has an eye magnet on the other side, like she's holding it up with some kind of string going through the plastic pane.

Then, the eyeball pops with a puff of smoke and a bang like a stuck balloon, making me cry out as little pieces of white stuff spray across the room. The TVs in the cells short out. The whole trailer rocks and shakes and groans like some sort of sick bulldozer.

But just like that, the plastic panes on the front of the cells fall forward, slamming loudly on the floor in front of us. Josefina the back-up Warden walks out looking frightened as O'Dea staggers out of what's left of the trailer and puts a hand to her forehead, and honestly, I feel it too, this little fear that has me wondering . . .

"What kind of spell was *that*?" cries PJ, stunned.

"A really old one," coughs O'Dea. She raises her head and nods at the door. "Come on."

Outside, everything's gone totally nuts. There's a whooping noise, low and intense, like a car alarm got really, really ticked off and went totally crazy, and then we're running through the compound, ducking between trailers and huts, and I'm trying to listen for footsteps and shouting but I can't hear anything over the mixture of screaming alarm and moaning zombies. When we do finally see people, they're not searching for us, they're running back to where we were before, back to the zombie trailer.

I catch a soldier-looking dude on a walkie-talkie say the word *infection* before the gunshot rings out. Then he drops the little black box and sprints off.

This is getting out of hand. I had hoped the adventure had come to a close when we reached Danny Melee's compound, but I've just done more awful stuff in the past five minutes than I'd ever dreamed of. Exploding eyeballs and jarred zombies aren't at *all* how I hoped this would go.

"What now?" says PJ.

"We must leave this place at once," says Josefina.

Okay, next step, *find Kendra and leave this place at once.* I scan the compound around us and finally land on a solution.

"That ladders on the walls," I say, pointing to an abandoned guard ladder rising up the gray block of the wall. The minute I say it, my own stupidity stings me hard, like a missed pass that slams you in the back of the head. "Well, it *is* a way out. Just, you know, with lots of zombies on the other side."

"That can work," says Josefina. "I have a terrifier with me. It scares them. As long as we're quick, we can outrun them. Let's go."

"Wait," says O'Dea suddenly, holding out a hand. "You go. I'm staying."

"*What?*" I find myself saying at the same time as PJ.

"Josefina," she says, "can you think of a way to imprison these creatures back under water, in the sunken cruise ship you were telling me about?"

Josefina furrows her brow but nods. "Carve a new seal from the sacred tree," she says. "But it will take some time—"

"Go find your grandmother," says O'Dea, looking worse than I've ever seen her, like her wrinkles just grew wrinkles. "She'll know what to do. Besides, I've gotta find the third one, the girl. These guys need her—we all do. And honestly, I'm starting to think being out there with your grandma is safer than being here with these psychos." She nods to PJ and me. "Don't worry about them, anyway—they're Gravediggers. They're just arrowheads that have to find their points, is all.

"O'Dea, you need to tell us what that means!" I shout. "How do we fight these things?"

"You'll figure it out," she says. "Sometimes, you're so surprised by the garden, you forget the spade is in your hand. That's all."

"Yeah, *that* helps—"

"HEY!" One of the guards stops in midrun and turns to us, looking confused behind his aviator shades and cigarette. "Wait a minute," he says, reaching for the gun on his hip, "who're you?"

Those're his last words before O'Dea leaps forward and puts a solid right hook into his jaw, sending him flying. She turns to us, her face back to the mean old snaggle-toothed hate stare we're used to, and snarls, "GO NOW."

Just like that, I'm climbing up the ladder, taking the rungs two at a time, scaling the wall—

And stopping, feet half over the edge, staring down into just . . . just the worst thing I've ever seen.

They stretch out some ten or twelve rows deep, a rainbow of gray rot that ranges from dirty tooth yellow to bloated mottled aquamarine and almost entirely swallows the green of the jungle around them. Now that they've been out of the water for long enough, their gooeyness has turned congealed and rotten, falling away to reveal dark strips of rotting muscle. And the whole time, they come at the wall, shoving into one another, slapping their weak claws at the concrete reinforcements and gurgling into the hot jungle air. Some are missing eyes and scalps and limbs, but each shuddering shape has two rows of teeth fluttering open and closed, trying to suck down its prey out of the air. Behind the wall is a barrier of sharp, biting stench and buzzing flies that buzz through the air before re-landing on their undead meals. And their outfits—swim trunks, sarongs, bikinis, water wings, boating blazers, sunglasses dangling from their necks—just make it worse. Like we're onstage at the spring break in hell.

"Get *MOVING!*" screams the almost-a-Warden chick.

But I can't. Once again, my legs turn to ice and my whole spine fuses into a solid piece, and my mouth just opens and closes, opens and closes. I'm useless.

"*Idiota,*" she moans, and leaps past me, flying like a ninja into the crowd of riled-up corpses, who all extend their skeleton hands toward her, and for a second I get ready for it, the sight I've always dreaded, when the zombies finally get hold of one of us and we watch them eat human guts.

Instead, there's a noise like a, what's-it-called? A

maraca, and then the zombies all clutch their ears (or holes or whatever, given their general lack-of-dangling-face-parts thing) and lurch back from the girl, who stands totally unafraid in the middle of them, like she's used to being surrounded by zombies. In her hand is some sort of small black ball that's making the rattling sound as she shakes it.

"Jump!" she cries.

"Please don't make me—"

"You gotta jump, Ian!" screams PJ behind me. "It's the only way! It'll be fine, I promise."

"*Fine?!*" I scream. "Look how many of them there are! I can't—"

"My arm hurts," snaps our new high-maintenance witch-girl, shaking her rattle harder. Around us, more and more zombies are noticing our presence and closing in around us, and some of the ones closest to us are extending their filthy fingertips and snapping teeth toward us despite the maddening rattle.

Before I can say another word, there's a sound, a crack that cuts through the noise all around us—a gunshot. That's when I feel PJ's hands on the small of my back and hear him mumble, "Sorry, Ian," and then he gives me a hard shove and I go tumbling off the wall.

I manage to land decently, and then I'm right in the middle of them, their shriveled claws scratching at their rotting ears and their white eyes spinning in their

sockets. The terrible waves of smell and heat and buzzing flies that come off them make dizzy, like I'm getting
a charley horse right through the very middle of me,
making me bunch up and ache and dry heave.

PJ lands nearby and grabs my forearms. He starts
pulling me through the zombies and to Josefina, saying
something that involves "sorry" and "not normally like
this."

"Move," says Josefina as we reach her, and then she
turns and cuts through the horde with her rattle held
high, the zombies around us falling to their knees like
they're praying to her.

"What about Kendra?" I manage to gasp out.

"She's in O'Dea's hands now," says PJ. "What else
can we do? We have to trust her judgment and go find
this Warden."

I'm not sure I feel the same way about O'Dea anymore, considering that she's the one who sent us out
to frolic among the zombies, but he's right, we've gotta
think on our feet here.

After we pass the thickest part of the groaning
swarms of writhing dead bodies, I can run without PJ's
help, and we march behind Josefina at a brisk pace, turning far-off zombie heads as we crunch our way into the
swaying green forever of the jungle.

CHAPTER FOURTEEN

Kendra

While Danny's antique illuminated copy of the *Der Hexenhammer*, the German witch-hunting manual from the 1400s, is fascinating in its intricacy, the gunshot from outside tears me away from its detailed illustrations of the Devil and his Sabbath. Something about the sound of a gun firing brings about an unrivaled sense of urgency, followed immediately by a blinding fear—unless you're on a shooting range or a hunting trip, such a report means trouble is on its way.

When I burst out of the library hut and into the muggy tropical air, the compound is in chaos. Guards in fatigues fight to run in the same direction that a surge of lab technicians, their white coats billowing out behind them, is fleeing *from*, faces ashen and eyes bulging. In the distance, screaming and the rumbling of machinery mix in the air with the moaning revenants outside the compound walls.

My brain is suddenly gripped with apprehension—the boys are nowhere in sight. In my estimation, a catastrophe that involves panicking adults has a 60 percent chance of involving Ian Buckley.

My feet carry me alongside the soldiers, brushing scientists out of my way as I jog. As I turn around the edge of a trailer, I glimpse Danny and Dario with a small group of guards surrounding them, both of their clothes and hair stained with some type of slimy fluid. Under one of his brawny arms, Dario props a man in a lab coat with a deathly pale face, who clutches his bleeding hand wrapped in a reddening wad of bandages; the look on the scientist's face is one of total hopelessness. Danny stands before a guard, his hands on his hips, appearing considerably peeved.

"And which one hit you?" says Danny.

"The old one, sir," says the guard with a wet snort. "The witch who washed up ashore. She took my walkie-talkie, too. I'm sorry."

An old witch who washed ashore, Kendra? That's O'Dea they're talking about. She's been here!

"Did she go over the wall with the other three?" asks Danny.

"No," says the guard. "That's why I shot at her—she's still in the compound. I swear, sir, I'd never fire a gun at children."

"Over the wall?" I say, causing every head to turn to me at once. "PJ and Ian . . . went out *there?*" Danny's eyes settle on me and switch from confusion to what appears to be terror. For a moment, there is complete silence, with Dario looking angrily at Danny, before the video game prodigy's face slides into an expression of sadness and sympathy. He slowly approaches me and places a hand softly on the side of my shoulder.

"I'm afraid there's been an . . . accident," he says.

"And what was he saying about O'Dea?" I ask. "Danny, *what happened here?*"

He opens his mouth as though to speak, and then does something PJ says I often do—stops, blinks hard, and assesses the situation. In that moment, my fear increases tenfold. Either he's reaching into his mind for the proper answer to my question, or he's attempting to put a spin on his answer that won't cause me panic.

"Your Warden friend somehow busted into the compound with the help of Jeniveve, the island's Warden," he says. "And it looks like she convinced your friends that it was safe to go back over the wall. They just made a jump for it."

"We need to go get them!" I shout, pushing against his hand, trying to move forward and reach the wall in some vain attempt to reverse what has already occurred.

"Kendra, it's useless," says Danny, grabbing my other shoulder and holding me back. "There's no way they made it past that many zombies."

"Sure there is!" I shout, feeling desperation creep into my voice and crack it. "Ian's very strong and fast, and PJ is so much braver than you'd expect! They might have fought their way out, or found a way to melt these zombies, or—"

"Kendra, cut it out," says Danny, "and listen."

For a moment, I want to scream at him to let me go, but when I quiet down, my ears take in the sound of excited gurgling and moaning that rules the air, cut only by crunching footsteps, slapping appendages, and humming insects. It is a constant dull roar beneath every other noise, like the crashing of waves in some starving, mindless, carnivorous ocean.

He's right, Kendra. If there are as many zombies out there as there appear to be, they would've been caught the minute they landed in the crowds. And then—

My mind clouds up with a series of anatomical images, and my field of vision blurs and twists. The cold sparks on my skin dig deep into my waist and legs, numbing them. The path between my stomach and mouth goes dry and feels dangerously short.

"Whoa, whoa, okay, there we go," coos Danny as his arm wraps around my waist, my body feeling cradled and safe in his arms. His voice sounds far away, as if through deep, murky water. "Deep breaths. I know, it's terrible, it's absolutely terrible."

"The bodies," I manage to gasp out. "I need to see . . . make sure they . . ."

Danny grimaces warily, but nods. "Let me figure things out here, and then we'll try to send someone out to scour for . . . remains." He grunts with the effort of holding me up and looks over his shoulder. "Dario, a little help?"

Dario trades the lab-coated doctor off to a guard, who looks reluctant about touching the bleeding man. Then his huge silhouette appears next to me, and his massive hands take me out of Danny's comforting arms, my heart deflating as the smell of Danny's hair and skin is replaced with that of chemicals and gunpowder. "Where would you like me to take her, sir?"

"Bring her to the office," says Danny. "Let her lie down on my couch for a bit. This must be a massive shock to her. Then get back here immediately. We need to assess the situation."

"Of course," says Dario, and then he's lifting me up, moving, the compound moving past me like dreams. For a moment, I'm self-conscious about being carried around by this man as though I were a baby and try to announce that I can walk fine myself, but then the vision returns of Ian and PJ being overwhelmed by the horde of sickening creatures out there, and it just makes my head light and my stomach spasm to the point where I'm grateful to not have to rely on my own center of gravity. Glancing back, I see Danny huddling in close to the lab tech with the bleeding hand, the guard next to them looking suddenly worried.

We reach the cool confines Danny's office, where only hours ago I was happily sitting with my two best friends, and Dario lowers me down on the beanbag across from Danny's desk. He walks back out the door, then stops and glances at me over his shoulder, a broad, calm smile spreading below his mustache.

"It'll all be done soon," he says in a voice much softer and smoother than his normal gruff baritone. "Then you'll be at the front line, where you belong."

"What?" I mumble, but he's already gone.

How long I lie there I can't really say. For a while, all I can do is watch the ceiling spin, and contemplate the road ahead of me.

Ian and PJ, my only two friends, torn to pieces. But more than that, there is the rest of my life. A life without the only two people I have ever felt an emotional connection to. For weeks, I have felt annoyed that I haven't had enough time to reconnect with my internet friends, yet now, staring into the hole where Ian and PJ once occupied in my life, I would never touch another computer again if it meant that they were still here. Ian, the rough-around-the-edges loudmouth who somehow saw through his stupid prejudices enough to like me for who I am. PJ, who could always tell what I was feeling, who had only kind words and good advice for me no matter which way we turned. My eyes sting, and try as I may to be calm and reasonable, the tears begin flowing. Gone. My only friends are dead, taken out of my world, leaving me once again in the place I swore to myself I would never return to: loneliness, complete and terrible solitude.

And their families . . . When I return to the resort, I'll have to tell the Wilsons and the Buckleys that their sons are no more. I will have to look into Kyra Wilson's eyes and explain to her that her brother was torn limb from limb. I alone remain to tell our story. And what story is that? *Zombies* won't do us much good. Mr. Buckley already heard us cry "zombie" during our last skirmish with the undead. He'll probably think I had a nervous breakdown and bashed their heads in with a rock. It doesn't matter that we are actually at war with the undead, that there are hours and hours of security footage around here showing that zombies are real, that we became friends with a zombie-herding witch on a mountain—

Stop, Kendra. Hold that thought. Forget your tears, forget the aching inside yourself. Fire up your brain once more. Consider what you've just said.

O'Dea. That guard said that O'Dea was in the compound somewhere. And if you remember correctly, there are security cameras everywhere here. All you heard from Danny and that guard were word-of-mouth testimony. But if there's one thing you've learned in your life, Kendra, it's that technology doesn't lie.

Suddenly, I'm sitting up and moving to the desk, my eyes focusing on Danny's desktop computer. My fingers fly over the keys, but a warning panel comes up over and over again asking for a password for user: MeleeDLuxe. When I attempt to switch on the screens hanging on the far wall of the hut, the ones that played security footage earlier, a box appears on each asking for the input code. Obviously, they're wired into Danny's personal computer somehow, and I don't have the password for it.

But you have access in the laboratory, Kendra. Danny made you a profile today, after all. He's thoughtful that way.

Danny's ID card lies on his desk, and after a moment of deliberation, I decide he would want me to use it for an inquisitive purpose and slip it into my pocket. If I get the answers I'm looking for, I'll have it back to him in no time.

Outside, guards and lab technicians dart across the rubber walkway, *careening* (five, but who cares?) through the compound. The words I catch are "outbreak" and "unlucky." For the first time, I see how strange this whole set-up is, with a video game designer surrounded by scientists and soldiers. These men don't know the first thing about computer graphics.

A pang of guilt strikes my chest.

PJ and Ian saw it first, Kendra. They took the time to tell you that this place was all wrong, and you couldn't get out of your own head for the five seconds it would have taken to hear them out.

Retracing my steps, I weave between huts and trailers over walkways and coils of wires until I find my way back to the trailer marked LABORATORY, outside of which two lab technicians smoke cigarettes and chatter. Some instinct yanks me behind the edge of the trailer, allowing me to eavesdrop.

"Think they'll catch that so-called witch?" asks one.

"Beats me," says the other. "She's probably gone already. I don't want to hang around here much longer myself, with the new specimen that Melee's working on."

"I know," says the first. "A real shame about Sean."

"I hear he's getting some kind of experimental new treatment, but we didn't get much more than that," replies the second. "Come on, let's go get some lunch." They walk off, leaving me to stare at their white-coated backs.

The new specimen Melee's working on? Do video games have specimens, *Kendra?*

Inside the trailer, it's the same lab as before, though now it feels creepy, menacing. The chemistry equipment around me looks like glass tombstones, still and erect. The computer monitors, all in sleep mode, stand in dumb silence, almost worse than the zombies outside, with green and red lights glowing from their consoles like eyes in the darkness.

I lower myself into the chair behind the one illuminated monitor and begin to type.

"Vocal recognition?"

My nerves ricochet around inside my body as I jump, looking behind me, to either side. The room remains empty.

Calm yourself, Kendra. It's the computer, nothing more.

"Good to be here."

"Invalid entry. Please try again."

Think, Kendra. Computers don't believe in Close Enough. Be exact.

"*Great* to be here?"

There's a pause, in which I can hear computers hum and motherboards click. Then: "Ms. Wright. What can I do for you?"

"Ms. Redfield, can you show me the recent security footage involving a breach of the compound walls?" I ask.

After a pause, the voice says, "Yes, Ms. Wright."

The screen where Danny had showed me his Melee spore flickers to life with security camera footage. For a moment, there's simply a guard watching the ladder, and then he looks over his shoulder, and someone wiry leaps out of the shadows and sucker punches him—

O'Dea. That's O'Dea. I'd know that hair, that silhouette, anywhere.

On camera, the boys and a third person, a girl I've never seen before (she looks young, maybe our age or a little older), come rushing out of the alleys between the trailers and go bounding up the ladder. The girl vanishes, but Ian freezes at the very edge before PJ shoves him in the back and leaps over after him. Their disappearance over the wall pulls the breath from my lungs, and, hands gripping the edge of the desk, I nearly shout, "Switch to exterior camera!"

The screen switches to a bird's-eye view of the horde of zombies parting, thrown into agony like they were by O'Dea's totem sticks up on the mountain. PJ drags Ian by the arm, and the boys and this new girl go sprinting past the disabled masses and into the jungle.

My lightheadedness is replaced by manic excitement as I stand, shove my chair back, and rewatch the video over and over. Sure enough, my friends escaped the zombies. A flicker of the previous camera shows O'Dea snatching something from the guard's belt and darting back into the compound.

This is huge, Kendra! Absolutely epic. They're alive! Danny was wrong.

I gulp down a lump of fear that fills my throat.

Unless he was lying to you, of course.

No, he wouldn't do that, Kendra. He showed you his private research, right? For his upcoming game about the realistic world of zombie killers. Though at no point did he ever mention specimens.

Think, Kendra. You're in a lab—use the scientific method. Hypothesis: Danny Melee is lying to you about something. Next step: test said hypothesis.

"When . . . ," I ask, considering the facts I've been told, "when will research be completed for the new game?"

"Research and launch for *ZA One* remains scheduled for the end of August, or once the game model specimen meets requirements," says the computer. "Shipment of game models begins shortly after." A map pops up on the big screen—Puerto Rico, the mainland, with Isla Hambrienta appearing next to it like a satellite. Lines arch out of the island, landing in different parts of Puerto Rico with large red X's at each touch-down point. Slowly, the red from the X's spreads out, covering the entire island.

In my gut, the nameless organ I've come to trust during situations like these, I sense the incongruity of this. Unless Danny is beta-testing this game just on the island, there should be lines traveling to major distributors around the globe, not to Puerto Rico alone.

"How close is the game model to meeting requirements?" I ask, still unsure what all this means.

"Bringing up game model versus current model," chirps the computer.

The big screen lights up with two images. On the left is the zombie Danny showed me before, skeletal, slumped, husklike, its silhouette illuminated with clusters in its spine—the so-called zombie fungus, the Melee spore, that Danny says is the answer to all of the Wardens' *superstition*.

On the right is . . . something else. A different kind of zombie, eyes endlessly black, mouth agape, fingernails grown out into pointed claws. The glowing clusters in its body show the fungus concentrated in its skull, in the shape of a brain. This creature, this neozombie, has a malevolent sneer on its face, and appears in a semi-crouching position, as though it wants to chase rather than stalk, and pounce rather than shuffle.

This is unbelievable. It's like some sort of zombie evolution. Do these horrible new creatures exist?

Wait a minute. *The specimens that Melee has planned. Work in progress, needs rewriting.*

"What are the requirements for game model?" I say, the breath catching in my esophagus.

The big screen zooms in to a close-up on the zombie

on the right, on its wild feral snarl. "To meet traditional standards and fit consumer expectations, the zombie fungus must be genetically altered," hums Ms. Redfield. "Anticoagulants and hemoglobin steroids will be added to help game model retain traditional red blood for 'gore' effect, while fungal concentration must be raised into the cranium for the player to achieve traditional head shot. It is believed that without these alterations, players would be disappointed by both the zombie's physical appearance and lack of easy killing method. The steroidal mutation also promises a fast, more frenzied model, which will present players with an increased challenge."

My head reels, taking it all in. "What . . ."

"Our tests show that viewers enjoy the easy-kill swarm mentality of the cinematic—"

"Ms. Redfield," I yell, cutting off the computerized voice, "what does *ZA One* stand for?"

"*Zombie Apocalypse First Wave.*"

"*Zombie . . . Apocalypse?*"

"Yes. The first live-action zombie survival game."

Live-action? Meaning real people? "What . . . is the objective of the *ZA One?*"

"Survival."

A cold, dry wind blows over my mouth and into my heart. The map of Puerto Rico floats into my head as horrible, black understanding settles into my heart.

Because it finally all makes sense. Danny's disdain for the Wardens, the heightened security, his fascination with the zombies . . . it's all for this. His final project.

He's not designing a game, *he's turning the world into some kind of . . . apocalyptic zombie theme park. And all of Puerto Rico's going to suffer for it.*

My hand finds my forehead. I lean on the desk, measuring my breath, imagining San Juan full of new superevolved zombies barreling down the streets with the speed of Olympic track stars, chasing down people and eating them alive. My stomach cramps again, threatening to jettison its contents.

My mind wheels through our last interaction with the zombies, trying to pinpoint the moment when things seemed solved. We got lost on the mountain, we found the cabin, we found the zombies, we escaped them, PJ found O'Dea, we found O'Dea . . .

Find O'Dea. You've gotten too distracted by this boy, Kendra, by his sinister plan and his research. From now on, your only goal is find your Warden. She'll know what to do. Everything else comes second.

"Ms. Redfield," I say, trying to keep my voice steady, "the woman in that security video, who punched the guard . . . is she still in—"

The door opens, and I spin in my chair to face Danny, Dario looming behind him. Looking into Danny's face, I see nothing of the boy who was so kind to me earlier today, the boy who I couldn't look away from and couldn't stop thinking about from the moment I met him; instead, there is only cold suspicion and base anger behind those eyes.

For a moment, this change makes me think about the zombies—it's the same body as Danny Melee, but something dark, cruel, and hungry has replaced the part of him that I had wanted to know.

Act natural, Kendra. If Danny is planning to release zombies on the mainland, chances are he'll do worse to you if he finds out you know about his plan. Be clever, be cool, and you can get out of this unscathed.

"What are you doing in here?" he says, his voice frosty and flat, like cardboard, like a stone floor.

I open my mouth, but the excuse I'm attempting to conjure up is nowhere in sight, and the truth blurts out: "I know what you're up to, Danny."

"Oh, really?" he says with a sneer.

Bravo, Kendra. Your cunning is masterful. That's two, now—falling for the evil genius and failing to tell a lie. As long as you're occupying this hole you so quickly dug for yourself, you might as well take decisive action.

"Ms. Redfield," I shout, "delete all files concerning *ZA One* now!"

"You are not authorized to do that, Ms. Wright."

Three for three, Kendra. It was nice knowing you.

"Ms. Redfield," says Danny, "delete Ms. Wright's

account immediately. She won't be using the network here anymore."

"Account deleted," says the computer.

After a pause, Danny shakes his head and lets out a laugh like a rattlesnake's tail. "You know, I thought we really clicked, Kendra," he says. "I felt like we had a really good dialogue going on, and that, I don't know, that maybe you were going to help me realize my vision. This is the kind of behavior I expected from the other two, but you, I thought, were better than this. I guess not, though."

"Danny, please listen to me," I say.

He waves a hand at me. "Nah, we're done with that. Dario, grab her."

CHAPTER FIFTEEN

PJ

Time and space are different in the jungle. With the sheer amount of vegetation and the level of humidity, every minute is an hour, every yard is a mile. Everywhere we go, another insect scuttles along the ground or a huge flapping bird goes sailing a few feet from my face. Every time we break through another curtain of leaves, vines, and bugs, I pray that the ocean will appear, its white sand and blue waters greeting us with the hope of a way out, the memory of the vacation I'm not supposed to be on. Instead, it feels like there's no end to the new layers of green, thriving hell we pass through—thick green leaves, twisted trunks that stretch out of the ground at impossible angles, flitting bugs and birds the color of candy. . . .

And who could forget, zombie tourists.

Not a yard goes by when we don't hear a throaty gurgle or see some pale, waterlogged hands reaching out at us from between the trees. The undead tourists come in all shapes and sizes—fat ones, near skeletons, towering lifeguards, tiny toddlers—but each one comes with the same slow, steady footsteps and straining, agonized hunger, bodies falling to pieces as they drag themselves between rough bark and over jagged rocks. Behind them lie trails of muck-caked tourist items: cameras and sunscreen bottles and half-corroded flip-flops.

None of this fazes Josefina, our new tour guide. The occasional lurching nearby zombie will make her jump back or utter a soft, surprised cry, but a quick shake of her rattle—a "terrifier," she called it—sends the living dead assailants to their knees, their hands clamping over their ears and their gurgles turning to cries of pain. She moves fast, familiar with the winding jungle terrain, so all Ian and I ever get to see is her straight black hair and long brown legs stomping off into the bush, rattle held high in front of her. Her attitude makes me think of O'Dea's—no-nonsense, superconfident, but angry at her situation, maybe at us.

It's hard to look away from her. You have to

understand, we're from a small town in Wyoming. They don't make girls like this back home.

"Another one," she cries, her hand running across the trunk of a nearby tree where a beautiful sigil has been slashed out with two broad knife strokes. "The masks, the sigils . . . *Dios*, he did everything he could to free them from their prison. He is a madman."

"He told us your grandmother was to blame," I say. "That she was the one who destroyed that tiki out in the water—"

She turns on me, her eyes large and shiny with hurt. "It's been *destroyed*? I assumed he'd just removed it and drawn them out! This is terrible!"

"Yeah . . . sorry" is all I can come up with. "He sort of blew it up. There's nothing there but a blackened stump."

She shakes her head. "We must fix this, and soon. As long as that seal is broken, more of the cursed will come onto our shores." Her eyes flick to Ian and me. "For now, at least, you can help lower the numbers. Where are your weapons?"

Our what? I look to Ian, who just shrugs and runs his hand through his sweaty blond hair. "No one gave us any weapons," he says.

"But you've done this before," she says, her shoulders falling. "Your Warden said you had—and besides, she said you were Gravediggers. You cannot simply choose to be a Gravedigger—it is shown to you when you faced the cursed."

"About that," I say. "We're very behind on what being a Gravedigger requires. All this spades-and-arrows talk doesn't make much sense to us—"

"She is saying that you are inexperienced," says Josefina. "That you have the ability in you, but that you have yet to discover how to use it. You have to wield it with a steady hand."

"Okay," I say. "And how do we do that?"

"Well . . . how did you defeat them before?" she asks, agitated.

"We outran them, mostly," says Ian, "and tricked them into killing each other. But we never actually, you know, fought them hand to hand."

The look in her eyes kills me—this perfect blend of disappointment, fear, and anger at herself for believing we might help for a single moment. It's like something out of a movie, and I find myself staring into those eyes rather than looking away, even though they make me feel like I've just let her down.

"Very well," she says, turning back into the jungle. "You are not Gravediggers, simply children who wandered into something you don't understand. Your Warden made a mistake, that's all. Let us find my grandmother. She will know what to do. Follow me."

She keeps moving through the jungle but has lost some of the swiftness in her step. As I trudge after her, Ian sidles up next to me.

"How does she know we *aren't* Gravediggers?" he says.

"She's a Warden in training," I offer, trying to see her side of this. "And we're surrounded by zombies. She's probably—"

"*Nnnraaaagh!*" A cold, wet hand closes around my biceps, and I scream. A female zombie, no older than sixteen when she died, wearing swimsuit tank top and cutoff shorts and dragging a horribly broken leg, lurches across the jungle toward me. Her rotten breath, her steely grip, and her eyes, those livid white eyes, make my face feel like it's full of hot needles and yank the air out of my chest.

"GET IT OFF!" I hear myself scream.

But when I look past the monster I'm grappling with, Ian's frozen in place, mouth open but nothing coming out. And Josefina? She's just staring at me.

"Do something!" cries Ian between gasps. "Use your rattle!"

"Wait," she says, matter-of-factly.

"HELP ME!" I shriek, feeling my throat go raw. The zombie pushes her face close to mine, and I plant a hand on her clammy pale forehead and try to shove back her persistent dead weight.

"You have the spade in your hands," she says. "Use it."

The zombie begins chomping her remaining teeth with a wet slapping sound, now inches away from my ear, but all I can do is watch *her*. Her eyes never go to Ian or the zombie, they just rest on me, brown and hard and glittering like stars.

Spade in my hands. The point of the arrow.

Everything slows down. My breath holds in my lungs; the jungle leaves slow their lazy swaying to a halt; insects float midflutter in the air between us; the dead woman grabbing at my wrists ceases her moaning and hangs in space, mouth open greedily. Even the breeze seems frozen solid in midpush. For the first time in ages, my panic and rage vanish entirely—like when I have a camera, only stronger, faster, cleaner, without the slow fade that comes with queuing up a shot. I can feel every joint in my body, every drop of blood in my veins.

Then, it all clicks together in a blinding instant.

"I'm sorry," I say.

My hand slips over the top of the zombie's scalp, through her matted filthy hair and onto the knob of the back of her skull. My feet pull me aside, and I use her own momentum to toss her past me, sending her face-down in the dirt. Her bones jut out from her back in bulging lines, and without a moment's hesitation, my right foot cocks up and comes down in two hard stomps onto her back, splitting flesh and bone. The zombie shudders, lets out one last gasp, and then a long, sorrowful hiss comes out of her mouth, and her body seems to sag into a pile of garbage.

Suddenly, the focus wears off, sending me reeling. The comedown is hard—everything spins, zooms in and out, turns weird colors. I try to count to ten, but my breath feels like it's catching on something in my throat and tearing open, letting all the oxygen out. Without thinking, I fall to the ground, my head spinning.

"Calm yourself," says a soft, deep voice, and suddenly the world slows down and holds still, and the jungle starts moving at a normal speed again. Josefina squats in front of me, her hand wiping the sweat from my brow. As my panic attack dies down, I feel tears tickling my cheeks. Across from us, Ian stands backed into a tree, eyes bulging at the ruined zombie lying in the dirt nearby.

"Sorry," I whisper to the big brown eyes floating in front of mine.

"Do not apologize," she says, letting go of me. "That was impressive. Forgive me for doubting you. I think you are a Gravedigger after all." A moan echoes around us, and I look up to see a handful of corpses slouching their way toward us through the underbrush. Josefina stands and shakes her rattle, and they collapse in a screaming heap. "For now, though, taking on the lot of them might be overdoing it."

"Sounds about right," I say, hand to my forehead.

We keep powering through the jungle, past overgrown thickets and slow-turning corpses. After a moment, Ian sidles up next to me, still looking completely flabbergasted. My heart is still a complete whirlwind, though, and try as I may, I can't look him full on in the eyes yet.

"*Wow*, dude," he says. "How are you feeling?"

"Scared," I blurt out. "Confused. But also . . . good. Like I had it there, for a moment."

"I'm . . . look, man, I would have helped you, it's just—there's something—"

"It's okay, Ian." I finally look at him, and he's staring straight ahead, lost in embarrassment. "Don't even worry about it. Everything turned out okay."

"It's up ahead," says Josefina, pushing through a massive grove of clawlike leaves. And she's right. It is up ahead.

Suddenly, I wish I had a camera. Not because I'm having a panic attack, but because I've never seen anything this weird before.

A few hundred feet away sits a small bamboo cottage, its roof a plateau of thatch and tile hastily painted with bright red sigils, swirling mixtures of crop circles and runes. Around it loom at least fifty zombies, their swaying, stinking bodies blurring together into a great ring of gleaming white eyes, snarling black mouths, and bruise-gray flesh. And there, on the roof of the building, sits an old woman in a brown dress, her head bowed, her eyes closed. She sits cross-legged with her hands resting on her knees, and from her mouth rumbles a steady stream of droned monotone Spanish that somehow rises above the moaning undead and buzzing flies. A machete lies across her lap.

Magic throbs through the air in a way I don't quite know how to describe. There's no halo of light around this woman, no crackle of electricity, but somehow I can feel that the words she's saying, the thing she's focusing on, is keeping the zombies away. They can't cross whatever barrier she's creating right now.

My stomach churns, but it's as though killing that first zombie helped. Though honestly, I'm not sure I could look away if I wanted to.

"*¡Yaya!*" calls out Josefina.

"Are you kidding me?" whispers Ian, frantic. "You're going to bring them our way!"

"She has them in some sort of trance," says Josefina. Then, even louder: "*¡Yaya! ¿Estás herida? Necesitamos ayuda—*"

The old woman's head snaps up, and her eyes flare out at Josefina, huge and dark and glowing with power. She stops droning on and shrieks a string of Spanish at Josefina, who takes a step back, eyes wide. At the same time, the zombies break out of their weird catatonic state, and the ones in front begin banging their fists on the walls of the cottage, making the Warden on top of it vibrate.

Suddenly, one on the edge of the crowd—male, late twenties, stubble, no left ear, barnacles peppering his tribal tattoos—turns those dead white eyes on us. He groans and extends a hand our way, and others, drawn to his cry, follow him.

The old woman screams out, *"AY!"* She snatches up the machete in her lap and rears it back, and then there's a *wunk!* and the butt of the giant knife wobbles a few inches from my face, the blade wedged in a tree. The Warden goes back to her droning, but not in time to get all the zombies, the few coming our way still trying to fight her magic, get to us, and dig into some fresh meat.

Without a word, Josefina nods, wrenches the machete out of the tree and ducks into the undergrowth, Ian following close behind her. For a moment, I consider standing my ground, trying to stomp some more spinal cords, but I can't lose sight of them, and I'm not sure I could pull it off without Josefina here. For now, I swallow my pride and jog after them.

"What'd your grandmother say?" Ian calls out as we trail her.

Josefina stays quiet for a moment and then rubs at her eyes. "She asked what I was doing here and told me to go carve a new seal before she had to come down here and thrash me," she grumbles in a cracking voice.

"What?" says Ian. "She's not going to help us?"

"We must follow her instructions," she says, trying to keep her face hidden.

"That's not good enough!" shouts Ian, running up next to her. "We've got more zombies around here than we know what to do with! She's not even going to get off her house and—hey!" Ian grabs Josefina's wrist and spins her around. "O'Dea told us to get her! We have to go—"

"*Never* touch me!" yells Josefina, and she raises her machete, brandishing it in Ian's face and sending sparks through my blood.

"Whoa, enough!" I shout, leaping between the two of them. Josefina's lips are trembling, and she's squinting hard. Ian's literally shaking, his teeth gritted, his eyes focused on the blade a few inches away from them.

"Let me take this for a second," I say, pulling the machete out of her hands. Slowly, staring at them, I get an idea, a way to kill two furious birds with one stone. "Josefina, is the path to wherever we're going overgrown? Is there a lot of jungle in our way?"

"Yes," she mutters, shrugging. "Things grow larger the closer we get to our sacred tree."

"Good." I turn to Ian and hold out the machete, the blade gleaming in the light. "Ian, we need a path chopped for us, and I know she and I aren't strong enough to do it."

Slowly, he nods, and something like a smile crosses

his lips. He snatches the machete from my hands, turns to the jungle, and suddenly he's Ian the human lawn mower, hacking his way through the treacherous underbrush with loud cries of exertion, "HA!" "YA!" "GET SOME!"

We begin walking behind Ian, making steady progress and managing to weave around single wandering zombies with ease. With her deep brown eyes, Josefina watches Ian swing the blade. She wipes at them, and then they turn on me and the skin prickles on the back of my neck.

"I'm impressed," she sniffles. "It was like you could read his mind."

"If Ian's being a jerk, it's usually because he's got nothing to do or he feels inadequate," I say. My cheeks burn hot. "Are you okay? What did your grandmother actually say to you?"

"What I told you she said," she says with a sigh. "But . . . I have been in that cell for two weeks, kidnapped, missing, and the first thing she can say to me . . ." She shakes her head and sniffs. "No matter. That is what Wardens are meant to do, take action. I should not need her instructions. It was foolish of me."

"I can understand feeling bad, though," I tell her.

"You cannot," she says. "Wardens are taught, Gravediggers are chosen. I must be the best, at all times, or people will die. Your strength was given to you."

"I'm really not that strong," I admit to her, feeling a stab in my chest. This isn't the kind of thing you're supposed to say to girls, is it? But here it is: "I mean . . . I have a lot of panic issues. I get scared easily. Kendra's the brains of the operation, and Ian's the athletic one, so he never has to be worried—"

"And yet, you are the one who can do his duty, while he freezes up at the sight of one of the cursed," says Josefina, crinkling up her brow. "You must be the heart of your team. Always the strongest."

"The heart?"

She nods as we walk through Ian's wake, a trail of minced jungle salad. "It is not uncommon," she says. "Most Gravedigger groups come in threes and are divided as such. Like Las Matanzas, in Mexico, as I'm sure you know."

"Uh . . . not really, actually," I tell her. "Honestly, we kind of fell into this thing a few months ago, when we ran into some zombies on a mountain. O'Dea just speaks to us in riddles and, like . . . propaganda."

She shakes her head. "It is only because Grave-diggers occur out of necessity," she says. "That confuses Wardens. When there are dark times, and containment is threatened, Gravediggers appear, somehow prepared to stop the cursed from overrunning the land, as if from nowhere. Las Matanzas were the same way. They were a trio of Gravediggers from Guatemala who fought the darkness all over Mexico in the late sixteen hundreds. They cleared out Mayan temples full of mummies and took down hordes of reanimated Spanish colonists. Mexico was a dark place at the time, heavy with bad karma after the Aztecs were conquered and smallpox ravaged the land, and so there was much trouble, many cursed spots. Las Matanzas kept the countryside from being overrun. There were three of them—Matias, Armando, *y* Don José. Matias was a great fighter and was favorite among the ladies, and Armando had a mind sharper than steel, but Don José was the one everyone remembers."

"Why?"

"Because he had great heart," she says. "For every demon he put down, he would bless their bodies, for they *had* been human, and their bodies deserved his blessings." She smiles at me. "I see that in you. A, eh..." She wheels a hand in front of her, deciding on a word. "A quiet power."

I can't help but laugh. "I don't mean to contradict you," I say, "but did you see me back there, against that zombie? I wasn't *powerful*, or incredibly *quiet*. My *heart* nearly gave out back there!"

"And you overcame it," she said. "You meditated, in your panic. You apologized to the cursed one as you put it out of its misery. It takes more than a little muscle to do that."

Is this what I am? Was that the tool O'Dea claims I'm holding, somewhere within me? Staring at the luminous brown eyes, hearing her accented words spoken in a calm, smooth voice, it feels right. She has a point—why *did* I apologize to that zombie before I killed it? How did I know what to do? For a moment, the pressure of our whole horrific situation lets up on me, and I feel my cheeks go rosy as I consider my heart, the power it has. When I look up at Josefina, she's smiling at me, and against all reason, I smile back, like I'm in on the joke.

"Yo." We come to a halt as Ian steps back, blocking our path. He's now in full-on jungle hero mode—face streaked with sweat and dirt, clothes covered with bits of leaves, T-shirt sleeves rolled up to shoulders that rise up and down with panting. It looks like any moment, he's going to fight the Predator. He must have had a lot of steam to blow off.

"Something fishy about this?" he asks, sounding like an eleven-year-old Clint Eastwood. "We haven't seen a zombie in ten minutes. Before, they were everywhere."

"That's because they avoid the sacred palm tree," says Josefina, pointing ahead of us. "The tree is blessed by the powers that be. That is why the seal we carved from it could hold so many of them in the sunken ship—it was made of holy wood."

"So—what?" asks Ian. "We just get to the tree and hack off a piece of wood, then get whittling?"

"Not exactly," says Josefina, pushing on ahead. "The tree is powerful and rare, and so it is guarded."

"By who?" I ask.

We follow her out into a clearing lit golden by the afternoon sun, and in its center sits a tree, a huge palm leaning to one side and swooping into the air, its bushy head spreading out in a lazy green explosion. This is, no question, some ancient sacred tree—its ropy roots snake along the ground around it, and its bark looks especially tough and brown with centuries of age. When the breeze touches it, a sound like crashing waves and soothing whispers shuffles through the air. From beneath its leaves, huge pod-shaped fruits dangle over the jungle floor, swaying gently.

"That's the tree," says Josefina.

"You don't say," laughs Ian.

"And those are the guardians," says Josefina, pointing at the tree again.

I open my mouth, about to tell her that I don't see any guardians. My mouth stays open, though, as one of the fruit pods shifts, twists, and spreads wide its leathery wings.

CHAPTER SIXTEEN

Ian

I don't like bats.

I don't know what's happening with the zombies. I don't know why they choke me up and make me feel sick like a chump. But it's not that, with bats. It's not a PJ thing, either, like I'm worried they're going to give me rabies, but . . . there's something about them. It's the way they look, mostly, like a wasp and a squirrel had a baby, this in-between thing, where it's all leathery and pointed and hairy at the same time, that just . . . *ugh*. They give me the willies. And right now, what I need is *Kendra*, telling me that bats do this and that for the ecosystem and there've been *blah* many bat attacks in the

US this year, because that turns them into something simple that you can put into a cage instead of . . .

Instead of *bats*. Flapping, swooping, biting *bats*.

And here, on this tree, are about five of the biggest bats I've ever seen, dangling like giant black pears.

When the first one unfolds its wings and we realize that the magical guardians of the special tree aren't blue kangaroo people or ancient ghost warriors but a bunch of *bats*, it's like a bad taste gets into my mouth—again, not like the zombies, but like the *smell* of the zombies, where I'm just grossed out by how little I want to be around it. The Warden chick obviously doesn't care, because they're her secret guardians, and PJ nods, ready for anything, which kind of gets to me. That kung-fu zombie kill was beautiful, the kind of thing that would get you a pat on the back from Coach Leider. So here I am, suddenly, totally unable to get my Gravedigger on. If there was ever a time to prove myself, it'd be now. Question is, can I?

"What's the plan?" I say, tightening my grip on the machete.

"You must knock one of the nuts off the tree," says Josefina. "Then I will carve it into a totem. They are up in the branches, so you will have to climb."

"What about *them*?" I ask, pointing to the giant bats, and I mean *huge*, man, almost as big as PJ, who gives me a dirty look, but whatever, this girl is telling me to waltz up to a freakishly large bat like it's no big deal. Uh-uh. "Why can't you go get the magic nut or whatever?"

"I am not yet a true Warden," she says. "I have not learned to speak to the creatures yet, so they will not allow me near the tree. But they will see that you are servants of good karma and let you pass. You must go without me."

Part of me wants to rage at her, because this whole explanation just sounds like a chance to get good ol' Ian Buckley to maybe get his face eaten off by a giant bat while Josefina the half Warden hangs back and files her nails. But then I remember the monkeys saving PJ, remember that voice on the walkie-talkie telling us that the animals respect us, and I realize she's probably right. Honestly, I just really don't want to have to deal with bats.

"Are you sure this will work?" I ask.

"Yes," she says. "Quickly. There is not much time."

Okay, game face: on. I look at PJ and give a nod toward the tree, and then we crouch low and leave the comfort of the tall grass, jogging out into the clearing where the giant palm tree stands.

At least I have the machete. If one of these bats comes at me, I can scare it off.

As the tree gets closer in our field of vision, PJ whispers, "All right, man. You've got this. Quick and simple."

"Right," I tell him.

"You're the man, Ian."

"I got that." *Ugh.* PJ is so see-through, it's not even funny: if I'm feeling superconfident, I won't freeze up. No way, man. I will not, I repeat, *will not* be babied by PJ Wilson. Not happening. I'd rather *eat* one of those bats than let him make me into the scared kid. That's *his* job. *I'm* the crazy headstrong jock, right? Just because I'm having some kind of issue with the zombies doesn't mean I need someone to change my diaper. All this means is that there's something wrong with me, and I need to keep at it until I've figured it out.

The tree is shaped like a big hook, a question mark leaning back, so I can actually walk up it like a balance beam for most of the climb. The trunk is huge and thick at its base, and it supports me pretty easily as I baby step my way onto it. PJ runs up behind me, but I motion with the machete for him to get under the leaves so that he can grab one of these coconuts when I knock it down.

As I inch my way up the trunk, I keep my eyes on the black drop-shaped forms hanging from the tree. They look just like speed bags at a boxing gym or something, totally harmless, and then one of them opens up its folds, and there's a quick flash of something—claw or ear or nose—before it vanishes again.

"Be careful!" hisses PJ from below me.

"I know what I'm d—" Of course, the minute those

words leave my mouth, my foot slips and I almost fall. "Whoa!" I cry out, jabbing the machete into the trunk and balancing myself.

And I'm not sure if it was the yelp or the machete in the tree, but when I look back up, they're all *staring at me.*

Five pairs of black, glittering eyes split by short stubby snouts and fleshy, triangle-shaped noses. Their ears are like leaves, long and perfectly pointed. Every time I try to focus on the task at hand, I look up to see bat eyes, quiet and huge, watching me move, and it's like they're judging me, sizing me up. My palms sweat like crazy, and my throat goes dry.

And now the tree hooks back up. So I have to climb for real.

The bark is rough and flaky, digging into my skin as I wrap my arms and legs around it. Slowly, I remember the rope climb in gym class and shimmy my way up toward the top of the tree. Soon I'm up near the leaves, and the bats are either leaning their heads impossibly far back to stare at me or peering out at eye level, faces obscured in their wings. The whole time, a feeling something like worms crawling under my skin runs along my body, and I do my best to focus. They're like the spectators at a game—just pretend they're not there.

Exactly like Josefina said, in the underside of the treetop hang huge round green-brown coconuts pushed up deep into the foliage of the tree, smooth and green instead of brown and hairy. I almost reach out to one, but the machete in my other hand isn't giving me much of a real grab on the trunk, so I reach out the blade, using it to tap the nearest nut. Nothing—it stays perfectly still. I tap it again, harder, sending a vibration through the tree and a shudder through the huge hideous night creatures dangling around my head like nooses.

"Try to pry it out!" shouts PJ. "Put the blade in by where it meets the tree!"

When I sink the blade in near the base of the coconut, the leaves are soft and yield easily. Slowly, painfully, I start to pry the machete outward. Sweat itches down my forehead and stings my eyes, and my hands are slippery with it, my shirt is soaked between me and the tree, and there are still those eyes, beady and creepy and focused on my every movement.

There's a snap, and the nut falls free. PJ lets it fall to the ground with a thud, then rushes over to it.

"I've got it!" he calls. "Good work! Come on down!"

A wave of relief starts washing over me.

And then one of the bats opens its huge wings and shakes itself out, and I *swear* it starts crawling toward me, and without thinking I rear back the machete—

"NO!" shrieks Josefina, running out of the bushes. "DON'T HURT THEM!"

That's all it takes. Their wings unfold, and suddenly

each black velvet pod is six feet wide and baring its teeth and shrieking at the top of its lungs, and I'm screaming along with them, dropping my machete and waving an arm in front of my face. They drop from their roosts and take to the sky, flapping in a wide circle and then swooping down toward Josefina. The whole sight makes me freeze up again, just turn about as wooden as the tree, and once I'm all rigid, my sweaty body slips—I feel my shin get skinned hard—and then falls off the trunk entirely, my arms flapping in the air like one of these freakish bats.

"I'VE GOT YOU!" screams PJ. "I'VE GOT YOU! I'VE—"

WHOOF! I land in PJ's arms, but since he's running and I have about twenty-five pounds on him, we just land in a big twisted pile of bumped elbows and bruised knees. Immediately, though, he scrambles to his feet and goes running after the girl, leaving me to climb to my feet and brush the bark and leaves off me.

The bats are all over her, either flapping in her face or doing wide arcs into the air and then dive-bombing her. She's waving a hand in front of her, trying to keep them at bay, but she's being overpowered, and her arms are already marked with small cuts from hand to shoulder. PJ runs to her, jumping and shouting and trying to scare them off, but while they don't attack him, they don't let up much on her.

He whips around and looks at me with these accusing eyes and snaps, "Ian, what are you doing? Help us!"

And the sweat hangs on my face, and pain burns down my bleeding shin, and my tailbone throbs, and my mouth is so dry it's like sandpaper, and here's PJ, my friend, snapping at me like I'm a jerk because he knows how to kill zombies and I can't bring myself to do it, and I've had it with this, I've *just had it.*

The machete feels good in my hands. The soreness in my legs pushes me forward. PJ and the girl grow in my field of vision, and then my arm swipes them away, tosses them to the side, and I look at this cloud of flapping black in front of me and raise my machete and I *scream*, with all my might, with every bone in my body. My throat stings and my chest burns and my face aches, and the noise that comes out of my throat is a roar, not like me but like some giant monster, like something that was never human in the first place.

And it works. The bats swoop off like I've sprayed them with a fire hose, do a couple of circles high in the sky, and go back to hang from their branches again.

As I'm standing there, breathing out loud, the whole island alive and bursting with terrifying things and situations, it's like I've got it *down*, like I can actually feel a sharp point coming out of me, just like O'Dea said. This is it, I know, this feeling is the pick and hammer that breaks the ice freezing me up. PJ may be all zen, apologizing to zombies, but not me, I *am* the spade, the point, and the machete. Here, now, this rush moving through me, I *am* a weapon against the dark, and I can *live with that.*

As the haze of red dies down, I turn back to PJ and this Warden girl, and they're both staring at me with these bug eyes.

"What?" I say.

"You okay, man?" asks PJ.

"Yeah," I tell him. "Why?"

"Why don't you just . . . give me *that*," says PJ, reaching out and taking the machete from me. He hands it off to the Warden chick, then slowly heads back over to the tree to get the giant coconut. First she gets the machete, then I do, then she does again. Notice how PJ never holds on to it.

"You all right?" I ask Josefina. She nods, never looking me in the eyes. "You sure? Your arm's kind of scratched up. Those bats' claws can't be clean." She shrugs, rubbing her arms, still looking away. "Was it the screaming? Is that it? You're freaked out by me."

"No," she says softly in a way that definitely tells me *Yes*, but then she says, "You are coming into your own, as your friend said you would."

Before I can say *You better believe it, sister*, PJ trots back to us, giant nut tucked under his arm like a football. In the background, the black winged shapes twitch and refold themselves. "I got it," he says. "It's pretty heavy. Are you sure you can carve it?"

"I'll be fine," she says. "I will start carving the tiki. Then we must return it to its spot in the water."

"Can you carve it on the go?" I ask.

She bites her lip in worry, but nods, finally. "Yes. I can do that."

"Now wait a second," says PJ. "There are no zombies around the tree. Maybe we should wait here."

"What about O'Dea and Kendra?" I say to him. "And her grandmother? If Josefina's not a proper Warden, she won't know exactly what to do. We need to get our team together and get these zombies back in the water for good."

PJ looks frantically at Josefina, and she nods. "He's correct," she says. "We must go get them."

"Then let's get walking," I say.

We head slowly into the jungle, PJ tiptoeing at my side, as though he'll be able to slip past the zombies. Behind us, the long, dry scraping sounds of Josefina carving the skin off the coconut ring out in the air.

"Are you okay?" asks PJ.

"Never better," I say back.

"Because you're acting *really* intense," he whispers. "And you're being really hard on Josefina. I know you're . . . having a hard time with fighting the zombies—"

"PJ," I say, facing him and trying to sound as simple

as possible, "earlier today, I had to drag your limp body through the jungle after you fainted. I just finished climbing a tree full of giant bats. It is seven million degrees out, and we're fighting a fifteen-year-old nut job, not to mention four hundred something violent dead cruise ship passengers. So I'm going to roll with this. *You* need to be calm. I need to be intense."

His brow furrows, and I'm ready to get some lecture from him about not going overboard or how I should take a deep breath, but instead he nods and says, "Okay." The look on his face and the tone of his voice tell me that it's the truth, that he thinks it's right for me to just go with it. It's like we understand, for the first time, that we're totally not the same person, and that's how it has to be, and *that* is okay.

As we crash out of a screen of fanlike ferns sticking out of the ground, a crew of zombie tourists greets us, three of them, all in faded and tattered swimwear. The minute I pop into view, their heads slowly turn like security cameras, and they switch direction and baby step toward us. There's a massive fat man with a bushy gray mustache, his gut shaking and shivering, and an old woman, hunched and drooping, who is missing a good quarter of her skull on the one side, revealing a bloated hunk of gray-green brain hanging out of her head. The third, a white-eyed man in a sagging linen shirt, raises his hands at us and lets out a sudsy moan.

But it's like the scream I let out at the bats has

shaken something loose in me, something hot and fast and *angry*, and every muscle I've got tenses up and starts moving on its own, and then I grab the machete out of Josefina's hands and go flying at them. There's this satisfying shudder down my arm as the blade bites into the waist of the old woman, and with a deep wet crunch she splits in half. My whole body spins and whacks into the fat one's belly, sending him reeling off and his gut spilling a tidal wave of Really Don't Wanna Think About It.

Before I can turn to him, the third zombie's got a cold bony claw wrapped around my machete hand, but just before his yellow teeth meet my arm, PJ comes around with a felled tree branch looking like some knight in a joust and smashes it into the side of the zombie's stomach, sending him flying.

We stare at each other, panting, angry, and he kind of half smiles and says, "I think we're going to be okay." But I don't feel okay, even if I can kill the zombies now without stiffening up. I feel angry and sad and sick, like the minute I stop swinging this machete, I'm going to have some kind of breakdown.

There's a crunch of leaves, and over PJ's shoulder I see another small group of zombie tourists, four or five, come limping through the woods, drawn by the sound. Nearby, the upper half of the old woman I just chopped starts crawling toward us leaving a slimy black trail. PJ's eyes go wide slowly and steadily, and I know we're in trouble.

"There are more behind you," he says.

"You too," I say, and we begin turning around and, yup, not just behind us, but on all sides of us, a mob of them is coming together. From each direction they come—only three or four at a time, but slowly building in numbers, closing in the ring around us.

"Now would be a good time to use that rattle thing," I tell Josefina.

The young sorta-Warden reaches into her shorts pocket, and her face falls. "Oh no," she whispers to PJ. "My terrifier is gone. I must have dropped it while I was saving the guardians from your friend."

"Whoa, whoa, whoa," I snap, "saving *them* from ME?!"

"This is *the* rule in zombie movies," whispers PJ. "Never get surrounded . . ."

This new unrestrained energy that I'm feeding off only gets stirred up by the slow-approaching crowd, moving forward like the shadow of a cloud, more just a wave of pain than an actual group of people or things. There's so much skin visible around their swimwear that it doesn't even look like a group of people after a while, just a wave of gray, like worms in a piece of meat writhing into one another. One of them, a teenage kid whose chest and ribs are full of gaping holes, has a piece of coral jutting out of his chest.

"Now what?" I yell at Josefina.

"You must fight them," she says.

"Way too many," says PJ hopelessly. "Look at them. We're really outnumbered."

"You must," she says. "There is no other way. If we had my terrifier or my drums, then maybe I would be able to stop them, but—"

PJ and I exchange a glance, and I can tell we're thinking the same thing—those weird drums earlier, in the jungle, when we first got here. "What do the drums do?" I ask.

"They are a beacon," she says. "They draw the demons, so that we may put them to rest or keep others from harm."

"I thought the zemi was the beacon," I say.

"The zemi is the seal," she says. "The drums are the beacon."

"Wait," says PJ. "I think I saw some drums on Danny Melee's desk. Maybe if we could get someone to play them—"

"And how will you contact them?" says Josefina.

The woman's upper torso coming at us reaches PJ's foot, and he smashes his branch into the back of her neck with a squishy crunch. "We need to think of something fast," he says, motioning to the ring of zombies closing in around us.

And that's when I save the day. My hand goes into

my pocket and comes out with the walkie-talkie PJ and I found earlier. When I pull it out, they both stare at it like, *Whoa*, and I nod like, *Yeah*.

"Get on the horn," I say to PJ, tossing it to him, and then I turn to the coming horde, brandishing my machete and swinging it at the first outstretched gray-green hands that reach us, hacking into more and more zombie flesh.

"Hello! Anyone!" screams PJ over my shoulder. "O'Dea, we need help! We're in trouble! O'Dea, Kendra, *do you read me, do you read me?!*"

CHAPTER
SEVENTEEN

Kendra

"We need help!" crackles Ian's voice from the walkie-talkie on Danny's belt. "I repeat: *we need help—*"

Danny flicks a switch, and the voice cuts out. My pulse skyrockets.

"I'm surprised they made it this long without getting eaten," he says.

"Danny, please don't let this happen," I say.

Dario grunts, and the ropes around my wrists tighten. My feet already throb from where my ankles are lashed to the chair legs, but I don't seem to feel the rope. The scene unfolding before me is too gruesome to be distracted from.

Danny stands in the middle of some kind of secondary lab, a room I hadn't seen before. The monitor he's bent over throws a ghostly blue-white glow over his face and makes his eyes shine with electric light. Next to him, a man and a woman in long white lab coats holding electronic tablets mumble instructions to each other while tapping in information. Behind me, Dario finishes tying me to a chair. And before all of us stands a huge transparent tube, inside which kneels a shirtless man, the bleeding lab tech from earlier, chained to a metal pole behind him, his face a mask of complete and utter despair. He shivers slowly, his skin sweaty, his cheeks pale.

"Whatever you plan to do," I yell at Danny, "it's a mistake. People are going to get hurt."

"You're underestimating me again," says Danny. "You need to learn not to do that." Turning to the man in the cylinder, he says, "Dr. Sean Marten, we have your paperwork signed. Now's your last chance to back out."

"No," says the man in a steady, brave voice. "I've been bitten. I'm dead anyway. You're right, Mr. Melee— I might as well be useful."

Useful, Kendra. That's what Danny Melee thinks of a dying man. You deserve this sense of shock, of betrayal. You got this one dead wrong.

"I appreciate it," says Danny. All around us is the humming of machinery, the clicking of computer equipment, and faintly, above it all, the soft thud of the zombies pounding at the walls outside. Dario finishes behind me and pats a massive hand on my shoulder almost lovingly.

"You'll be finished with this indignity soon," he says. Then he moves over next to Danny. "Everything's set, Mr. Melee. Whenever you're ready."

"Danny, listen to me!" I shout. "You're playing with fire here! I know you've isolated some kind of spore, but trust me, there are powerful forces at play here! The curse that came to this island—"

"Enough with the *curse* talk!" says Danny, finally looking up at me. Now I see what PJ must have caught in his eye—an unnatural glow, the flare of madness. "There's no magic here, just science! It's a *fungus*! It can be *harnessed* and *controlled* if someone just has the fore-sight and brains to go ahead and do it!"

"So you can *what*?" I shout. "Release it into the gen-eral populace? Cause the end of the world? My *father* is in Puerto Rico, Danny! All of our parents are!"

He closes his eyes, laughs, and shakes his head. "*End of the world*. Listen to you, Kendra. You think I'm some kind of, what, supervillain? *Zombie Apocalypse* is just a great phrase, rolls off the tongue. It'll just be Puerto Rico—contained, great landscape, large but not too central to the world economy. Once we've released the specimens and it's overrun, I'll swoop in with a bunch of money to contain the disease, massage some government officials, and then we'll begin contacting possible players. I've already gotten interest from two Oscar winners and a multiplatinum rock star who want to do twenty-four-hour survival tours." His eyes blaze open again, and he holds up his hands, framing a shot in the air like PJ. "Imagine it—*ZA One*. The first *real* first-person shooter, fully interactive, complete with live ammo and real monsters. It's just that the zombies were wrong. That's why we mutated the fungus so it would cluster in the head and keep the blood red. Say what you want, Kendra, but I'm dedicated to my audience."

"Mr. Melee," says Dario.

"You think these zombies are something you can control," I cry out, "but I swear, Danny, these creatures are supernatural! The Wardens utilize *magic* to keep them contained!"

"Baloney," he says, shaking his head. "The Wardens just know something, some part of the equation we haven't figured out. Yeah, we *had* to torch that zemi with a guided missile, but *why*? When I met you guys, I was hoping you could teach me. I wanted to help you discover the secret *behind* being a Gravedigger and then let you in on the action. I'm talking *major* roles in *ZA One*—these three zombie-hunting kids." He rolls his eyes. "Though I thought you three would be a little less difficult to deal with. You and your buddies have a real talent for tossing wrenches into gears."

"Danny, you're talking about killing *thousands* of people for this . . . morbid safari," I cry out.

"You make it sound worse than it is," he says. "Look, you can't have zombies without dead people, and the ones who are already reanimated don't take to the mutation. And besides, that kind of real-life drama draws in an audience: Who gets bitten? Who survives? Will the players make it out alive? That's why it's *ZA One. Second Wave* will happen once some of the zombies have been taken out, and only the really tough ones have survived, and we'll up the ante with some downloadable content. I'm talking new weaponry, survival methods . . . even a cure!" He clasps his hands together in front of me. "We're so close, Kendra! If only those Wardens would give up the science behind all this—"

"Mr. Melee," drones the woman in the lab coat, "it's getting late. Dr. Marten's infection is spreading rapidly."

"Right, sorry," he says, ducking back to his computer monitor and typing in a long string of code. "You'll see, Kendra. People don't want to sit around and live their stupid, normal lives. They want excitement. They want fear, and they want power. And I'm going to give it to them."

"Danny, you don't know what you're—"

"Ms. Redfield," he barks, "begin Updated Zombie Model, Trial One."

"Beginning Trial One," hums the computer, "now."

From the ceiling of the tube comes a whir, and a small robotic arm descends into the tube, its tip adorned with a thick hypodermic needle full of dark red viscous fluid. The chained scientist doesn't even look up as the needle descends toward his throat.

"Injecting subject with mutated fungal concentrate," says the man in the lab coat. "Mutated reanimation should occur within thirty seconds."

There's a click, and the needle jabs into his neck and plunges its contents into him. He convulses hard . . . and then his head falls forward and he lets out a long, wheezing breath.

After a few seconds, Ms. Redfield announces, "Subject One is deceased."

My stomach goes cold. My wrists ache as I strain against my tethers, which loosen with a creak. Slowly, a wave of horrible dumb numbness settles through me. I am not aware of the tears falling down my cheeks until they hit my pants with a soft patter. A low sob comes out of my throat, calling out to the poor slumped lab tech.

There it is, Kendra. You made it pretty far without having to witness it, but at the end of the day every adventurer has seen it. You thought that as a researcher, a lover of science and discovery, it would be easy, something you could handle. But no, you didn't know a thing. It's as crushing as anything has ever been in your very short life.

That's what it's like to see someone die.

"Wait for it . . . ," says Danny Melee. "*Wait for iiiit. . . .*"

We wait for thirty seconds, during which the silence of death hangs over us unbroken, save for the steady thump of the creatures swarming the walls of the compound. Finally, Danny Melee lets his hands drop by his sides and pouts.

"It looks to be a failure, Mr. Melee," says Dario.

"Yeah, I *got that*, Dario," whines Danny. "*Thanks.*" He snorts, then turns back to his hulking assistant. "I need those Wardens back here, okay? Both of them. There must be something I'm doing wrong, something that stupid handbook won't tell me."

"You'll never catch O'Dea," I croak.

Danny glares at me over his shoulder and rolls his eyes. "After that, we need to rework this fungal injection. I don't know what went wrong here, but there has to be an answer—"

A bloodcurdling scream cuts through the air. Everyone jumps, terrified by the unexpected outburst.

The man in the tube is looking at us.

His eyes are deep and black, the pupils dilated to the point of taking over the orb entirely. His waxy skin glistens, beaded with sweat. Throbbing veins grow more and more visible in his forehead and jaw by the minute.

A low growl comes out of his throat, and when his lips peel back, a rush of blood runs between his teeth and down his chin, tickling my gorge. My mouth curls into a similar rictus of unease as his head slowly scans the room, taking us in one after another as though we were insects.

"Amazing," whispers Danny, peering into the creature's shiny black eyes with ghoulish fascination. "The mutation took. Look, look at the fluid moving up to his head, and the *red* coming from the mouth!" He grins hideously. "Catherine, Louis, congratulations. This is exactly what I'm looking for—"

"*EEEYAAAAAAAAAAAH!*" shrieks the mutated zombie. He begins banging his cuffs hard against the pole he's lashed to, eyes fixed on Danny's assistant, Dario. He thrashes again and again, and his cuffs meet the pole with repeated clanks that I can almost feel in my teeth. As he swings his head around wildly, flecks of foamy red spittle hit the clear surface separating him from us.

"Wow, look at this," says Louis, the male scientist. He shuffles up to the wall of the tube and points at the spit droplets. The plastic where they spattered is bubbling, smoking. "It appears as if the creature's saliva is acidic—"

As if on cue, the zombie lurches forward, and a jet of red goo flies from his mouth and slaps against the plastic. The vomit begins smoking and bubbling, and great chunky pieces of the plastic tube fall away, letting trails of red smoke pour out into the trailer. The scent of burning plastic and sulfur stings my nostrils, and I try to rear my head back. An alarm begins whooping while Ms. Redfield screams, "BREACH! BREACH! BREACH!" over and over.

Danny presses against the wall, stunned. Dario cracks his knuckles and keenly observes. Louis stumbles backward, with only enough time to shout, "We need to abort!"

—before another cough full of red mucus hits him in the face. With an awful hiss, he runs screaming through the door and into the fading tropical light, clawing at his eyes.

"INFECTION," booms Ms. Redfield. "SPECI-MENS MUST BE TERMINATED IMMEDIATELY."

"Come on!" shouts Dario, barreling out after the shrieking scientist. Danny sputters, dumbstruck by the sudden turn of events, before he and Catherine, the lab-coated woman, follow hot on his heels.

"Don't leave me here!" I shout, but it's no use. My voice is swallowed by the whooping alarm and their cries for help. Suddenly, I am alone.

Alone with . . . *it*.

Not "him," certainly—"it." The undead creature, this *science zombie* in the slowly dissolving tube, no longer has a gender. Every moment, it becomes more and more repellent. Its hair falls out by the second, its fingernails grow longer, its face becomes a cobweb of veins. It stares at me through obsidian eyes, studying me, its mouth a gore-coated grimace. Even the zombies retain their gender, male or female corpses brought back to life. This thing is just a reanimated mutant, nothing more. The very concept makes my flesh tingle in horror.

Outside, there are shouts and gunfire. Tears prickle my eyes.

Deep breaths, Kendra. Try not to panic, even if the world appears to be falling apart.

It coughs two gouts of blood at me, trying to splash me with its acid spit, but the angle is odd and the fluid can't reach me, thank God; it just splashes everywhere, burning the tubing, the floor, the robot needle arm. I scoot the chair as far back into the corner as possible, listening to the creature snarl and bang away at its shackles and feeling my heart pound, my stomach knot.

It's going to get out of there eventually, Kendra. And then it's going to hurt you in ways you can't imagine—

"Girl." My eyes fly to the door of the lab, and my spirits soar. O'Dea stands there, a scarecrow outlined in daylight, eyeing the science zombie in disgust. It leans out in the passage directly between us, leaking acid from its hungry, mindless grin. "What in the name of the Holy Mother is *that*?"

"It's a mutant zombie," I yell to her. "Melee has found a fungus that causes reanimation, and he's mutated it. He's trying to release these things onto Puerto Rico and turn it into some kind of zombie conservancy where people can hunt them."

"*Fungus*," she says rolling her eyes. "Stupid outsiders with their scientific theories. There's this Warden in Russia who always—""

"O'DEA!"

"Right, right," she says. "What's with all this smoking red crap on the floor?"

"It spits acid," I tell her.

"Of course it does," she says. "How to get past it is the thing."

"It's been altered to die by head shot," I say. "If you cut its head off, or stab it through the eye somehow—"

"No," says O'Dea.

"*What do you mean, NO?*" I scream, feeling betrayed by O'Dea's calm. I make my chair hop in my furor. "I'm tied up here, O'Dea!"

"It's our way," she says quietly. "I'm a Warden, that's a zombie. I'm sworn to keep the balance. I can't kill it. That's *your* job." She closes her eyes and holds out a palm, and after whispering a few syllables, she tightens her hand into a fist. There's a sharp snapping sound, and then the bonds loosen around my hands and feet and slither to the floor in a pile.

Rubbing the ache out of my wrists, I rise and press myself against the wall. "Thanks," I say, "but how do I get past this thing now without it immolating my face with acid?"

"If it's a zombie, I should be able to put it in a trance," she says. "Then, while it can't protect itself, you can kill it."

"Kill it? Right now?" I say, stunned. Such a concept hadn't crossed my mind.

"Of course," says O'Dea. "You're a Gravedigger, Kendra. You're the blade of light that rends the thundercloud open to feed the land."

Of course, Kendra. That's what she's been saying all along: you're a sunbeam.

"Wait a second—"

"Hush," says O'Dea. "I need to concentrate." She crouches down and puts her hand to the floor, then begins droning incomprehensible syllables in a steady monotone. At first, nothing happens, and I'm sure that we'll be totally unable to get past the zombie—

And then, the air gets thick, heavy with some kind of energy that seems to permeate the air with a certain electric humidity. O'Dea's chanting seems to fill the room, to shake the walls around us with a kind of deep resonance, almost like powerful bass notes from a subwoofer. The zombie's eyes roll back into its head, and its body goes into violent spasms, red froth dripping from its maw and its cuffs rattling against the metal bar. But her spell works—as I near the creature, its shivering form responds in no way.

Once I'm positive the creature is comatose, I hop over the smoking puddle of zombie saliva and approach O'Dea, overjoyed to see her alive. When I put a hand on her shoulder, she stops chanting with a strong exhale. As she rises to her feet, I see a drop of scarlet running out of her right ear.

"O'Dea, you're bleeding!" I say.

"That . . . wasn't what I expected," she says with a heavy sigh. "That thing . . . it's an abomination. It's not like the normal zombies. Took all my power, and when I connected with it . . ." She shudders. "This is more evil than I've ever felt."

The room shakes as the science zombie reawakens, eyes rolling and wild, mouth foaming red. Startled, I jump back, colliding with O'Dea.

"You've got to destroy it," she says, gently pushing me toward the smoking tube.

"I . . . I can't," I finally say, pushing through a wad of pride and mortification that seems to clog my throat. Suddenly, a reality sets in on me: "I don't have any weapons, O'Dea, and I . . . I just can't."

O'Dea shakes her head and grunts. "You're going to have to get used to the idea eventually," she says. "Come on, we need to get out of here."

Outside, all is chaos. Lab techs and armed guards run across the center of the compound, shouting orders or yelling for help. Trails of blood spot the walkways between trailers and huts. An alarm whoops somewhere. The pounding of hands against the walls is even louder, and every few dozen yards, on the ladders that line the walls, guards stand, blasting at the hordes of undead with machine guns. The air is full of a million sights, smells, and sounds, all of them hostile and jarring.

Think, Kendra. Break through all the stimuli. What's next?

"We need a walkie-talkie," I tell her. "The boys are—"

"Way ahead of you," says O'Dea, pulling a small black square from her pocket. She flicks it on, and as it crackles to life, a shrieking voice is emitted from it.

"O'DEA, PLEASE, SOMEBODY, JUST HELP!"

"PJ!" I say, grabbing the walkie-talkie. "PJ, it's Kendra. Things are going crazy here. Where are you? Are you guys okay?"

"We're out in the jungle!" he pants. Behind his voice, Ian yells, and a chorus of gurgling moans fills the air. "Listen to me, Kendra. In Danny Melee's office, there is a set of drums. They're magic. We need O'Dea to play them."

"I remember those," O'Dea says. "He forced this girl I was being kept with, Josefina, to play them. Started asking all these scientific questions about them, if they had a *unique frequency* that was *in tune with zombie DNA*."

My mind flickers back to when I first met Danny, and I see the drums perfectly—a small set of bongolike things, covered in swirling dark designs.

"Come on," I say to O'Dea. We dart across the compound, over the central walkway separating the huts and trailers and toward the thatch-roofed hut where I was first brought, back when I thought Danny Melee was anything but a psychotic madman.

"YOU TWO—STOP!" booms Dario's voice behind us, and we pick up speed, barreling headfirst into Danny's hut and slamming the door behind us. Immediately, I'm at his desk, but the drums are nowhere to be seen, and panic begins to overtake me, drowning me in panic and inner *cacophony* (I've got to add that to the list) and adrenaline. When I tug at his desk drawer, it's locked.

"O'Dea, I need an unlocking spell," I shout.

"A little busy," she says, putting her shoulder into the door as a fist bangs on it from the other side.

"KENDRA!" screams PJ through the walkie-talkie.

My heart races. Everything is a tidal wave of noise and fear, of monsters of all sorts bursting out of every possible space. The panic that's in the air is being generated from every guard and prisoner and lab tech and millionaire visionary within these walls. And as O'Dea braces herself against the door and a deep voice from the other side bellows order and guns fire and Ian screams, I find myself overwhelmed, unable to think beyond the wave after wave of horror bearing down on me.

Without thinking, I place my foot on Danny's desk and pull with all my might at the handle of the drawer. It creaks, strains, and finally flies open with a crash, revealing a small set of weathered drums, their flaking wood inlaid with intricately beautiful sigils. My mind a blur, I yank them into my lap and commence slapping my hands on the grainy animal hide that coats them.

And something happens.

EIGHTEEN

PJ

There is a moment when I'm positive we're going to die. The circle of zombies around us has closed in, and Ian and I are standing back to back, with Josefina huddled near us. The tree branch I've taken on as my personal sword has become caked with slimy black blood and bits of gooey gray and green skin. Ian's machete drips with dark gore, sending great globs of the stuff flying everywhere each time he cocks it back. But the zombie tourists keep coming, usually only falling backward or stumbling into one another and then shuffling slowly back into place.

With my joints sore, my head swimming, and my

lungs on fire, I'm absolutely sure that this is it. Eventually, one of them will get past us unscathed, grab hold of my arm, and drag me into the roiling ocean of gooey pale limbs and gnashing watery mouths before us.

Then, the drums.

They come from deep in the jungle, but they might as well be right next to us, playing at some kind of low, heavy frequency that sinks down into the bones in my jaw. At first, the zombies still come, their moaning as loud as ever and their grasping claws dangerously close to us . . . but then, one by one, they lower their outstretched hands and freeze. Slowly, the ones farthest away from us turn their heads, stare off at the sound, and then lurch their way off toward the rhythm. Their arms don't extend the way they do to grasp meat, but they lead with their mouths, drifting ghostlike through the underbrush.

The ones closest to us don't leave for a while—it's as though they're comparing their hunger for our flesh with their longing for the beating of the drums. For a moment, I worry that they've come too far, that seeing us this close up will let them break the Warden's musical spell and come flying at us . . . but then they turn and crunch off into the jungle. Even the ones that are broken in half or hobbled at the legs drag themselves along the rich dirty forest floor in the direction of Danny Melee's compound.

After a few uneventful minutes, I drop my branch-club, feeling a wave of relief surge over my sore muscles. Ian still brandishes his machete wildly, as though the power of the drums might wear off at any moment.

I pull the walkie-talkie out of my pocket and flick it on. "Kendra, keep it up," I say. "They're being drawn to you guys."

There's a crackle, and O'Dea's voice comes in over the horn. "Good to hear," she says. "Kendra's playing her heart out, and it sounds like a new wave of zombies has distracted all the cretins trying to kill us."

A second blast of gratitude surges through me, knowing my two friends are all right and aren't about to be tied up and fed to the living dead. "Well, keep it going," I tell her. "You're ridding us of zombies entirely."

"Good on Kendra," says Ian, whipping the blood from his blade.

"Impossible," mumbles Josefina. When we glance back at her, she stares hard at the shaved coconut in her hand, sweat glittering on her brow. "Something else must have drawn them."

"Listen," I tell her, pointing to the air. "Can't you hear those?"

"Only a Warden should be able to play those drums and make any real sound with them," she says, carving a huge round eye out of the bullet-shaped thing in her hands, the smooth dark green skin now peeled away to reveal the flaky light-brown ball underneath. "Your friend has not had the proper training in the magical arts. She could not have drawn in away."

"Maybe by being a Gravedigger, she has the same powers," says Ian.

"Gravediggers are masters of combat and destruction, not containment and distraction," she says. "These are the rules, the way it has always been."

Uh-oh. *Rules* is a word that normally sets Ian off, and his Jason Statham routine has me worried. But surprisingly, he doesn't say a word, just shrugs and wipes his machete clean on his pants. "What's next?" he says.

"With the cursed drawn away from us, we must return to my cottage," she replies. "My grandmother will assist us with the carving of the new seal."

We make our way through the jungle, lush green plant life jutting out at us from all sides. Zombies still stalk the forest, moving face-first between the thick-trunked trees with the low-hanging vines, but the dead seem far more focused on the beating drums than on us, and dodging around them becomes easy enough, even if one or two of them reach out a hand and give a gurgling moan in our direction. Jeniveve's cottage reappears in the distance, and seeing it makes us shift from a march to a jog; even in this relatively quiet moment, the need for shelter, for a *base*, is overwhelming. When we're a few yards away, Josefina's grandmother comes bursting out of the door in a flowing green dress that billows around her. She speaks in a string of sharp, snappy Spanish, taking the sacred coconut from Josefina and giving her the quickest of squeezes on her shoulder before immediately vanishing back into her cottage.

"My yaya says that we have done well," says Josefina. "She has told me that she will try to use her abilities to communicate with your friend O'Dea and guide her to the cottage. She has said that you two should go up on the roof and look out for her and your other friend. If you see them from up there, you should attempt to grab their attention and draw them here." Josefina points to a wrought-iron ladder attached to the edge of the house. "Quickly," she says, and then vanishes inside and swiftly shuts the door.

Ian and I climb the ladder, and as we crest the top of the roof, I feel something wonderful inside me, something warm and human that I haven't felt in a while—the appreciation of a view, a shot. From up here, we can see the island stretch out before us in a sea of lush, glossy green, with the setting sun hazy and orange behind a thin veil of clouds, bleeding a ruddy red light into the sky. The view fills me with something sweet and a little sad, a deep love of beauty and the world and the rare opportunity to see something like this.

But then there, in the distance, are the walls of Danny Melee's compound, jutting out of the organic perfection of the green forest like a zombie itself. From here, the massive crowd of corpses lurking outside is visible even through the trees, stretching back into the jungle and undulating like a body of water, its shifting mass the color of an upset stomach. Over the walls, guards lean forward and shoot into the undead crowds, the blasts from their guns crackling through the air. Their numbers have grown so high that even this far off, the thud of their combined hands banging on the walls can be heard over the pounding of the drums.

It kind of reminds me of the lines at a toy store around Christmas. The insanity, the hunger. *Everything must go.*

"I wonder how Kendra and O'Dea will find their way out of there," I say to Ian. "It's pretty surrounded."

"What? Oh. Yeah." When I look back at Ian, he's sitting back on his haunches, staring at the blade of his machete. There's very little actual concern coming off him, mostly anger and exhaustion. Part of me is dying to help him, to say or do something that will make him smile and quell his bad mood, but another part of me just doesn't know how to do that. Either he's freezing up around the zombies and his confidence is gone, or he's a zombie-killing machine and acting like the whole world's gone to hell. There's no middle ground for him.

"PJ?"

The walkie-talkie crackles to life in my pocket,

O'Dea's voice buzzing out of the speaker. I press the button, and say, "We're here, O'Dea. What's up?"

"Well, we've got good news and bad news," she says. "The good news is, it seems like everyone here is caught up in their own issues and has forgotten about us. But that's also the bad news."

As she says it, there's a sound, a great crack that seems to split the air in half. Before my very eyes, a section of the wall surrounding Danny Melee's compound falls inward, collapsing with a resounding BOOM that shakes the cottage beneath us and sends Ian leaping to his feet.

The bottom of my stomach drops out as I watch the swarm of zombies go surging into the compound. Suddenly, the gunshots increase a hundredfold, and screams begin emanating from inside the walls.

The drumming stops.

"O'Dea, the walls have been breached! They're coming!" I cry into the walkie-talkie. No response. "O'Dea, do you hear me? You need to get out of there! Grab Kendra and *run*!" Still no answer.

Fear, cold and harsh, crawls up and down the skin on my arms, sends sparks through the hair on the back of my neck. Already, the horde on the edges of the walls has thinned out, the majority of the huge mob of walking corpses swarming into the compound. If O'Dea and Kendra don't get out now, they're as good as doomed.

"We've got to go save them," says Ian, pointing his blade at the compound. "Come on. If we run, we might be able to make it in time to fight our way in—"

But I know—I feel, in my heart—that that's not right. Somewhere, through all the sadness and fear at seeing the walls broken down, I hear the insanity of what Ian's saying and think of how O'Dea would respond in this situation. It's not fun, and it's not adventurous or brave. In fact, it tears me apart even having to say it.

"Ian, we can't," I tell him. "We've got to get this seal finished and have it replaced. Going back there is just a chance for *us* to get attacked."

"Sorry, man," says Ian, shaking his head hard. "Now's not the time to wimp out. We've got to get over there and save them. Case closed, end of story."

"Ian, please listen to me," I say, trying to make my voice express the yearning I feel inside. "There's no way for us to save them by going back there. There are way too many zombies, not to mention guards with guns."

"Fine, then *I'll* go," he says. He turns and walks toward the ladder, but I manage to dart in front of him and block his path. "Get out of my way, PJ."

"No," I say.

Ian's eyes drip hatred as they take me in. The muscles around his jaw twitch, and he tightens his grip on the machete. Some portion of me is screaming in my head to back off, that trying to square off against Ian in his current state of rage and violence is suicide, but I know I can't budge.

"PJ," he says in an intensely calm voice, "either you get out of my way, or I put you out of my way."

"Then you'll have to move me," I manage to say. "I'm sorry, man, but earlier today you told me not to give up. You saved me earlier, so I'm saving you now."

"And killing Kendra."

"Kendra has O'Dea. You have me."

He blinks at me. The machete quivers in his hands, but I know he won't use it. Finally, he exhales sharply, and the point of the blade lowers to aim at his feet. In the quiet between us, the gunshots and screams in the distance might as well be the breeze in the palms around us. Ian takes a step forward and puts his hand on my shoulder, and I put mine on his. It's as though we're feeding off one another, letting all the obstacles and arguments of the day drift away.

O'Dea would be proud, because I know. This is who I am—the guy who reminds us of who we are.

"I ought to throw you off this roof, you nut job," he says with a dark smile.

"Yeah, just try it, Buckley," I answer, and he cackles.

"Guys, you there?" This time it's Kendra's voice coming out of the walkie-talkie, sending Ian and me scrambling for it.

"We're here," I say to her. "What about you two?"

"We've escaped the compound," she pants. Ian and I both lower our shoulders, a sigh of relief coming out of him. "When the wall came down, everything went nuts, and we managed to escape through one of the gates on the opposite side from where the zombies broke through. What's your current status?"

"We're on top of a cottage a ways away from you," I say. "We've met the Warden for the island, and she's in the process of carving a new seal to keep the zombies in the water. We can come down and find you—"

"Wait." There's a pause, and a crackle of noise. "O'Dea says she can hear the Warden chanting to her in her mind, if such a thing is possible. She says she'll lead us to you. Sit tight and remain where you are."

"Got it," I say. As I put the walkie-talkie back in my pocket, I say to Ian, "Great. Fantastic. See, we don't even have to risk our lives trying to get them. They're on their way."

Ian nods, staring at his feet, but then he looks up into my eyes and his expression is pleading, almost sad. "For the record, man," he says, "I'm trying to figure all this out as much as you, or Kendra, or anybody." Then he brushes right past me and takes the ladder so quickly, he might as well have jumped off. Before I follow him, I take a moment to stare at the crumbling compound in the lush tropical jungle, a plume of black smoke now rising from within its walls, and think about Ian's words and Josefina's story earlier. Always three of us, each one with a purpose.

As I climb down off the roof, Josefina comes out of the cottage, brushing wood shavings from the front of her shirt, a large sharp hunting knife in one hand. "We heard the noise," she says, "and could see a smoke cloud from the window. What happened?"

"The zombies trashed one of the walls to Danny's little research hangout," says Ian. "The whole place is overrun. But O'Dea and Kendra are on their way, apparently, so we're pretty much good to go."

"I know. My grandmother says she has reached the mind of your Warden friend. She draws near."

Josefina's grandmother emerges from the cabin, clasping the coconut in her hands—only this isn't the nut we rescued from the tree. It's been carved into a bullet-shaped head of sorts, its face painted into a ghoulish grimace with giant hollow eyes and a mouthful of blocky teeth. Sigils swirl up the sides of it like fire, the swirling rings and strange curving shapes chiseled into its surface with careful and practiced grace. How they could carve such a thing in such a short period of time is beyond me, but I suppose that's why the Wardens are so necessary.

Suddenly, there's a crunching in the woods, too quick, too heavy-footed to be a zombie. We all hear it, our eyes turning to the expanse of thick lush jungle to the left of the cottage. Suddenly, there's a static burst from the walkie-talkie, and I hear Kendra's voice, panting and husky, shouting between clips of white noise.

"Kendra, we didn't get that last one," I tell her, "but we can hear someone running in the jungle. Is that you?"

There's more static crackle, and I get two phrases between the squawks of electronic noise: "not us . . . found him . . ."

From between the trees, a shape appears, charges through the jungle in long awkward strides, and bursts into the clearing surrounding the cottage, his face glistening with sweat, his eyes bulging. He skids to a halt with a cry, the heavy black duffel bag draped over his shoulder swinging hard and almost dragging his scrawny body with it.

"Well well *well*!" shouts Ian.

"Please," cries Danny Melee, his speech a series of gasps and pants. "Please don't hurt me. I didn't know it would be like this."

Seeing this kid again, now fleeing like a rat from his own sinking ship, hits me with a feeling of anger and disgust. At once, Ian, Josefina, and I all circle around him and begin closing in on him, my eyes staying on Ian. I don't want to see a machete used on a live person. As much as it hurts me to do so, I might have to intervene.

But before I even get the chance, the sound of another

set of speedy footsteps grows in the distance, and suddenly Kendra, our intellectual computer nerd friend, comes barreling out of the forest and tackles Melee like a lion bringing down a gazelle in a nature documentary. They hit the ground with a loud grunt. Danny barely has time to roll over and put his hands up before Kendra has him by the front of the shirt and begins throttling him over and over, slamming his back into the ground and shrieking at the top of her lungs.

"You *idiot*," she snarls, shaking him by the shoulders.

"Ah," says Josefina, "the third Gravedigger has arrived."

"It was horrible," he sobs. "Please. They got some of my staff. They ate whole bodies, the meat, the bones. They ate their *teeth*."

"You *twit*," shrieks Kendra, slamming him around the chest and shoulders with her fists. "I *trusted you*."

"I didn't know," he bawls, shielding his face. "I thought we could control it. If I'd known—"

"If you'd known *what*?" she snaps. "That turning thousands of people into zombies might have some consequences? That people who make monsters usually end up being *killed by them*?"

"What's she talking about?" I ask, the phrase *turning thousands of people into zombies* sticking in my craw.

"PJ was right from the start," she says, rising from

on top of Danny and wiping some of the leaves and debris out of her hair. "Danny's team has concocted a new form of zombiism using a spore he's found present in the zombies. His plan was to infect all of Puerto Rico and turn it into a sort of resort where people can hunt them in a post-apocalyptic world. A real-life violent video game."

"Let's just bail," gibbers Danny. "Seriously, guys. I own the island—I'll just make it illegal to come here! Put up some signs: ¡CUIDADO—ZOMBIES!"

"*¡Cállate!*" snaps Josefina. "You would leave our home in ruin? You would damn all of mankind by allowing the cursed to roam free?"

"But they're just on the island," he whines. "I haven't released them on Puerto Rico yet—"

"Of course you have," she says. "With the seal broken, many came onto land following the drums, but there is a chance some turned the other way, heading toward Puerto Rico. If we leave the seal broken, they will escape this place."

Oh, no. The look on Kendra's face tells me she knew this already, but the idea is expanding in my head like some sort of black, clammy explosion. Our families. The Buckleys, Kendra's dad, my parents.

My sister.

That's what's waiting for these zombies in Puerto Rico, as well as another three and a half million souls who don't deserve to die. This is what this kid was planning all along—a human sacrifice in the name of the game.

The air grows heavy with hostility that seems to press down on Danny Melee, forcing him into a curled-up ball. But as much as he infuriates me, as much as his twisted little plan makes me loathe him and everything he stands for, I can't let this happen. As terrible a human being as he is, Danny is still a teenage boy.

Slowly, I kneel down next to Danny, grab a handful of his greasy hair, and yank his head back so that his watery bloodshot eyes stare helplessly into mine.

"I think Melee Industries has work to do," I say. "Like making sure this mutated fungus never gets out into the world. And giving Josefina and Jeniveve their island back. Right, Danny?"

He blinks for a second, and his hair-dusted upper lip twitches in what I can tell is an urge to tell me to go jump in a lake, but then he gulps and slowly nods. "Yes. Fine."

"Promise me," I say to him, doing my best to make my voice sound like rock.

"I promise I'll clean up this mess and leave you people alone," he says. "Just, please. I want to get out of here."

"Good," I say, letting go of his hair and rising to my feet. "Atta boy." In the jungle, shadowy and mysterious with the coming evening, a bony silhouette steps out from beneath a tree. As she enters the clearing, sunlight falls upon her, revealing a set of sigil-adorned drums in her hands and a warm joyful smile bunching up the wrinkles of her face.

"Look, a creepy witch woman!" I say.

O'Dea nods. "Yeah, yeah," she says, "and some movie nerd who finally took a hint and started listening to what I've been telling him."

For a moment, my eyes stray to Josefina, who wears a similar smile to O'Dea's. Her story of Don José, the blesser, the one with the big heart, flickers into my head. Maybe there's some sense to this—to being this thing, a Gravedigger, whatever that means.

But if I'm a Gravedigger, I'm not just here to forgive. I'm here to put the living dead back where they belong.

"Now that we've got everyone," I say, "let's get this zemi out in the water and get these zombies back in their cruise ship."

"Our boat is still a short hike away," says Josefina, "and with the drums no longer playing, the remaining cursed might advance upon us. You will need weapons."

"I can help!" squeals Danny, kneeling. He unzips the duffel bag and dumps out its contents—two huge knives in holsters, two crowbars, a long black nightstick, and another machete, a modern version of Jeniveve's— glittering curved blade, ribbed rubber handle.

Ian whistles, tossing the old machete to the ground and picking up the new one. "Yeah," he says, "this'll do just fine." He leans over and offers me the nightstick. "Not a tree branch, but I bet you can make do." As I take its weight in my hand, I feel how right his words are—like the branch I was wielding earlier, there's a heaviness to this that makes it feel powerful, like a tool of judgment.

Kendra hefts a crowbar into her hand and lets it lie flat across her palm. "Balanced and utilitarian," she says, wrapping her hand around it.

We stare at each other for a moment, not at O'Dea or Josefina or the whimpering pile of Danny Melee in front of us, but at one another, Ian, Kendra, and me. The hostility from before returns, but there is a hope to it, a clean feeling, that there is nothing now but us and what must be done.

"Well," I say, "what are we waiting for?"

CHAPTER
NINETEEN

Ian

Okay, fine. You want Gravediggers? Here's Ian Buckley, the Gravedigger.

We haul into the jungle, me in the lead, Kendra and PJ on either side just behind me, the Wardens on their tail, and Danny Melee whimpering like a little wuss as he takes up the caboose. Josefina's big realization has kicked us into overdrive—it's not just us at stake, it's the main island. It's our families. And look, my dad's a pain in the neck, but that doesn't mean I want him to have any part of this.

The jungle in front of us, which seemed totally insane and overgrown and unbeatable earlier today, is now just a series of things to trample, hurdle over, or hack down with my fancy new Melee Industries–brand machete, which feels a little less cool because of its safety handle but is a ton sharper and better at slicing through things than Josefina's grandmother's. As I tear down vines and feel the crunch of roots and heavy fern leaves beneath my feet, it's like I'm the most powerful thing in the jungle, not a wolf, like Coach Leider likes to call us on the team, but a lion.

"Turn right here," calls out Josefina from the back. "Our boat is on the western side of the island, away from the zombies' beach."

There are still some zombie tourists wandering the jungle, latecomers from the cruise ship who are now moving aimlessly without the drums to draw them in, and we make short work of them. When the first group of them attacks us, I get this short, sharp shock of that horrible feeling, the thing that had me hyperventilating and pressed against the wall like some yellow-bellied dork, but instead of letting it freeze me up and paralyze me, I take it and use it like fuel, make it control the movements of my arm and send me shrieking at them, machete raised. The first one to come at me is a kid about my age in swim trunks, his eye sockets empty and black and his tongue half eaten away, and when he reaches out for me and my insides feel like they want to jump out of my mouth and turn into butterflies so they can fly away, I force everything I have into the muscles in my arms and swing my machete with all my might, taking out one of his legs and then hitting him hard while he lies on the ground. It's gross—there's cracking and hacking and black stuff everywhere—but when it's over, we're one zombie closer to saving our families.

Looking up, I see Kendra and Ian going to town, but it's each in their own way. Kendra goes clinical, snapping a balding male zombie's knee with her crowbar, then sinking one end between his shoulder blades and pries out two of his backbone discs and sending them tumbling into the dirt. PJ's got the night stick held in one hand and gives three sharp cracks to the lower back of a bloated green female zombie, who goes falling to the ground. He makes sure to say, "I'm sorry," like he did before, and by the look on his face, I can tell he means it.

As we stand panting over the whupped undead, I feel the urge to get this over with and get away from this island as soon as possible. We move quickly and keep coming upon zombies, mouths open and hands outstretched. Some, like the teenage lifeguard in a red polo shirt with her caved-in skull overflowing with barnacles or the old man with his nose dangling by black meaty threads, lose their appendages and keep gurgling at us as we pass their slow-crawling bodies. But for the first time, there's no running away from any of them.

Every walking corpse that lurches up to us or comes popping out from between trees and grasps us with a wet pale hand gets its world rocked hard. The smell of ocean water and rotting meat follows us as we walk, and I notice the Wardens behind us flinching every time they hear metal collide with meat and bone.

At some point, the gang of monkeys that saved PJ and me starts running in the tree branches alongside us, chirping and shrieking a nice in a cheerleader-y sort of way.

After I spot a security camera, its lens still and its red light dark, I glance over my shoulder at Danny Melee, this seasick-looking jerk with his hand clasped over his mouth, walking on tiptoes to try and avoid stepping in dirt and zombie remains. When Kendra first told me about his nut-bar plan to turn the real world into *Total Wasteland* and put our families in jeopardy, it was the hardest thing I've ever had to do to not just kick him in the face until he couldn't pronounce his name. Now, watching him scurry behind us with this terrified look on his face, I don't even think he's worth it, like it would be a waste of strength. Beating him up or tossing him to the zombies is like fouling the kid on the opposing team who made fun of you, just something you're going to regret later.

Josefina suddenly stumbles, crying out. Another zombie, this one a chubby dude in a Speedo with his legs gone from below the knee, has a hand gripped around her ankle and drags it toward his mouth, and of course, Danny Melee is right behind her but just stands there with his hands on the side of his head and his mouth open, and for a second I think that that's how I must have looked when I got all freaked out by seeing the zombies earlier. I lunge over, whip my machete over my head a few times, and pretty soon the thing is a pile of crud. Looking at Danny, I point at the zombie's remains with my blade. "Use that for your research," I snap at him. Danny chokes back a scream and expertly steps around the mess in front of him. Kendra raises an eyebrow at me and PJ gives me that sad look I was getting up on the roof before. But I don't care. That felt good, though not really. It just felt gross and cruel and got a rise out of Danny and that's what seems to be driving me to kill zombies right now, so whatever.

Finally, the sound of crashing waves begins to grow louder, and between massive overgrown trees and dangling bunches of vines, I catch sight of greenish blue with white foam on top, until finally I chop aside a massive palm leaf hanging before me and reveal the ocean stretching out into the horizon, lined with hard brown rock that leads in a sort of natural staircase to where the red wooden motorboat rises and falls in the surf, tied to a metal spike sticking out of the rock. The whole view is beautiful, something out of a brochure, with these huge discs of misty cloud hanging around a blood-red sun as it goes down into the water, which stretches all the way into the sky even as it sucks and slaps at the jagged rocks in front of us. This could be a scene from either some pirate story or a nature show or infomercial about a tropical vacation—

—but it's not, I remind myself as I try to shake some of the caked flesh and black stuff off my machete. This place is beautiful and exotic, but it's cursed; I can't let my guard down, even for one second, or we're toast.

Jeniveve and Josefina hop down the jagged rocks and into the boat like it's nothing, and my body's used to jumping and climbing enough that I join them after a few seconds, but the rest of them take their sweet time. Finally, O'Dea half climbs half falls into the boat, and we all sit there for a moment, rocking with the surf.

"Last chance, amigos," says Danny Melee, suddenly looking excited. "Let's just forget this ever—

"We fix the seal," I say, "and we do it now. Josefina, get that motor running."

Josefina yanks the cord on the boat motor, and it sputters to life with a rumble and a puff of smoke. Jeniveve yanks the rope at the ship's front from its spike, and we putter out into the water.

The boat drifts slowly around the edge of the island, and I begin seeing things I recognize: the white beach, the blown-up pieces of buoy bobbing up and down in the distance. Josefina guns the motor, and we go skipping along the waves, our bodies bouncing in the air with each hard slap and bump. Kendra's knuckles go white as she grips the edge of the boat.

Finally, we pull up somewhere between the beach and the buoy, and Josefina stops the motor. She nods to her grandmother, who nods back and takes the drums from O'Dea, resting them in her lap.

"So what now?" calls PJ over the water slapping the boat.

"My grandmother will begin playing her drums and draw the cursed to the water," says the Warden in training. "When they first begin walking into the sea, we will go to the chain anchored in the wreck of the *Alabaster* and draw them there. Then, all three of us magic users must bind the seal with a holding spell, and the cursed will be forced back into the wreck by the karma being given off by the seal."

"And you're sure they can't attack us?" I ask. "They can't swim?"

"If they do somehow get to us," says O'Dea, "you can take care of 'em. You've obviously figured out your part in this."

O'Dea's words leave me confused, because on the one hand, I hate this idea of my role, like all I can be is Ian the Human Blender, but on the other hand, I know exactly what she means, like once I managed to zone in on that sharp shock that rips through all the cobwebs and worries in my brain, I'm unstoppable, doing exactly what I'm supposed to be doing.

Jeniveve closes her eyes and takes a deep breath that seems to take her old form an extra size up, like a balloon being filled. Then her hands drop onto the surface of the drums, and she begins to play. Her rhythm is different from the ones we heard earlier, especially Kendra's. That beat was sloppy, persistent, more about banging on the drums than playing a song of any kind. This is a practiced rhythm, slowly speeding up, twisting and flapping and sending these deep hypnotic sounds into the air that I can feel behind my eyes and in my teeth, like she's playing the rhythm of my heart like a drum.

For what seems like a century, we watch the shore in our bobbing little boat, waiting for something, anything, to happen. After a while, I'm wondering if we're being chumps and if the zombies are even hearing the drums.

"Wait," says Josefina softly. "Soon."

And then, wouldn't you know it, the treetops begin quivering, and there's this loud sound of a million chirps and animal calls that gets louder and then goes silent at once. Before my eyes, the jungle grows dark, that dim space between the trees and bushes going super dark, totally filled with shapes like people to the point where there's just that front line of palm trees against the sand of the beach and then this giant black shadow behind it.

And then, they show up.

The first thing that comes to my mind is snakes, not the animals but those crappy fireworks you get when you light a black disc on fire and a snake of ash trails out for a while, only here the island is the disc, and the snake isn't ash even though it's the same color. It's a snake of tight-packed, loud-voiced dead people.

There's first a line of rotten faces, then a thick, never-ending outpouring of rotten pale gray flesh and gnashing teeth, spilling out from the trees like the jungle is throwing up a mouthful of the nastiest sardines you've ever seen, which makes sense because they're so tightly packed together that their expressions have turned into nothing, just a smear of gray-white meat, this faceless parade of the dead. They stampede right into the water like they don't even see it, and pretty soon, there's not even a line of zombies, just a growing dark cloud in the bubbling sea that's spreading out into the ocean.

Josefina fires up the motor again, and the boat launches out to sea, cutting through some waves and skipping over others like a stone. Somehow, Jeniveve keeps up the drumming as we bounce and splash our way across the murky water.

"There's the buoy," yells PJ over the wind and motor, pointing to the blown-up wooden cigar butt drifting in the waves a few feet away. Looking at it, I realize how much smaller our zemi will be compared to the old one, and I hope and pray this will work.

"Perfect," yells Kendra. "How long do you think it will take to get the new totem in place?"

"I'll have to say a spell," says O'Dea. "And Josefina, you'll have to help me with some of your own—"

There's a sound like someone dropping a phone book, and we all catch major air as the boat hits a hard wave. Suddenly, the zemi goes slipping off Josefina's lap, hanging in the air for a second as straight-up panic crosses all our faces—and then it goes splashing into the surf behind us.

"NO!" screams O'Dea, but before Josefina can even let up on the motor, my legs spring hard and I'm in midair behind the boat. There's no thinking, no feeling, just the zemi, the water, my friends, and in a blur I'm splashing into the ocean, which was warm with the sun earlier today but now in the evening is unexpectedly cool against my skin. I put one hand over the other until I feel the etched surface of the buoy slap my palm. For a moment, I open my eyes to make sure I've got it, and yeah, there it is, floating inches away from me. . . .

And then I see the cloud, dark and rippling in the sea beneath me, spreading out toward me.

"Here!" I scream, tossing the zemi to a surprised Josefina, who barely catches the slippery object. For a split second, I admire my spiral—maybe I need to look into football next year—and then I swim like crazy.

There's this type of running called *lion running* that Coach Leider talks about. There's a lion behind you coming at you as fast as it can, and if you slow down even the *tiniest* bit, it's going to slam its claws on your shoulders and bite you in the neck, so you just push yourself until you feel your body about to break. He says that even athletes can't lion run for more than, say, ten seconds before collapsing. This is *zombie swimming*, the kind of stroke someone does when they realize that a massive horde of hungry dead people is coming. My lungs burn and I swallow great big mouthfuls of ocean water that stings my throat, and none of that matters because I can almost feel cold dead bony hands nipping at my ankles like the claws of some giant lobster trying to drag me down.

I'm swimming so fast that I jam my fingers on the edge of the boat when I collide with it, but that's the kind of pain you get used to doing school sports. The minute PJ and Kendra yank me, dripping all over the place, into the boat, I go grabbing for my machete.

"They're down there," I say between loud coughs that send up gross mouthfuls of salt water.

"You three get ready," says O'Dea. "With us performing this spell and Jeniveve drumming to get them all gathered below us, one or two might make their way up. They get attracted to magic." She turns to Josefina, who raises the pieces of the old totem out of the water, then unhooks a chain attached to its bottom, tosses the burnt tiki end aside, and jams the hook at the end of the chain through a hole in the bottom of the new zemi, creating a new buoy.

"You good to go?" asks O'Dea, rubbing her hands together.

"Yes," says Josefina, even though she doesn't sound like she believes her own answer. She clears her throat and then begins to mumble softly in Spanish. Both women put their hands to the wooden head, and slowly, they lower their heads, close their eyes, and begin to chant, Josefina in Spanish and O'Dea in some kind of other language, something strange and probably super old that I've never heard before, with lots of grunting noises thrown in. Soon, Jeniveve joins in with even *another* language, something ancient and creepy that sounds like throat clearing.

At first their voices are separate, new layers on top of Jeniveve's drumming, and then slowly they mix together with the beat and spin into this one solid sound in my ears, a strange droning noise that makes the air feel hot and full of energy and gets the whole ocean beneath us bubbling and splashing.

Only it's not just the Wardens chanting.

"Here they come!" shouts PJ as the dark cloud seems to gather beneath us, concentrated into a single nasty black spot that fills the ocean like a bruise. The water begins churning, going all foamy and white up near the edges of the boat. My hands close around the handle of my machete, and I glance behind me and see PJ and Kendra gripping their weapons, waiting.

The hands come first, rising out of the foam and clamping down on the edges of the boat with their green-white gnarled fingers. Slowly, the zombies pull themselves out of the bubbling sea, their mouths wide and gushing with water and black goo. Immediately, we start going to work, aiming for their hands and faces, sending the first wave of awful gooey wet corpses flying backward and sinking back down into the sloshing water. But then there are more of them, pulling at all sides of the boat and sending us rocking back and forth. Not just the boat, either, but each other—the minute one's pale gasping face comes into view, another rotting hand slaps on top of it and uses its brother's head to lift itself out of the water. And that's when I realize that they're not swimming, they're climbing, that, oh geez, there are enough zombies that there's a tower of dead people rising between the crashed cruise ship and the surface, which just gets rid of any remaining glimmer of hope that we can fend them all off.

At first, I focus on individual zombies, taking them one at a time and trying to hit them hard enough to hurt their spines or chuck them off the boat, but after a while I'm just swinging wildly, slicing and dicing at anything in my way and sending big hunks of meat and fingers and all types of zombie debris flinging everywhere, but still they come, more and more of them reaching out from the white foam. Spit flecks my mouth and I have a snot bubble going the size of an onion, but I'm just swinging away until my arms burn. Because, I decide, this must be our last stand, so I'm going out swinging.

And as a cold hard hand reaches out and grabs the front of my T-shirt, I just hope, *all* I hope is, that my parents understand I died fighting for my friends. That is, if they're not eaten alive by zombie tourists.

That's when the chanting and the drumming and the weird blur of Warden sounds seems to grow louder than any other noise, filling the air, until with four hard slams on the drums and a single grunted syllable, they stop, and a feeling like a balloon made of wind popping blows across the ocean.

The growing tower of dead limbs and hungry decayed mouths freezes, just stops moving. For a second, the zombies just stand there in midattack, like someone's used a remote to pause them.

"The curse is sealed," says O'Dea softly. "The garden may grow."

"The shadows recede," says Josefina. "The balance returns."

Slowly, one by one, the dead close their mouths with soft, rippling moans, then they release the boat and begin sinking back down into the water, white eyes glazing over with a look like they got a bogus penalty called on them, like we're not playing fair, and this feeling of relief washes over me as I see my enemies sink into the water.

But the corpse holding my shirt doesn't let go, and all of a sudden I'm fighting a whole mess of dead weight pulling me over the edge of the boat.

"Guys!" is all I manage to scream before a couple hundred pounds of homicidal dead guy drag me over the splintery lip of the boat and into the water.

CHAPTER TWENTY

Kendra

Things that live deep under water have always been supremely upsetting to humanity. During my research into these islands, I found myself shuddering as I observed photographs of fish and cephalopod life that dwells in the deeper trenches of the ocean floor, creatures like vampire squid, frill sharks, and of course the hideous snaggle-toothed angler fish. My initial deduction was that these animals were simply terrifying because of their odd appearances, usually caused by their dwelling in areas with incredible amounts of pressure and very little light or energy. However, I have begun to wonder if it is not just the dwellers of this inky environment that are so jarring to us, but the environment itself. Perhaps it is not the fear that these creatures may confront you, but that they will drag you deep into a place so unlike the human world, somewhere suffocating and quiet and crawling with other beings that appear built by a twisted madman.

Which is why, as Ian goes over the edge, I feel as though I am electrically shocked and find myself jumping in after him. It defies all logic—Ian is stronger than I am, and even if he doesn't free himself from the zombie's grip, there's no point in me being pulled down into the waters with him. But there is something in me that snaps on when he screams "Guys!" and goes overboard, something that knows the only thing that makes sense in this world is to follow him. I cannot let him sink to those depths—not alone.

Water soaks me, sending chills through my skin though it is warm, tropical seawater. My hair becomes a dead weight, swaying in a manner that makes me think of half-cooked ramen noodles. Ian is just below me, and though my eyes sting in the salt water, I keep them open to see his shape sinking in the waves. My arms stretch out and wrap around his waist, attempting to pull him toward the surface. The weight of the zombie gripping his shirt is impossible for me to lift, and much to my dismay we both begin sinking deeper and deeper into the ocean.

Suddenly, two warm hands enclose my ankles and pull hard. Our descent stops with a sudden jerk, leaving us dangling down in the water, my face buried in Ian's hair.

Through his thrashings, he manages to stab at the hand clutching his chest, finally prying it open. Suddenly, the extra weight pulling us down into the cold lets up, and Ian swims up and away from me, back to the boat. For a moment, I hang facedown in the ocean, my eyes open.

How will I ever describe what I see?

How to even begin, Kendra? The murky mountain of writhing bodies crumbling apart and descending all the way to the coral-studded ocean floor, where it scatters in a slow-motion collapse. The wreck of the Alabaster, *deck, windows, and all, its enormous white hull covered in great fluttering tentacles of seaweed and algae, its pointed nose gashed open on one side with a jagged hole, through which crawls a horde of corpses like deep-sea insects, their pale eyes catching the beams of dying light through the water for a moment before they vanish into the ship. The zombie that had dragged Ian down flailing his arms as he falls off the pile of his brothers, hands still held out to us as dingy bubbles escape his mouth and he goes sinking into the abyss, into the watery tomb below us.*

This is a researcher's dream. A once-in-a-lifetime sight that any zoologist or paranormal investigator might dream of witnessing. But who would listen to you, when you told them about it? Who would want to?

Then we're rising out of the water, more hands clasping onto my ankles, my legs, and dragging me and Ian up onto the boat. "And *HEAVE*," shouts PJ as my ears break the surface, and suddenly there's a hard yank that leaves us dripping and coughing on the rough floor of the boat, the sky overhead dotted by concerned faces.

"Are you two all right?" says PJ.

"*¿Le mordieron?*" snaps Jeniveve. "*Rápidamente, debo saber.*" (Were you bitten? Quickly, I must know.)

"No bites," gags Ian. "And it looks like they're climbing back into their little underwater prison."

"So . . . that's it, then?" says Danny with a sigh. "We're done? It's finally over?"

"I think so," says O'Dea. She looks over at me and manages a smile. "That was a pretty close one, huh?"

"Eh," says Ian through chattering teeth. Then his head falls back, his skull thumping loudly on the boat, and he emits a long, low groan. "I'm done with this vacation. Can we go home now?"

"We must first return to the island," says Josefina. "Yaya and I need to begin restoring the other barriers tonight—the sigils, the masks."

"That's perfect," says Danny, his voice high-pitched and giddy in a childish manner. "If we get back to the compound, we can get an inflatable raft, food, a phone—if someone didn't already take it, we can even use my helicopter! I've taken lessons, I can probably handle it." He gives me a grin, as though trying to make up for his past transgressions, but it only makes him look even more insane.

"Fine," Josefina says. "We will return to the video game laboratory or whatever that place is. But after you have found what you need, we will part ways. My grandmother and I have much work to do."

"Don't worry," I assure her. "We want to leave as quickly as you do."

As we ride back to land, I watch Danny Melee perch at the bow of the boat like some sort of excitable dog, drumming his hands impatiently on the side. His sudden turnaround from wailing and horrified to jittery with excitement only serves to make him more of a strange, bizarre creature in my eyes, a vast disappointment who would use his intellectual skills and massive financial holdings for all the worst purposes. . . .

And you, Kendra. He would use you—as a girl to manipulate and win over to his side, maybe influence your friends; as a Gravedigger to promote his wild park and keep his chemically altered zombie population in check. It seemed too good to be true, a boy as independent and brilliant as that listening to you, taking time with you . . . and then it just turns out he's a jerk. What a fool you were, believing your heart.

Suddenly, my thoughts go to my father and mother, how they must feel learning that what they had wasn't what they expected. They must feel as duped and foolish as I. I could only see the lack of logic, the incongruity of *We don't love each other anymore.* Now, here I am, logic having abandoned me, the pain in my chest hard-edged and deep. My eyes burn and cloud up, with tears or ocean mist, I can't tell.

As evening fades fast into night, the walls of Danny's compound grow in the shadowy distance. The gray concrete barriers, before seemingly impenetrable, now just seem grisly and depressing. Every inch of the wall from the ground up to approximately six feet is covered with gory handprints. A few crumpled zombie bodies lie at its base, trampled into permanent death by their companions. One section of thick concrete lies on its back, creating a gaping hole in the wall of the compound. Josefina leads us over it.

What was once an astonishing, thriving research facility is now both war zone and ghost town, sending a terrible pall over all of us. Pieces of clothing and equipment—clipboards, firearms, suitcases, bundles of notes—lie in thick crimson patches on the pounded dirt and flat rubber walkways throughout. Huts and trailers face each other silently, their doors open. Though we so eagerly rushed here to get the equipment we need, the seven of us, three Gravediggers, three Wardens, and a teenage maniac, walk slowly along the blood-streaked ground, the feeling of death and sorrow pressing down on me like a great weight.

"It's this way," says Danny Melee, pointing to the other end of the compound. As per his description, a black helicopter, its side stenciled with the Melee Industries *DM* logo, waits there. Seeing its blades hanging still in the air grips my mind with a thin but powerful feeling of hope.

Almost there, Kendra. Almost home.

"Wait a second," says Ian, using his machete to point to the ground in front of us. Following his blade, we take in a pile of bodies, rotten and waterlogged, dressed in tacky floral prints—zombie tourists, spinal columns gone, gaping gashes down their backs. They lie in a concentrated pile of mangled forms.

There's a bang of metal connecting with metal, and we all jump. The trailer in front of which the dead zombies lie is now open, and out of it appears Dario, heavily armed and entirely unharmed. Behind him, he drags a long steel box that shakes and shudders. With every drag, his neck becomes tight and wiry and the muscles in his arms bulge and swell. "Dario?" says Danny.

At the sound of his name, the huge man whips his head toward us and his hand goes to the knife on his belt, but when he sees us, his mouth becomes a light-hearted grin, and he straightens up.

"Ah, the young Gravediggers," he says in a thick, oily voice, so unlike the charming baritone he has used throughout the day. At my side, PJ gasps, and Ian's jaw and machete drop at the same time.

"What?" I ask.

"Earlier today, Ian and I found a walkie-talkie in the forest," says PJ. "The person on the other end knew about us . . . but he spoke in that voice, not Dario's. He knew our names, that we were Gravediggers—"

"I should!" oozes Dario, cracking his knuckles. "I've been following you for some time now, ever since my underground contacts first fed me the rumors of your little adventure on that mountain in Montana. I had to be sure, of course—rig your school raffle, spy on you in your local graveyard, even hire that poor whale-watching guide to bring out here just as we breached containment. And let me just say you three have been truly marvelous." He folds his beefy arms and smirks. "As for your karmic occupation, I'm certainly familiar with it. After all, my father was one of the last great Gravediggers, Joseph Savini. Surely Ms. Foree has heard of him."

"Oh yeah," growls O'Dea. Hatred emanates from her in thick, acidic waves. "I know Joe Savini. Yeah, now that I look at you, you have that funny-shaped head."

"A brilliant strategist and a brave warrior," says Dario

proudly. "At twenty years old, he single-handedly fought off a horde of thirty zombies at his home in Naples."

"And then, five years later," spits O'Dea, "he murdered a Warden."

"*¡Hijo de perro!*" snaps Josefina, along with a series of phrases in Spanish that I decide not to attempt in conversation with a teacher.

"A Warden who was unable to do her job," says Dario. His smile appears exponentially more forced by the minute, and his voice has reached a tone that leaves me feeling *trepidatious* (a classic vocab word if there ever was one). "Whose zombies, once freed, devoured his sister. He had every right to take his vengeance out on a woman who no longer had any power over her flock."

"Just as the Wardens had every right to denounce the Gravediggers after that," says O'Dea.

"They had *no right!*" snaps Dario, his face flaring red, his mouth flicking spit. We all involuntarily take a step back. "You know the law. Wardens are taught, Gravediggers are *chosen*. You cannot *disband purpose*. My father understood the truth—that containment is *foolish* and *impossible*. But because some old women believed their magical power was more important than safety and action, they cast him out and cursed him. So he vanished. Left my mother and me without a trace."

My breath catches in my throat. Our predicament

is far worse than I could have imagined. This man isn't crazy, he's *driven*. There is no greater motivator than revenge.

"Whoa, where's this coming from?" asks Danny Melee. "You told me you were a poacher from Kenya!"

"The only way to deal with the evil is to destroy it," he says, ignoring his former employer. "Which is what I intend to show the world." He slaps the metal crate twice, sending the box into a new round of shaking and screaming. "With the help of Mr. Melee's finances and connections, I've created something that the Wardens will find themselves unable to contain—oh, they're not the ghouls my kinsmen fought, but I'm sure we Grave-diggers will be able to handle them. Dr. Marten here will be a perfect Patient Zero. I think I'll take him to Mexico City to start the infection—its large population and lawlessness are ideal for our purposes. And once the world erupts in chaos, and containment fails worldwide, the Wardens will have no choice but to turn power over to the Gravediggers. And we—myself and the three of you, and all others chosen to fight the evil—will have the world we deserve, where *we* rule and *they* follow. The way things should be."

He nods, his watery-eyed compassion leaving me in gooseflesh. All is silent, the sheer intricate madness of Dario's doomsday plan leaving us aghast. Finally, I realize that the horror that almost dissolved my face with acid is what bangs so angrily at the metal coffin by Dario's feet. The very thought of it fills me with disgust, but also with an undeniable conviction.

"If you think," I say, "for a *second* that we would help you with this . . . *villainy* of yours, then you're either stupid or crazy."

"Seconded," says PJ.

"Ditto," says Ian.

"Children," says Dario, unfolding his arms and extending a gloved hand out to us. "I make this offer only once. As a fellow Gravedigger, I respect your abilities in a way these witches cannot comprehend. Please, come along."

Wait, Kendra. Think. What about this feels wrong— not just wrong morally, but wrong logically? No matter how proficient you've become with a crowbar, you're still the thinker here. You're Queen Brain, according to Ian and PJ. What's the problem?

"But you're not a Gravedigger," I say.

Dario guffaws. "I assure you, Ms. Wright, my father was one of the greatest—"

"But you're not your father," I say, my argument picking up momentum within my mind. My mental processes snap together perfectly, framing the words as I say them with a border of righteous knowledge. This is my power at work—my mind, my great and easy ability to understand the facts and deduce. "You said it yourself, Gravediggers are *chosen*. Their abilities are not passed down through a bloodline the way witchcraft is. And no true Gravedigger, even your father, would take action to *help* the forces of darkness, even if they did kill a Warden. If Gravediggers occur naturally, then they must have a natural aversion to the undead. Meaning you're *not* a Gravedigger. You're simply a well-trained zombie killer with a chip on his shoulder."

The scowl of bitterness and contempt that crosses Dario's face is satisfying in the extreme. At my side, Ian chuckles meanly.

"That must have really chapped you, huh?" he says. "Dad's a Gravedigger, you're just a wannabe."

"You're no better than him," says PJ, pointing to Danny. Danny sputters an argument, but I don't hear it. The power surging between the three of us, pointed at this traitor to our cause, to what we are, is all I know.

"What a shame," says Dario, finally. "Since you're not with me, you must be against me. But seeing as I have no quarrel with you three, I'll spare your lives for today. However, if you'll excuse me, I have a helicopter to catch. You may have caught me this time, but I'm sure there will be another."

"Not so fast, jerkface!" shouts Danny, jabbing a finger at Dario. "You even *try* to steal my chopper and I'll get on the remote override system and send you into the ocean!"

"Oh, you'll be too distracted to do that," says Dario, leaning over to his metal crate. He undoes a heavy padlock on one side before giving us a final wave and jogging off between the rows of trailers and huts, heading in the direction of the helicopter.

"After him!" shouts Ian, charging forward.

"Ian, wait!" I scream.

The lid of the silver crate explodes open with a deafening noise, and out bounds what I feared—the science zombie, a mutated creature beyond life and death. Its eyes are entirely black, its mouth drips foaming red, and its skin is a veritable roadmap of indigo veins that crawl up its throat and become black as pitch at its forehead. Every muscle in its body bulges with effort, its neck a mountain of taut lines, its clawed hands and bald head twitching like some breed of oversized fly. Its white lab coat, the tails tattered and stained with bright red blood, billow out behind it like a foul butcher's cloak.

Ian skids to a halt, arms windmilling in the air. "What the heck is that?!" he shrieks.

The mutant zombie responds with a deep guttural roar, and we all have barely a second before we can turn and run away, our day of accumulated bravery in the face of zombie slaughter vanishing beneath a tidal wave of pure, unadulterated fear.

Immediately, we split up, Ian veering right, PJ heading left, the Wardens scattering between the huts and trailers that make up the center of the compound. Of course, when I peer over my shoulder, I see that the mutant zombie has decided *I'm* the best candidate for the chase; whether this is because it recognizes me from earlier or has locked onto my appearance (curse my recognizable hair!) is beyond me. I hear a helicopter whup to life in the distance, and I feel a breeze as it lifts into the air, but I can't bring myself to care. All emotions other than fear leave me, and that raging terror pumps my arms, moves my legs, and begs me to put distance between this abomination and myself.

Obstacles, Kendra. This monstrosity may have speed on you, but one doubts that it's very intelligent. Don't simply outrun it, outthink it. Your brain is your tool.

I leave the rubber walkway, run down the middle of the compound, and dart between two large trailers, doing my best to hopscotch the plethora of wires and cables running along the ground between them. A glance behind me shows my strategy working, the mutant zombie snarling as it trips and stumbles on its way between the two metal containers.

As I round one of Danny's trailers, I throw my back against the rear of it, which is mostly occupied by dusty air vents and more wires sprouting from its tiny window. My breath heaves in my chest, my lungs burn, and helplessness grips me harder than I clutch the crowbar to my chest.

This is it—this is my chance. I need to make this count.

The growling nears from around the side of the trailer until it's right next to me, and then the bald head and black eyes come around the corner; the creature twitches uncontrollably. Its mouth sends flecks of steaming red spittle flying onto the cable-strewn dirt.

"HEY!" I cry.

The mutant zombie turns to me, its monstrous visage tightening as it lets out an inhuman roar. Mustering every ounce of courage and aggression within me, I rush forward, brandishing the end of my crowbar at its face—

—and planting it directly in the monster's mouth.

Not its brain.

The mutant zombie barely notices, shoving against the crowbar. Panicked, I put my whole body into my efforts, but the monster is stronger, and already the crowbar begins to bubble, smoke, and melt at the touch of its acid spit. Before I am aware of what is happening, the zombie wraps its hands around my throat, squeezing with incredible strength. As the air slowly seeps out of me, I stare into its glossy black eyes and gaping red maw, and with terrible resignation that sits cold and hollow in my gut, I foresee my doom.

And then, there's a wet stabbing noise, a *chunk* if you will. The zombie's eyes seize up, as does its whole body. The hands drop from my throat, and then slowly, it staggers, shudders, and collapses to the ground, a machete plunged forcefully into the back of its skull.

CHAPTER
TWENTY-ONE

PJ

The monster's roaring stops just as I find my night-stick again and get ready to head after Kendra. I cry out her name as I run between the trailers where I last saw my friend disappear. There's no reply, but the sound of a voice sends me racing in the right direction, praying that I don't find her or Ian with a gaping bite-wound in the neck. Instead, the scene I discover is somehow even more upsetting.

Ian and Kendra stand over the twitching body of the mutant zombie that Danny Melee built. Ian's machete is sunk into its head, red blood spilling out from the wound. Kendra's got her back to the side of the trailer we're behind, but Ian stands directly over the body, sobbing wildly as he points at the monstrosity over and over again.

"See?" he cries. His other hand claws at his face, his hair. "I got the last zombie this time, I did it, they don't scare me, nothing scares me, I'm a Gravedigger, a real Gravedigger, number one, the winner, Ian Buckley the zombie killer. . . ."

Not knowing what else to do, I dart over and throw my arms around him. I hold him still, and right then his gibbering cuts out, and he just starts crying, loudly. Slowly, Kendra steps over the zombie's body and puts her arms around the two of us, helping to cradle Ian as he shakes and weeps. Finally, for the first time since we've gotten there, it feels as though everything has gone silent, and we three are just friends, together, in fear.

"It's too much," cries Ian through a mouthful of spit. "All this killing and fighting. I don't want to do it anymore."

"It's okay, Ian," I whisper. "We've got you. It's over."

Kendra's adamant, and Danny Melee nods along with a hangdog look on his face. The science zombie's body is a biohazard—normal zombie corpses break down harmlessly, but the Melee's mutated version could get unstable. We have to burn it.

By the light of Melee Industries Night Chaser model flashlights, we roll the body of the mutant zombie onto a tarp and drag it out onto the dirt near the walls of the compound, leaving a red smear behind it as we go. Danny leads us to a hut marked AUTHORIZED PERSONNEL ONLY, where we find cans of gasoline and two missiles next to a launcher about as tall as me. Kendra glares at Melee, who shrugs sheepishly—"Dario said it would be the easiest way to destroy the seal"—but I'm far past caring about any discoveries we make. This whole thing has been awful. It's time to end this.

We douse the mutant zombie's body in gas, and Kendra lights a match and tosses it on. There's a *whumpf* as the whole thing goes up, sending out great clouds of inky smoke that carry a smell so awful, I nearly throw up. Danny leaves and returns with two canisters of red fluid and a massive notebook and tosses them all into the flames. We stand there for a moment. The blaze roars, and my friends' faces are painted with yellow flickers, like they're watching an old film.

With the helicopter gone, our only way off the island is Josefina's boat. We wrap one end of my nightstick with a piece of torn lab coat and use gas to make a torch out of it. Josefina takes the lead, and we follow her as she holds the blazing stick over her head, sending weird yellow light onto the looming dark shapes of the trees. At night, the jungle is incredibly spooky, with unfamiliar shadows being thrown off at all sides by our every movement.

As we near the beach, Kendra gasps and points, and Ian and I look up to see five heavy black podlike shapes dangling from a branch overhead, their eyes glittering in the torchlight as we pass them.

"Look at the size of them," she coos. "They could be the result of island gigantism."

"They have come to see you off," Josefina says, nodding toward the bats. "No doubt they appreciate what you have done here today."

How do you speak to giant sacred bats? "You're welcome," I finally say as we pass beneath them. If those huge leaflike ears hear me, their owners show no sign of it.

Kendra raises an eyebrow. "You know those bats?"

Eventually, we break through the thickness of the jungle and arrive on the beach. The ocean reflects the same pitch-blackness as the night sky, and the cold skull-white moon appears in the sea as a quivering white finger pointing at the island. One by one, we wade through the crashing surf and haul ourselves into the boat. Josefina starts the motor, which now sounds deafening in the intense silence after dark. Then she turns us toward the open water, and we cut through the waves and out into the night, the numberless stars overhead like the reflection of the hundreds of white eyes beneath the waves, like glowing pale blood splattered across the sky.

After waving good-bye to Josefina, we walk across the sand and into the lobby of our resort, which feels even more luxurious than before after our having been through hell. As we pad our way into the building, we get stares galore. The people behind the front desk look like they've seen ghosts. A family at the Information desk crinkles up their noses and takes a step back from us. As we make our way toward the elevators, a concierge—a toothpick of a woman with short blond hair and a blue pants suit—runs in front of us, blocking our path.

"No," she says. "No, no way, uh-uh. No begging, *¿comprende? No solicitar. No quiero llamar a la policia.*"

"We're guests here," says Kendra.

"Is that right?" scoffs the woman. "You five. Staying here. And with who?"

"With me," says Danny, raising his hand. "It's Rose, right? I met you when I hired you. You might not remember."

The woman glowers at Danny for a second, like *how does this guy know my name?*, and then her eyes go huge and she rushes forward. "Mr. Melee," she coos. "I'm so sorry, sir, I didn't see you back there. Are you all right? Welcome back."

A bad taste floods my mouth as it all comes together. Of course Dario put us up here when he decided to bring us in on his plan. Danny owns the resort—it was on the company dime.

If this is not the worst day of my life, it is definitely up there.

"Fine," he says. "Do me a favor: help my friends here get back to their rooms, and send up some room service, on me. And this is Ms. Foree—put her in the Dictatorial Suite. On me, also."

"Of course, sir," says Rose. "Oh, and it's good you're here. Your, uh . . . *Gloria* just contacted us to say she'll be arriving tomorrow afternoon."

Danny's face goes pale and stark, far worse than he's looked at any time today. He nervously tucks greasy strands of hair behind his ears. "Tell her I'm not here," he says. "I'll contact you about transferring me to a different hotel and putting more money in her account tomorrow. Give her whatever she wants, but have someone make sure she doesn't drink too much this stay."

"Who's Gloria?" asks Kendra cruelly as Rose scuttles off. "Someone you owe money to? Perhaps a zombie theme park investor?"

"She's my *mother*," Danny spits, as though it's a dirty word, and storms off into an elevator, glaring back at us as the doors close behind him. I watch him go, part of me filled with all the contempt and loathing I felt earlier in the day, but the emotional side of me can't help but pity the poor guy.

"Such a jerk," says Ian. "I'll never play another video game again."

"I get the feeling it wasn't the video games," I tell him.

Once we're showered up—and to put it lightly, I have never enjoyed a shower more in my life—we meet in the hotel hallway and go to find our folks, O'Dea staying in to enjoy her suite. ("What the hell is an Epsom salt?" she asks me over the phone.) At the front desk, Rose almost doesn't recognize us without the dirt all over our faces but eventually tells us our parents have a reservation at the hotel restaurant, scowling the whole time.

As we walk there and snake our way between tables of drunk tourists and their families, laughing and clattering their silverware, my mind can't help but wander, picturing them in tattered and waterlogged clothes, their lips eaten away, their skin sagging and green-gray, filling their mouths with forkfuls of—

Our families are out on the terrace, eating around a table by torchlight. At first, I hope that, given how we called home and are now cleaned up, our folks will just ask us about our day. It seems, though, that over the course of the longest day of my life, I have forgotten who my mother is.

"PETER!" she shrieks, leaping out of her chair and flying across the terrace stones like, well, a giant bat.

Within seconds, she's kneeling down next to me, alternating between holding me at arm's length, touching each part of my face, and yanking me to her shoulder. "Oh, sweetheart, I've been so worried all day! Honey, do you now how late it is? They said they saw smoke coming from one of the islands today, too! Oh, sweetie, honey—"

"I'm fine, Mom," I manage to say. By now, the Buckleys and Lennox Wright are also closing in on us, looking concerned, and my cheeks feel like they've turned beet red.

"We're getting you checked out by someone at the resort this *instant*," she cries. "Dennis, can you cancel our entrees? We need to head back to the suite—"

"Mom," I say, taking her by the shoulders, "I'm fine." I push her away from me, slowly but firmly. My heart aches seeing her so worried, tears welling in her eyes and all, but I just can't deal with this right now. Another time. "You guys have dinner. I don't want to upset you—I just wanted to say good night and let you know I'm okay."

"What happened to you three?" asks Kendra's father, taking a knee in front of her.

Ian, Kendra, and I glance at each other. My brain attempts to dredge up a story and goes blank—these kinds of things aren't really my specialty, even when I haven't been chasing zombies all day. I meet Ian's eyes, and I can tell he's thinking the same thing. Thankfully, among the three of us, there is a brain—my favorite brain in the world.

"While boating to watch the whales," Kendra says slowly, blinking hard as she takes the time to think of a plausible version of today, "we were hit by a large wave that capsized our vessel." So far, so good. "After swimming to shore, we found another, smaller resort . . . from which we called you. The resort owner liked us, and fed us . . . and then sent us out on a walking tour of the island." I grit my teeth. That part is a little flimsy; if I saw it in a movie, I'm not sure I'd believe it. "While out in the jungle observing some . . . rhesus monkeys, our guide slipped and fell down a ravine. He was all right, but we had to . . . find our way back. With the help of a local girl, named Josefina. Who then . . . fed us and boated us back here."

Our parents blink at us, stunned. For a second, I wonder if the story is just too convenient, and they're going to ask us what *really* happened. And in general, they don't totally buy it—the Buckleys stare at each other, stunned, and Mr. Wright twists his face into a smirk that suggests he's proud of his daughter's ridiculous answer.

"Why didn't you mention this earlier?" he said.

She smiles warmly at him. "I didn't want to alarm you. You should enjoy your vacation."

"I promise you," I say to my mother, "we're fine."

"Well . . . if you're sure," says my mom.

"We can get you guys some extra chairs, if you're hungry," says my dad, pointing to the table.

"I'm okay," I say to him. "I think I just want to get room service and go to bed."

"Bed," echo the other two with exaggerated nods.

Slowly, our parents rise, shrug, and head back to the table. My mother lasts the longest, kissing me three times on the forehead and making sure I know where the Claritin is. Slowly, we turn away from our puzzled families and head back inside.

In my suite, my sister sits in her bed watching the end of *Finding Nemo* with a resort employee, some babysitter who bails the minute I arrive. Her large eyes intently follow me, just like they did when I came in to take a shower. She never says a word as I brush my teeth and get into my pajamas, and soon it begins to get slightly creepy.

"What's up?" I ask her, just to break the silence.

"PJ," she says softly.

"Listening," I say. My mind flips through the probable options—can we order ice cream, can we walk on the beach tomorrow, can I read her a story tonight. "What is it?"

"When you disappeared today," she says, "were there . . . you know." She raises her hands in front of her and moans.

I see. My six-year-old sister, the most intuitive person I know. Every time I think she's just a kid, she surprises me.

"Yeah," I tell her as I climb onto my bed. "There were. We didn't know they'd be there, but . . . something happened. It got really crazy."

"But you didn't get hurt, right?" she says. Her eyes are big and soft, watching every movement of my face. "You're okay?"

Am I okay? That's an interesting question. It'd be easy to just smile and wave her off and laugh and say that everything's fine, but I'd be lying to her. As the past day flashes through my mind, I find myself amazed that we kept it together. The dead, hundreds of them, rush before my eyes, dressed in their tropical finest and clutching their beach pails and holding on for dear life. Danny Melee, grinning at us like he's our friend while planning to use us like some sort of sick power-up. Dario, rigging our lives like a game show, flashing us a psychotic smile as he released some kind of monster with bloody lips and black eyes. And my friends, Ian and Kendra, one terrified by how quickly he can do horrible things, the other entirely lost in her head. And me, PJ Wilson, still worried, still unsure, still pretty much scared of everything.

Maybe things won't ever be okay.

And then I see my sister's eyes, not wide with the

excitement of another ghost story but half open, shiny, pink with veins from crying. When she blinks, tears ball up in her lashes and drop quickly, splashing her red cheeks and pattering onto the floor.

"I'm okay," I tell her softly, with a slow, careful nod.

She bounds off her bed and jumps onto mine, her arms wrapping around my waist, her body shaking with sobs. I hug her to me, closing my eyes and shushing her as best I can.

"Don't get hurt," she cries. "Please, PJ. I get scared. I don't want you to get hurt."

"Never," I whisper. "I'm okay. I'm here. I'll always be here."

Maybe things won't ever be the same. Maybe our lives are like this from now on, dark and rough, all the time. But I can't let it get to me. So I'll be terrified—panicked and shaky and unstable—for the rest of my life. It doesn't matter, so long as they're safe: Ian, Kendra, O'Dea, Kyra, my parents, the people around me. As long as I can keep them safe, and keep myself safe for them, then the darkness doesn't matter. I'll take it as it comes.

That night, in my dream (somehow, I know it's a dream), Kendra and Ian and I are swimming over the remains of a sunken cruise ship. The ship looks perfectly normal and unharmed, but it's underwater. At first, I'm kind of frightened by it, but then I swim down into the water, and it's like I don't even need to breathe.

I wave Ian and Kendra down after me, and they follow, laughing. We swim down, past flickering gray fish with white glowing eyes, until we reach the deck of the ship. The only people here are us and a thin man in a black suit whose face I can never quite make out. He opens a door into the cabin of the ship and beckons us within. The other two hesitate, but I swim right ahead, and go sinking into the yawning shadows.

"And . . . open your eyes."

My eyelids crack apart to reveal Josefina on the beach, the turquoise sea and royal blue sky making it look like she's in heaven. But it's more than our location; it's a new view on the world, a new lens through which I'm seeing things. The tropical setting around me seems to glow with a shining brilliance that I'd never noticed before. The breath in my nostrils smells sweeter. The sand shifting beneath me is soothing, not irritating, not anything to worry about. All that matters is the breeze on my skin and the stillness in my head, the feeling of the air in my lungs.

"How do you feel?" asks Josefina.

"Better." I exhale, feeling a smile creep over my face. "Thanks. After you made me kill that first zombie on the island, I figured you might be able to help."

"The least I could do after you saved my yaya and me," she says. "If you meditate like this once every few days, you should be able to focus your strengths and conquer your darkest fears. It shouldn't be too hard for you." Her mischievous smile makes my stomach twitch in a not-unpleasant way. "You have a powerful heart, after all."

"Let's hope," I say. "Are you sure you don't need any help reinforcing the island?"

"Not to worry," she says. "We have everything under control. The worst part is that my kidnapper keeps trying to contact us, asking if he can come back and rate the value of *his* island. *Idiota*, understanding nothing but facts and computers."

"Can you believe he thought the zombie virus was a fungus?" I say.

"Oh, that part is true," says Josefina.

"What?"

"There have always been those who call the curse *the fungus*," she says, rising to her feet and brushing the sand off her cutoffs. She offers me a warm, soft hand, and I take it. "That is simply the method through which the evil is delivered. That was that fool's problem—he doubted the power of evil and so became evil himself. It is not uncommon among scientists." She nods. "Your friends approach. Should I stay?"

"Actually, if you don't mind . . ." Over my shoulder, I see Ian, Kendra, and O'Dea making their way out onto the beach, O'Dea's new floral-print shirt billowing around her in the ocean breeze. Kendra looks intimidated—since we got back from Isla Hambrienta two days ago, she and I have stayed inside the hotel, holing up with movies, room service, and the indoor pool rather than set foot outside. Only Ian has been running around outdoors, like Ian in overdrive; now that he's found his inner Gravedigger, he wants to try it out.

"What was that about?" asks Ian as Josefina walks away with a wave.

"She was just helping me meditate," I say. "She thinks it would be a good tactic to learn as a Gravedigger." I take a deep breath, preparing myself. "Which is actually why I called you all out here."

Ian and Kendra raise their eyebrows and nod, almost knowing what I'm about to say. O'Dea wrinkles her weathered brow. "What's going on, PJ?" she asks.

Here we go. Start positive. "First of all, O'Dea, I wanted to thank you," I say to her. "All your advice may have been as straightforward as a fortune cookie, but you knew what you were talking about. And it helped. You saved our lives again. Thank you."

Ian and Kendra nod along approvingly and mumble their thanks. O'Dea's eyes go soft, and she nods back at me. "Thanks, you three," she says. "You know, it was so great to watch you little warriors get your Gravedigger going out there—"

"However," I interrupt, holding up a palm, "I think you were a little unfair to us." She cocks an eyebrow, confused. It kills me inside to do this, but I have to.

"After we came off that mountain, you told us we were playing a part in a huge cosmic game, and then we barely heard from you for *months*. That can't happen anymore. We *need* you, because . . ." It requires a deep breath to say it, but I know it's right. "Because we're kids, O'Dea. We're just figuring this out. And if we're going to be the best zombie hunters we can be . . . heck, if we want to *survive*, we need your help and your knowledge." I look up at Ian and Kendra. "Right, guys?" Their eyes move from me to O'Dea and back again, and their heads nod hard. An understanding passes among the three of us, the agreement that my request speaks for all of us.

O'Dea opens her mouth, and the sharp, ornery expression on her wrinkled face makes me think she's going to go on an absolute tirade, with her telling me I don't know what I'm talking about. "I—you can't— I just—" she sputters, and then groans and shakes her head, letting the tensions seep out of her shoulders.

"Okay," she says after some time, nodding. "You are absolutely right. Let's start right now." Slowly, she lowers herself to the sand, and we follow suit, making a circle—three warriors, all different, and their teacher.

"So," she says with a smile, "what do you want to know?"

"Everything," says Ian.

The last morning is a blur of shoving our stuff into our suitcases and double-checking to make sure Kyra packed her iPod for the flight. I find myself in the front lobby sitting on my bag, waiting for the rest of our crew to make their way down, and once again, I wish I had my camera. There's a couple complaining at the front desk, and a group of frat boys in tank tops who already look hammered, even though it's only noon. It would be great people-watching footage, and besides, this front lobby is nice, all yellow tiles and bathed in sunlight. Maybe life is all scenes—the big stuff, even, or the scary stuff. I'm just meant to get them down.

As I'm using my fingers to frame a shot around a woman trying to keep her two-year-old son from taking his trunks off in the middle of the lobby, I hear a giggle behind me. When I look over my shoulder, Josefina smiles down at me. She wears a sleeveless shirt and cutoffs, and has a huge pink flower tucked behind one ear. Behind her, sunlight glares in through an open patio door, giving her a halo of light.

"Hey!" I say. "What brings you here?"

In response, she steps forward and presses a folded sheet of paper into my hands. "There," she says, "for you."

"What is it?" I ask. I start to unfold it, but her hands stop mine.

"Read it later," she says. She bites her lip and her eyes go sad, and I want to do anything in the world to make her smile again. "Just remember, PJ, that you must be the heart of you three. The strength of your spirit will help you all."

My mouth flutters open and closed. Her hands are so warm. "I'll try."

She squeezes my hands and nods, still looking sad. "That's all I ask." She opens her mouth, like she wants to say more, but then nods again. "I should be heading back. Good-bye, PJ," she calls over her shoulder as she leaves.

In a movie, I would run after her, take her in my arms, and stare deep into her eyes—

But I don't. This isn't a movie, that's not me. So I watch her go, my heart pounding, my hands sweating. Her shape enters the white-hot blur of daylight, and then she's gone.

"Dude?" Ian and Kendra stand behind me, loaded down with bags. In the distance, behind them, our parents are wheeling their luggage out of the elevators.

"You ready to go?" asks Ian.

"Definitely," I say, nodding away the blur of hormones in my head. "Never been readier."

Each family gets into a different taxi to the airport this time, and once I'm in the backseat, wedged between Kyra and my mom, I unfold Josefina's note. The first thing I see—look at *that*—is an email address, with *Keep in touch!* written beneath it, and my heart soars.

Then I read the message.

"PJ, what's that?" asks my mom.

And for once, I'm happy to not have Ian and Kendra around, to not be a part of a team but just one person, because my hands shake, my head swims, and suddenly all my excitement at seeing Josefina one last time turns to something else, something cold and electrifying and hideous, like the feeling of someone's wet hand slapping down on my shoulder and spinning me to look into their grisly face.

PJ, reads the note, *I wanted to give this to you alone because I don't know how you'll feel, and I don't know if you want your fellow Gravediggers to see this message.*

Knowing you has been very nice, if even for a couple of days, she writes. *But the truth is that if I have acted strangely since we met, it is because I felt that I knew you from somewhere. It was only a few days ago that I remembered where I'd seen you before: in one of the dreams I have been having for months now. To me, they are simply nightmares, but according to my grandmother, a far greater Warden than I am, they are visions, magical images of things to come.*

And if that is true, she writes, *then PJ, I have seen your future. And you are in terrible danger.*

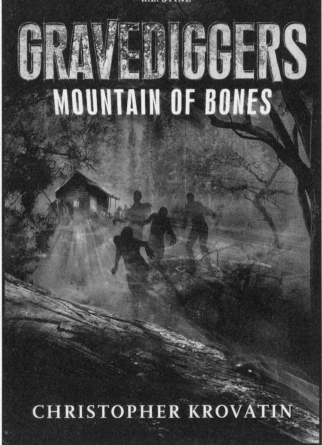